SMOKE AND MIRRORS (VIGILANTE JUSTICE SERIES)

Bristol Kelley Book Two

V F STREETS

Page Turner Books

For mom and dad, you've always been my biggest fans

SHE HAD WATCHED *him for two weeks, patient and meticulous as always. Her clients often tried to hurry her, but these things take time.*

Perfection.

Control.

Every Thursday, John Stevens had a drink at Ronnie's, the small bar below his apartment.

Ronnie's was a dump. The tables were always sticky, and the floors were littered with the same nuts that filled bowls on the counter.

Sometimes John would hit on a girl. He wasn't usually successful. But tonight he was going to get lucky.

The barstool beside him was empty. Fortunate, as the place was usually busy on a Thursday. Happy Hour, they called it.

Bristol plopped herself on the stool beside her mark. She ordered a fruity drink with a stupid name and leaned her elbows on the counter, making it easy for John to become interested.

She didn't know what he had done to piss off her client, but he was lucky they had hired her. She didn't kill people anymore.

"I've seen you hanging around lately. You new to town?" John said, leaning close.

"Yeah, just moved." She kept her voice light and airy and smiled at him in a way that told him she was interested in getting to know him better. It always surprised her how easily people got sucked into her ploys. She, on the other hand, was always on her guard. She knew how cruel the world could be and wasn't about to let it get one over on her.

John slid his glass closer to engage in a more personal encounter. It made it easy to slip the drug into his drink. She took a sip of her own and had to keep the grimace to herself. Sweet drinks like this were disgusting, but they spoke louder than words to what she was doing there. A girl out to have a good time. Whatever that meant.

After a few minutes of pointless chatter, John's pupils dilated, and Bristol offered to take the conversation somewhere more comfortable. He was so happy to accommodate, he didn't notice the fog that was quickly rising up the back of his head. Bristol knew he'd be unconscious in less than a minute.

In order to hurry him up, she made it clear what he was getting, so he half chased, half tripped up to his place, only getting as far as pushing the key into the lock before he slid to the ground.

Bristol dragged him inside. She only needed to get him somewhere appropriate, like leaning against the sagging couch that was closest.

All that was left was to put the needle and other paraphernalia in place and then let her client know they could anonymously contact the local police to come and find him using. They wanted to ruin his reputation, apparently. But from the state of his apartment, she was surprised he had any sort of reputation to ruin.

She pulled a syringe out of her bag, full of enough cocaine to kill a horse. After finding a vein, she inserted the needle. Once it was in position, she pushed the stopper all the way in.

Wait. No.

She wasn't here to kill him.

She wasn't a killer anymore.

Then what was she doing?

Chapter 1

BRISTOL JUMPED upright at the table.

"Whoa. You okay?" Cole asked as he set a steaming mug in front of her.

She blinked at him. "Was I just dreaming?" She scratched at the back of her head. "I only wanted to rest my eyes for a minute." She wrapped both hands around the mug. "Thanks for the tea."

She glanced over at a young guy in his early twenties who sat hunched over a laptop at the next table. His fingers were laced through his hair, causing it to stick up in several directions. His jittering leg and wide bleary eyes gave the impression he had an assignment due very shortly.

Bristol looked back at her tea and shuddered off the dream, reminding herself that she didn't kill John Stevens. She had put the needle in his arm and left.

This business with Silas Lincoln had messed with her head. Dealing with the worst of humanity was part of her job fixing crime scenes, but Silas was different. Silas was personal. And even though she knew he was behind bars, she couldn't shake the feel of him, and the knowledge that he had manipulated her. He had controlled her.

The vague pressure of a headache still swam at her temple.

She pulled her borrowed police jacket closer around her body and attempted to push her own kidnapping from her mind as Cole watched to make sure she was okay.

Cole. The man who saved her, in more ways than one.

The same man she nearly killed on Silas's command only a few hours ago. He surprised her in ways most people couldn't. After spending the dark early hours of the morning at the police station answering questions about Silas's child-trafficking ring, Cole had brought her to this café to unwind.

He reached out and put a hand on her shoulder, giving it a squeeze. But he pulled back when her shoulder dropped from underneath his touch. "You're hurt?"

"It's nothing."

"I wish you wouldn't do that."

"Do what?"

He shook his head. "What is it? A pulled muscle or something?" She hesitated to respond. Cole's voice dropped an octave. "What is it?"

"It's nothing. I told you."

He stared her down, but she stared right back.

Finally, he shook his head. "Fine. You want to make things difficult?" He reached over and pressed a hand onto the back of her shoulder again. She only allowed the passing of a grimace, but it was enough for Cole.

"Let me see," he said, pulling back her jacket.

She glanced around at the other people in the café. None of them were paying attention.

Still wearing the gown from her visit to the museum, there was no way to hide the raw skin as the jacket slid off her shoulder.

Cole's breath hitched, and he stared for a second, then he carefully pulled the jacket back into place and looked into her eyes. His own were menacing.

Bristol couldn't explain the sweep of shame that came over her, and it pained her to keep eye contact, so she swung her head away. "You look like a bull that wants to be let out of his pen." She was trying to lighten the mood, but Cole wouldn't have it.

"Why didn't you tell me Silas branded you with those damned linked circles?" His voice was irate, but the hand that now rested on her arm was gentle.

"Because it doesn't matter. I can get someone to fix it." But the truth was, it did bother her, being branded by Silas. She felt violated. And the knowledge that there would always be a scar hurt her worse than the burn.

She rubbed a hand down her face. If she wasn't careful, she'd lose it. She was too tired to guard against her emotions.

To push back the tears that threatened, she focused

on the truth that Silas had been caught in his own game. That memory twisted the lump in her throat and it came out as a rolling laugh before she could stop it, the fatigue draining her self-control.

"Better to laugh than cry?" Cole asked, concerned.

"Silas's face when you played that recording of him admitting to everything? It was worth all the trouble just to see him speechless."

"It was nice for a change, wasn't it?"

Bristol covered her face with both hands as a giant yawn overtook her.

"Drink up," Cole said, nodding at her cup. He took a big gulp of his own.

"You don't seem very tired. How can that be?" Bristol asked.

"I've had a lot of practice at not sleeping. And besides, I wasn't the one who was drugged. There could still be traces in your system."

Bristol frowned into her tea. "Wait, didn't I say I was going to buy the drinks?"

"It's too late." Cole grinned, and he reached for his phone when it buzzed in his pocket. "But if you want to argue about it — " He dropped his eyes to see who was calling and frowned when he saw the name Richard Beverly.

"Who is it?" Bristol asked, panic rising at the look on his face.

"It's just my dad's lawyer, but I should probably get this."

Bristol nodded, relieved, but she still took a strand of hair and twisted it around her finger.

Cole turned his body away from her and answered. "Richard, good morning. Bit early for a phone call. Is everything okay?" As Cole listened, the creases in his forehead deepened. "I see." He licked his lips and looked up at Bristol. "I'll get on the first plane … Right, see you shortly."

He hung up the phone and watched Bristol knot then unknot her hair one-handed. "That was my dad's lawyer."

"Yeah, you said. Everything okay?"

"My dad had a massive heart attack last night."

Bristol's fingers stopped mid-tie. "Cole, I'm so sorry. Is he all right?"

"He's dead." He said it so matter-of-factly that she was unsure how to respond. "I've got to fly to Chicago and take care of a few things."

"Of course."

"I'm sorry. I really wanted to have this coffee with you."

"No, Cole, your father … you have to go. Let me know if there's anything I can do."

He reached across the table and took her hand away from her hair, holding it firm. "I'm not happy leaving you after what's happened."

"I'll be fine. I've been through worse. And don't forget I've got Eli to look after me." She rolled her eyes.

"Right, yeah." Cole didn't catch her sarcasm. He let go of her hand and pulled out his phone. "I'll give him a call and ask him to look in on you."

"Cole." Bristol slid a hand across the table, tapping it lightly on the table to get his attention.

He looked at her, then shook his head to clear it. "Sorry. I just … my head's all over the place right now." He put the phone back in his pocket.

"I know." Bristol watched him. He was staring at the table now.

She stood, hoping to help him get moving. He stood in response, and she stepped around the table toward him.

"It'll be okay," she said, but wasn't sure what to do next, so she hugged him. She wasn't expecting not to want to let him go, but with her face pressed into his chest, she could have stayed there for a while.

Her body relaxed into his and her eyelids fell, so she attempted to push away before she didn't have the strength. But as she moved back, Cole fortified his grasp. She was tempted to let him keep her there as long as he liked, but it could be a long time and his dad had died. He needed to go home.

"Cole." She pulled away harder, and he finally let go.

"I can give you a lift home," he said, tucking her hair behind her ear.

Bristol looked at the guy at the next table who was still absorbed in his work, then her eyes lifted to the employee behind the counter who was pretending he wasn't paying attention to their exchange as he absent-mindedly wiped a mug, looking everywhere but at them.

The surrounding air suddenly felt stiff as she became painfully aware of how intimate they must look. Her arms dropped to her side, and she stepped back. Cole glanced at the guy too, and half his face hitched in a grin. "Not a fan of public displays of affection?"

She shrugged. "It's no one's business but ours so why put it on display." She quickly changed the subject. "You'd better get going. You've got a plane to catch."

He let out a big breath, considered her for a second, then grabbed her face and kissed her hard and fast.

Heat coursed through her, but she told herself it was embarrassment. She glanced at the employee again.

Cole, on the other hand, didn't take his eyes off her. "Don't worry about him. Just tell him my dad died. You're allowed PDAs when your dad's just died. Can I call you?"

"What?" She asked, still looking at the counter.

Cole put a hand on her cheek and turned her head toward him. "Can I call you, from Chicago?"

"Uh, yeah, sure, of course."

Cole turned and rushed out the door before he could change his mind about leaving her. His dad had a way of ruining the best things in his life.

Bristol didn't move as she watched him go, except to pull her coat more tightly around her. Finally, she turned toward the counter. The man behind it was now smiling. She walked over to him. "His dad's just died."

"Oh. That's terrible. I'm sorry."

"Yeah." She had no idea what the appropriate next thing to do was, so she smiled awkwardly, turned, and hurried out.

She scowled when she was back out on the street.

She could handle a murder scene, but not a friendly exchange. As she lifted a hand to hail a taxi, she remembered her car was still parked at the museum a few blocks away. The idea of going back to where she had been kidnapped wasn't a pleasant one, but neither was shying away simply because she was afraid.

Chapter 2

COLE DROVE his rented BMW up to the gate of his father's estate. He glanced at the security camera as he pulled up to the keypad. Punching in the code, he watched as the sensors, mounted on the high stone fence, blinked in response, and the iron gate slid open noiselessly.

His father had been a very successful businessman, but Cole could never decide whether the man's paranoia was a help or a hindrance to that. As long as Cole could remember, the security on the property was always state of the art to the point of excess. Perhaps that's where Cole had gained his appreciation for the high-tech security he offered to his clients.

Putting the car into gear, he continued down the driveway, observing the noticeable increase in the size of the trees that lined it. They were a testament to how long it had been since he'd last been there. But as he pulled around the circle drive to the front of the house, it surprised him to find that the ornate fountain he circled seemed smaller than he remembered.

He got out of the car and walked over to it, remembering when he climbed on it as a kid. Just once. He could still picture his dad storming out of the house and down the steps. Cole had held his ground, knowing what was coming and knowing that if he ran, the punishment would be worse.

As a child, he could have sworn that there were flames flickering behind his dad's dark eyes and smoke pouring from his flared nostrils. When his father yanked Cole from the side of the fountain, his voice was quiet and condescending as he explained that the fountain had cost him a *bloody* fortune.

His dad had only a passing connection to any commonwealth countries but loved to use the British expletive *bloody* whenever he had the chance.

Cole chewed on his bottom lip as he pushed the memory aside and stepped up onto the lip of the fountain. He balanced there for a second, but it didn't make him feel any better. It didn't make him feel anything at all.

He jumped backward and turned on his heel, the white stones crunching under his shoes.

After pulling his bag out of the back seat, he decided to leave the car where it was at the front door. No one else would be coming, so there was no point putting it in the garage out of the way.

He pulled a small piece of paper out of his back pocket and unfolded it as he climbed the stairs. It was the house's alarm code that Richard had given him when he arrived.

After scanning the number, he crumpled it tightly in his fist, letting out a hiss. His birthdate. It wasn't like his father to be sentimental with something like that. He'd change it to something more secure after he settled in.

He shoved the key in the lock, but as he turned it, he could feel through his fingers that the lock wasn't engaged. It was very unlikely that Richard would have left the house open. Cole slid his hand under his jacket for a gun that wasn't there.

Before opening the door, he took a breath and pictured the layout of the foyer. It would be about ten steps to reach his father's study, where Cole could get to the gun his dad always kept in the bottom right-hand drawer of his desk.

He eased the door open, keeping his body as far to the side as he could in case someone was ready to shoot.

The entryway was empty. His gaze swept through the large space until he was fairly certain that the room was clear, then he quickly checked the alarm system to confirm it was disengaged. He considered alerting security that there was a breach, but decided he was in a fowl enough mood, he'd rather deal with this himself.

He darted silently across the hall to his dad's office.

The room was dark and stuffy, but Cole ignored his surroundings and went straight for the drawer with the gun. He slid it open noiselessly. It would be kept oiled for just such an occasion. For once, his dad's paranoia had come in handy. Except that the drawer was empty.

A bang came from the direction of the kitchen. Cole

grabbed a poker from the fireplace as his next best option and checked the foyer again before sliding out the door and moving back through the hall.

Rolling his feet along the floor from his heels to his toes, he took long slow breaths until he reached the kitchen door. He pressed himself against the wall and listened. There was more noise. A dish on the counter.

The door was partially open, but whoever was in there wasn't in his line of sight. Cole put a flat hand on the door and eased it open.

The door pulled open from under Cole's hand, and his muscles coiled to strike.

"Master Cole!" yelped a tall slim man in a black suit. The coffee he had been carrying was now soaking into the white shirt underneath his suit.

Cole let out his tension in a long, slow breath. "Brian." He leaned his weapon against the wall. "Brian, I'm so sorry. I wasn't expecting you to be here. I thought with my dad gone, he wouldn't need his butler."

Brian's face was serious, but there were laugh lines around his mouth. He smoothed his hand along his comb-over and a smile slid up his face. "It's good to see you, sir. My apologies for the mess."

"No, it's my fault."

Brian glanced down at the poker and lifted his eyebrows. "You've become a very capable young man. I'm pleased I wasn't an intruder." He flicked the cloth napkin out from underneath the empty cup with an expert hand and began dabbing at his chest. "I thought you'd like a coffee after your trip. I'll make another and then clean this mess."

"That's not necessary. I had one on the way over." Cole was actually dying for a coffee, but he didn't want to put Brian through the trouble. He had grown up with the butler in the house, but the man felt more like a friend than a servant. "It's really good to see a familiar face."

"I expect, sir, that you will see quite a few over the coming days."

"Then maybe I should add *kind* to that description."

"I rather think there are many who remember you fondly."

Cole harrumphed and looked around the room. "I expected the place to be abandoned."

"Mr. Beverly suggested I stay until the estate is wrapped up."

"Is he making sure you are compensated?"

"Yes, of course. Can I get you anything before I clean up, sir?"

"No, thank you. I'm going to go into the study and get a feel for things."

"Very good, sir. Let me know if you need anything."

"Brian?"

"Yes?"

"Can you call me Cole? I've been out of this world for a while and I find 'sir' makes me uncomfortable. You are a good man who works hard, and to me, we are on the same level."

Brian paused, then said, "Certainly ... Cole." Cole noticed a flinch in the man's face but hoped Brian would get used to it after so many years serving his father, who never would have let him speak so casually.

·   ·   ·

Back at the door to his dad's office, he paused this time before entering. Now that the threat was gone, a heaviness settled on him. This was where his dad spent most of his time. Growing up, Cole had rarely spoken to him outside this room. Most of their conversations here were cold and often filled Cole with a sense of rage or disappointment.

He pushed his shoulders back and stepped over the threshold.

Dark heavy curtains were completely covering the windows, and the room smelled like moldy books and liquor.

He went straight for the windows and pushed the curtains aside, letting in a wide swath of light that made rivulets of dust visible. He turned and looked at the disarray in the room, some of which had been hidden in the gloom.

"Brian," Cole called out. He heard the clack of footsteps across the marble floors.

"Yes, sir?"

"Cole."

"Yes … Cole?"

"Has anyone been in this room recently?"

"No, sir. Your father spent less and less time in here, and he requested that the maid no longer clean it."

"Do you know why?"

Brian hesitated. "May I speak honestly?"

"Please."

"Brutally?"

Cole brought a hand to his chin. "Yes, please."

"I believe your father had a lot of regrets. He saw this room as a purgatory of sorts, and he couldn't decide if he belonged here or not. He missed you, Cole."

Cole was doubtful. More likely, Brian's fondness for Cole clouded his judgment.

"Thanks for your thoughts. I don't think I'll need anything further today, so you can go home and change out of your wet clothes and take the rest of the day off."

"Thank you. I've already made sure there is dinner in the fridge if you are able to heat it?"

"I've been living on my own for a few years now. I think I got it."

Brian reddened. "Of course. Will you be staying here tonight?"

"I wasn't going to, but now, looking at everything I have to get done, it might be simpler."

"I will prepare your father's room before I leave."

"No, please, I'd prefer the guest room."

"Very well. I will be back in the morning." Brian turned to go but then stopped and turned back. "May I?" he said, pointing at the desk.

Cole nodded and watched as Brian wrote a phone number on a piece of paper. "This is my number. Call me if you need anything. Anything at all."

"Thanks."

Brian turned on his heel and went out of the room.

Cole watched him till he was out of sight then cast his eyes around the room, allowing them to settle on the desk. There were various piles of papers and two filing cabinets he'd have to go through and decide what to pass on to the lawyer and if there was anything family related he needed to deal with.

He walked around and sat in his dad's chair, running his hands along the well-worn surface. He rested his elbows on the desk, then linked his fingers, and rested his mouth on his fingers, blowing out slowly. This was going to be a long couple of days.

He pulled open all the drawers. The top left one had the revolver in it. He wondered what made his dad move it. Cole pulled it out and checked. It was loaded. He took the bullets out and laid them back in the drawer, then checked the one below it. There were some photos with a flask on top. He lifted the bottle, unscrewed the lid, and smelled it. Whiskey. He shuffled through the photos. They were family pictures mostly. Formal photos from when his mom was still around. There were also a couple of him he had sent to his dad when he was in training. He leaned back in the chair and stared at them, glanced up at the whiskey, then back at the photos. His jaw clenched, and he tossed the liquor back in the drawer. It bumped something at the back. He reached in and pulled out a small ledger with lists of numbers and initials with dates. He ran a finger down the page, then turned to the next one. It meant nothing. He tossed it back in the drawer and ran his hands through his hair. If he were a less responsible person, he'd get on the next flight to LA and leave it all behind.

He slammed his hands on the table just as the phone shrilled the noise he recognized as the buzzer for the gate.

"Shit." The last thing he needed was company. He

moved to the panel with a screen showing the gate. He could see the driver of the taxi but not his fare.

Cole picked up the phone to speak to the driver. "Can I help you?"

The back door opened, and a woman stepped out, waving with her fingers to the camera. Cole tapped the phone on his forehead and swore under his breath. "Come through." He pushed the button to open the gate.

He considered letting Brian answer the door, but it would be better just to get it over with as quickly as possible. He waited in the office until the doorbell rang. Brian appeared in the hall as Cole walked to the door.

"Don't worry, I've got it."

Brian stopped and waited, his face guarded. Cole smiled briefly as he reached for the door, thankful that Brian had his back, but didn't hold the smile when he opened the door.

There was an arrogance in the way the woman at the door stood, but her face softened when she saw Cole, then paled.

Cole clicked his tongue and sighed. "Hello, Samantha."

Chapter 3

"THAT'S NOT QUITE the hello I was expecting," the woman said, pressing a hand to her throat. She was trying hard to look confident, but her eyes were jittery.

Cole looked at Brian. "Thanks, Brian. I'll handle it from here."

Brian bowed his head and went back to preparing the guest room.

"Aren't you going to invite me in?" Samantha smiled with thin lips.

Cole stepped aside, and she ambled in, lifting her head to take in her surroundings. "In all these years, this place hasn't changed." She was dressed like money, but Cole saw the shabbiness in what she wore. It couldn't be called gaudy, but there was something counterfeit about it.

"Samantha." He punctuated the name. "Why are you here?"

"*Samantha.*" She sighed. "You can't call me mom?"

"I haven't seen you in how many years? And suddenly you're my mom again?"

Her eyes flitted about the room as she tried to ignore his question. "So, how are you?"

"Why are you here?"

"I thought you would know."

"Well, I don't."

She pouted like it was a bother for her to explain. "Your father just died."

"And?"

"*And,* I'm here to pay my respects."

"Uh-huh."

"And to see my long-lost son."

"I was never lost."

She opened her mouth to speak when a flash of fear crossed her face and was gone. She grunted with exasperation and walked toward the back of the house. Cole followed, and they entered the kitchen. She pulled a cabinet open then closed it and moved to the next. Cole crossed his arms and leaned against the island.

"Surely your father has wine around her somewhere."

Cole went to the other side of the room to a chrome door and pulled it open. "You still drink red?"

She turned with her hand still on a cabinet door. "You remembered."

Cole grunted and uncorked the bottle, pouring her a small glass. He slid it across the counter. She eyed the glass but didn't take it. Cole clicked his tongue, pulled the glass back and filled it halfway, then set the bottle aside to indicate he was done. Samantha picked it up, a tremor in her hand, and gulped it back. Setting it down, she picked up the bottle and filled it nearly to the top.

Cole shook his head. "You haven't changed much."

"You won't join me for a drink?"

"I don't drink."

Samantha's eyebrows shot up. "That surprises me."

"Why?"

"Well, looking at your father and mother … You obviously didn't get that gene. Or maybe it's because of us that you avoid it?" Her voice softened at the question. She was searching for an opening to connect, but Cole wouldn't give it to her.

"Don't flatter yourself. I made my own messes and made my own decisions to clean up those messes. I'm an adult and don't need to blame you and dad for my choices."

Samantha set her glass back down on the counter. "I'm glad." Her voice was low. "That makes me happy to know you're doing well."

"I'm not doing it to make you happy." He felt juvenile saying something so petty, but he was adamant he would not give her any leverage to get close to him.

She stared into her drink. Her hand shook again, and she pressed it into the counter. "Since you hate me anyway — " she said into her glass.

" — I don't hate you."

"What do you call it?" she fired back, but flinched. "I'm sorry."

"Why are you here?" There was a desperation to the question that Cole hadn't meant to let out.

"I — " She pressed her lips together, then lifted her

drink and didn't stop till she had drained it.

Cole couldn't help the cringe on his face. "There's no reason for you to be here. I'll call a taxi and you can show yourself out."

He turned and walked back toward the office.

"Cole, wait, I can't leave until — "

She marched after him, but then Cole stopped and she nearly ran into him. He turned angrily, and she jumped back. "I've got enough on my plate right now without having to work out your motives. Please, just leave me alone."

Her whole body sagged. "I'm sorry, Cole, I … " Her tongue was heavy. The wine was finding its way into her bloodstream, and Cole couldn't help but soften his voice. "Forget it. There's been a lot of water under the bridge. Just leave things as they are." He walked to a sitting room with her tailing behind. He pointed at the couch while he called a cab.

Samantha was picking at her lip when he hung up the phone.

"The taxi won't be long," Cole said, looking out the window and willing it to hurry.

She dropped her hands into her lap. "You have to know, I would have fought for you if I could have."

"What?"

"Your father never would have let me have you. I had nothing to fight with, and he had everything. He didn't care that you were only ten, and you needed your mother. He just wanted to hurt me."

"Mom. Stop. It doesn't matter."

"It does. You need to know I didn't leave you. Not

because I wanted to. But that doesn't mean it wasn't my fault." She closed her eyes tightly and clenched her fists. "I had an affair." Her face puckered up like she expected to get slapped.

Cole wouldn't give her the satisfaction. "That's why he made you leave." It wasn't a question.

"The man I got involved with used me to get to your father. At least, that's what he told me."

"I see. So I can take responsibility for my actions but you can't take any for yours?"

"No — that's not what I mean. Your father and I were struggling. I was vulnerable." She stood and walked over to the empty fireplace. "I'm not saying he forced me, but … he only did it to poke at your father. I was so stupid."

"*Poke* at him?"

"He's a man who needs to be in control."

"Why are you telling me this?"

"I didn't want to."

"Then why are you? It's actually none of my business, and I'd rather not know."

She frowned but didn't respond.

The phone shrilled in response to someone at the gate. Cole didn't bother confirming it was the taxi, he just lifted the phone and punched in the code.

"Taxi's here."

"There's something else."

Cole could tell by the lilt in her voice that the rest of the wine was working its way to her head. "Make it quick, the taxi is waiting."

She took her time and swallowed before continuing.

"It — it was with a man named Silas Lincoln." She finally forced out.

"Shit, mom. Are you kidding me?" The temper that had been simmering away burst out in an instant.

She was on the verge of crying. Pain marred her face. "I'm so sorry," she breathed.

Cole's face darkened as he got himself back under control. "How do you know that name means anything to me?"

"I'm … I don't."

It took him one big step to cross the room and grab her arm. "Tell me."

"I can't, Cole, please." The taxi's horn blared. "The taxi is waiting. I have to go." She wrenched her arm out of his grip and wobbled toward the door.

As Samantha walked away, Cole realized he already knew the answer. Silas had put her up to confessing this now, while his nerves were raw. He had used Samantha to hurt his dad, and now he was using her again.

He stood still with his fists clenched until he heard the crunching of tires on the gravel, then he went back to the window and watched the cab pull away. Telling him that had cost her a lot, although it shouldn't have. If she had slept with anyone else, it wouldn't have mattered to him. At least that's what he told himself.

"I'm going now," Brian said from behind, startling him.

Cole composed himself quickly. "Thanks, Brian. I'll see you tomorrow."

"Is everything okay?"

Cole shook his head. "No, it's not."

"Is there anything I can do?"

"Unfortunately not." Cole smiled. "It'll be fine."

Brian bowed and walked away.

Cole intended to go back to the office, but he couldn't face it. Instead, he remained in the sitting room and looked at the couch where his mom had been sitting.

What he wanted more than anything was for Bristol to be there with him. He pictured her sitting with him on the couch, curled up in front of a fire, but that picture created a longing he couldn't satiate.

He walked back over to the window and slapped a flat hand on the wall. He needed to take his mind off her.

He glanced over to where a couple of crystal decanters sat on a small glass table in the corner of the room. He walked over and took the lid off one, then put it back on, but took it off again and poured himself a small glass. He tipped it back in one swig and coughed at the burn. He poured himself another and knocked it back. He looked at the empty glass and grimaced.

"Walk away," he said to himself. He set the glass down and went to his room. He was thankful to see there was a TV mounted on the wall. Making himself comfortable on a pile of pillows, he switched on the news and allowed himself to drift. The swirl of alcohol in his brain after so many years helped.

In what felt like only a moment later, his ringing phone ripped him out of sleep. He sprang out of bed and jumped for the dresser where he had left it, hoping it was Bristol. It wasn't.

"Andrew, hey."

"Cole, I'm outside your house, where are you? Are you with Bristol?" He sounded distressed.

"Unfortunately not. My dad just died. I'm in Chicago."

"Oh. Cole, I'm sorry."

"It's fine. I wasn't that close to him if you remember." Cole rested his head in his hand. The alcohol was making his head fuzzy.

"I know, but that doesn't make it easy. And I'm afraid to say I'm calling with bad news."

Cole groaned. "Bad news is the last thing I need. Is it important bad news?"

"That's why I'm at your house. I'd rather speak to you about it in person, but I guess that's not going to happen. I've got a friend in the DA's office. I've asked him to keep me apprised of what's happening on the inside."

"Don't tell me."

"Silas's lawyers are trying to get your recording of Silas's confession thrown out."

Cole slammed his hand on top of the dresser and started pacing the room. "They can't do that. What's the argument?"

"That you were trespassing and an ex-cop should know better."

"Son of a bitch."

"Yeah. I told you before he was a slippery devil."

"Does your friend at the DA's think they have a shot?"

"Unfortunately for us, it's with Judge Lions, and he's

been on a crusade against evidence that's been improperly obtained. So, yeah. It doesn't look good. You'll need to let Bristol know."

Cole wrenched his arm back, intending to throw the phone against the wall, but stopped himself at the last second. He put it back to his ear. "Thanks for letting me know. I've gotta go. I'll call you later." He hung up on Andrew before any goodbyes and slammed the phone on the dresser, storming out of the bedroom

"God dammit!" he bellowed at the vaulted ceiling. He grumbled his way into the sitting room and poured himself another drink. It was enough to take a couple swallows to finish, and he nearly choked on it. After he drained the glass, he hurled it into the fireplace. The glass exploded and sent shards skipping along the floor in a cascade. Cole flopped onto the couch and hung his head. The anger coursing through him was undoing him. He knew the feeling well, which did nothing but add a sliver of guilt to the pile of emotions he was already trying to restrain.

He went back to his room and fumbled through his bag for sweatpants and a sweatshirt. He'd go for a run and work the liquor out of his system. The cold air would do him some good.

But first he had to make a phone call.

Chapter 4

BRISTOL SAT in bed against the wall, picking at her fingernail. She had managed only a few fitful hours of sleep before jumping awake, expecting to be locked in a cage.

After saying goodbye to Cole in the early hours of the morning, she had found herself at loose ends and spent several hours watching movies. Or more accurately, staring at the screen while the movies played.

Cole sent her a text around lunch to let her know he had arrived, but she hadn't heard from him since. She reached for her phone now to check for any messages that she already knew wouldn't be there. She unlocked the phone and brought up his number, her finger poised over the call button.

She practiced her greeting. "Hey, Cole. How are you … Hey, how are you feeling? Hi, Cole. What have you been … Ugh." She tossed the phone down on the bed beside her and drew a disgusted breath. She'd seen how silly some women could be around men. She never thought she'd be one of them. There was something developing between her and Cole, but if it meant that her brain would become a pile of goo, it wasn't worth it.

She threw the blanket off and jumped out of bed, but as she attempted to stand, her head started spinning and she sat back down.

Despite having been in countless awful situations over the years, she was still shaky from her abduction the other night. As she scrubbed a hand down her face, it occurred to her that it wasn't the other night. It was last night. It should have faded into the background like everything else, but with Lila and Cole involved, it had taken its toll. Not to mention her fear of being controlled by Silas. The thought brought bile to her throat.

She reached her hand to the back of her shoulder, prodding the raw wound gently. Getting over that experience would not happen in a couple of hours sleep. She couldn't imagine what Cole must be going through, dealing with his father's death in the middle of it. At least he wasn't the one kidnapped.

"Although I did shoot him," she said to the wall.

She hadn't had a choice, but if he hadn't been wearing that vest … she shook her head and tried to stand again. Taking it slow, she headed for the shower.

As she stood under the spray, she pushed the picture of Cole lying shot on the ground out of her head and instead pictured him at the café before he had to leave, which reminded her of his kiss. Her face flushed, but she couldn't deny that she felt good about him. Everything else had been hell, but having him there in her mind soothed her. And that kiss. It lasted only a second, but still lingered.

She turned the water off. These thoughts would not do. She'd have to keep herself busy. Pining after Cole was not an option.

She got dressed quickly and got her usual tea to go. She needed a friendly face.

When she arrived at Eli's gym, the evening sun turned the sky to shades of purple and orange. She scanned the room before walking in. There were a few people scattered throughout the room working their way through various routines. Eli was hanging off the ropes talking to a couple of young guys wearing headgear and boxing gloves. They were leaning toward him, listening eagerly. Eli had a way with young people. She had idolized him as a teenager. She still did, in her own way. But he felt more like a dad these days.

Bristol walked over and leaned on the rope next to Eli.

She recognized Sam, Eli's latest protégé, with his hair poking out in every direction through the small holes of the headgear.

"Hey, guys," she said, dropping an arm over the rope.

"Huhh wif — wif." Sam was trying to talk through his mouth guard. He spit it out into his glove. "Hi, Bristol," he finally managed to get out.

"Hey, Sam. How are you? Feeling better after I kicked your ass?" she teased.

He laughed and started bouncing on his feet. "I want a rematch."

"Any time little fella'." She winked at him.

The other guy punched Sam in the arm. "She kicked your ass? You wuss."

Eli cleared his throat. "Sam's downfall, Brennan, was that he underestimated his opponent like you're doing right now. If it were you and Sam in a match against her, all my money would be on her."

Brennan sized her up. "She doesn't look that tough to me," he said, knocking his gloves together.

Bristol rolled her neck. "Oh please, Eli, may I? It's just what I need after the day I've had."

Eli looked up at Brennan. "Now look what you've done." He turned to Bristol. "He's got a lot of talent, so try not to break him permanently."

Brennan started bouncing on his feet and moving around the ring. Sam separated the ropes and climbed out, allowing Bristol to climb in. "It's your funeral, man. I'm going to enjoy this." He tapped Bristol on the arm. "Don't go easy on him like you did me."

Bristol smiled wickedly.

"You don't want any gear?" Eli asked.

"Won't need it. This won't take long."

Brennan jumped toward her then back, an insolent smirk on his face. "You're not even dressed for a fight."

"No? When I'm out on the street kicking ass, I'm not usually dressed for a fight either." Bristol didn't bother jumping around. She sidestepped lightly, one foot behind the other, her arms hanging by her side.

She circled around Brennan until he took an experimental jab at her. She swept her arm up, swatting it away. He took another more forceful jab that she avoided, then she reached up and slapped him on the side of the head.

The smirk left his face. "At this rate it'll take all night," Brennan said, slowing down. She took the opportunity and reached out, slapping him in the head again before he could block. "So it's gonna be pissy little baby slaps is it? It'll take more than that to bring me down."

"Will you stop talking and fight me?" She slapped him again and watched his countenance change from insulting to angry, which is what she was aiming for. Emotion was a brilliant tool to use against your opponent. She had always been very good at it, until Silas.

The memory of Silas distracted her enough that she didn't fully avoid the right hook that bloodied her lip. She almost laughed at the look of triumph on Brennan's face. She touched her tongue to her lip. The metallic taste brought her back to herself and cooled her blood for the fight.

She went in for another slap, knowing he was waiting for it and that he'd block it. When he did, her leg shot up and caught him on his side, hard enough that he stepped back and scowled.

"Here we go," she said under her breath.

He came at her then, overzealous as expected. She used his uncontrolled momentum to send him into the ropes. When he swung back at her she did a roundhouse kick that sent him to the mat. He got up fast and threw himself into her at waist level, flattening her. He raised a glove to punch her in the head, but she hauled her legs up and flipped him over the top of her, then spun around on top of him, pinning him to the ground. She wasn't strong enough to restrain him for long without stunning him, and she didn't want to hurt him so jumped up quickly and retreated.

Brennan got up a bit slower than before, but now he was full of rage. Eli saw it and stepped into the ring. "Time," he said, spreading his hands between the two. "Bristol, I'll see you in my office. I want to have a word with Brennan."

Bristol nodded and held out a hand to Brennan, but he batted it away. Eli would have a long road with him. Sam was a good kid with a light inside of him. Brennan, on the other hand, he was angry. But then so was she. If anyone could teach him to control it, Eli was the one to do it.

Bristol made herself at home on the couch as she always did and waited. When Eli came in, he looked discouraged.

"You think you'll be able to work with him?" Bristol asked, hopeful.

"I knew he was a handful, but your fight with him showed me a bit more of what's going on under the surface. I'll need to wait till he cools down before I can find out whether or not he's malleable."

"You always did know how to pick 'em. I seem to recall a young girl in your care who had some anger issues."

Eli shook his head. "Yours were different. You were hurting and didn't know how to handle it. His has a sadistic edge that I'm unsure about. Anyway, what's going on with you?"

"What makes you think something is going on?"

"Like Brennan said, you aren't dressed for the gym. You never come not dressed for the gym."

"Today I just need someone to talk to. Although getting in the ring helped me work off some stuff. "

"Okay … so what's going on? Does this have something to do with Cole?"

Bristol looked at him suspiciously. "What makes you think that?"

Eli laughed. "You never come to me just to talk."

"Should I go?" she teased.

"No, I'm impressed with the change. It just made me wonder if it was related to someone in particular."

"Well, maybe, but a lot has happened since I saw you last."

"I'm all ears."

She put her feet up on the coffee table. "I actually had a really horrible night last night."

"Then why do you seem giddy?"

"I'm not giddy," Bristol growled.

"You got this weird smile on your face when I mentioned Cole."

"Did I?"

"It's Cole."

"Okay fine, but that's not what I'm here to talk to you about, so get that smug look off your face."

Eli pinched his lips together to stop smiling and cleared his throat. "So what happened last night that was so horrible."

"Well, to start off with, I was kidnapped by a child-trafficking ring."

Eli sat up straight. "You're serious?"

"Yes, but I mean, obviously it turns out okay 'cause I'm here." Eli just stared at her, so she continued. "Cole found me and together we stopped the guys who were doing it, but not before I shot Cole." Eli's eyes widened. "He's okay. He was wearing a vest, but it turned out this guy — "

"Wait, wait, wait. You shot Cole? On purpose?"

"Only because I didn't have a choice."

"Did you know he was wearing a vest?"

"You always ask the worst questions. No, I didn't know."

"But you shot him anyway?"

"It was complicated. But you ask Cole. He was fine with it."

"I'll take your word for it."

"But the bad guy, Silas Lincoln, he was going to get away with it, but Cole recorded his conversation, so now the guy's been arrested and it's all fine, but then Cole's dad died so he had to go to Chicago. So here I am, trying to rest, but after everything I've just been through, I'm finding it difficult to settle down." Eli continued to look at her, saying nothing, but with his mouth hanging half open. "Aren't you going to say anything?"

"Cole's dad died?"

"Yeah, he just had a massive heart attack last night. I guess a lot happened last night."

"Is Cole all right?"

Bristol shrugged. "He wasn't very close to his dad, but, you know, it's still his dad."

"Wow, okay. You're right. A lot has happened since I saw you last. So, how did you feel after shooting Cole?"

"Why are we going back to that?"

"Because that's what's bothering you."

"No, Cole is fine."

"But you're not."

"Weren't you listening? I said everything is okay. I am a little shaken up. That's why I'm here. You're my friendly face. But I'll be fine. I just need some time and some sleep."

"Have you spoken to him since he left? How's he doing now that he's in Chicago? Especially if last night went how you say it did, he must be shattered."

Bristol dropped her head. "Yeah. I don't know. I haven't spoken to him."

"You haven't spoken to him?"

"I'm not going to call him. I don't want to bother him. He can call me if he wants to talk to me."

"That's the stupidest thing I've ever heard."

"Hey, I barely know the guy."

"If it were me, I'd want my wife to call."

"But that's because she's your wife."

"I mean before she was my wife."

Bristol shook her head. "We aren't at that place. I'm not going to call him."

"Okay, it's your choice." Eli planted his hands on his legs and used the momentum to stand.

"Yes, it is."

"You're welcome to hang out here for a while. I'm going to go back out and see if I can't knock some sense into Brennan. Make yourself at home."

"Thanks, Eli. I will."

"You're sure you're okay?"

"Yes, I am now. I'm here."

He looked at her again before walking out the door and shook his head with a smile.

"What?" Her voice was raised in mock indignation.

Eli laughed. "Nothin'." Then he left the room.

Bristol leaned her head back onto the couch and counted the tiles on the ceiling. She was completely spent from the inside out, but her eyelids refused to budge. Every time she closed them, they popped back open. The sounds from the gym were strangely soothing, and knowing Eli was out there eased her mind a fraction more than it had been.

Her phone rang, startling her. When she saw who it was, her stomach flipped, which was irritating. She let it ring a couple times before answering. "Hello?"

Chapter 5

"BRISTOL ... "

She listened to him breathing. "Cole? You okay?"

"It's so good to hear your voice." He was sluggish.

"Yeah, you too. Everything all right?" she asked cautiously.

"I just … I wish you were here."

She did too but wouldn't say it. "I'm not sure there is anything I can do." She remembered Eli's words. "But if you need to talk."

"Just you, Bristol. Just being you, but here. I wish you were right here."

"You … um … you sure you're okay? You sound a little odd."

His voice went sharp. "Why, because I'm telling you how I feel? You've always had a problem with that. Is it because I kissed you?"

His sudden change in tone startled her more than the mention of the kiss. "No, Cole. I — "

" — If I could have, I would have kissed you a thousand times by now. You're just cold sometimes, Bristol. You need to lighten up."

"Uh … "

Cole sighed loudly into the phone. "I got some bad news from Andrew."

"Okay."

"It's Silas's lawyers. Sounds like they're throwing out my recording of Silas."

Bristol jumped up. "They can't do that!"

"They can and they will. I'm — I think I'm gonna go for a run. God, I just want to smash his head in."

"Cole … " Bristol's stomach plummeted as she suddenly recognized what was off about him. "Have you been drinking?"

"What makes you say that?"

"You have."

"I'm not working."

"I don't think that's the best way to handle this situation."

"No? How would you handle your father dying after you stopped a madman and then having that man go free? Not to mention finding out that your mother had an affair with the aforementioned madman?"

"Your mom?"

"Forget it."

"That would have been hard to hear. I'm so sorry. How did you find out?"

"I said forget it."

"You say you want me there, but right now I'm really glad I'm not. It does make you different. The alcohol. And I know you'd handle this, all of it, better without having your judgment clouded."

Cole was silent for a moment. When he spoke again his voice was low and hard. "I'm sorry, Bristol. I forgot how good you are at handling everything difficult in your life." Cole laughed laconically. "I'll take a leaf out of your book, push everyone who cares about me away."

"I think you're doing a pretty good job at that right now."

"Not really. I said I need to push away the people who care about me. I'm not sure that you do."

"Of course I care about you, Cole. I'm just trying to help."

"Well, I'm just doing the best I can."

"I'm sorry." Bristol's eyes were burning. She closed them, trying to clear her head. It wasn't working. "So what do we do now?"

"How the hell should I know?"

"What is wrong with you? You know, you're a real asshole when you're drunk. Call me later." She hung up the phone so she didn't have to listen to him anymore. She had been giddy, like Eli said. Especially when she saw it was him calling. Now she felt sick.

Silas going free should have bothered her the most, and while that news created a black hole in the bottom of her stomach, her conversation with Cole stung clear and deep. Maybe the kiss was a mistake. She should have known better than to let someone get into a position where they could hurt her. At least with Silas, she knew where she stood.

A clutter of emotions grabbed at her throat. She hugged herself around the middle, not willing to let it out, but in the end she couldn't hold it. She slid to the floor where she was sure no one could see her and cried until her eyes were swollen and her insides felt like they were on the outside. Then she hoisted herself back onto the couch and lay down on her side, tucking her arms tightly against her chest, and when she closed her eyes, this time, they stayed closed.

When Cole finally managed to pry his eyes open, the curtains glowed with the morning sun. He was sprawled across the bed, still in his sweats. The night air had done him good last night, even though he hadn't been able to go far in the state he was in, his head whirring with the alcohol. When he lay down after his run, he hadn't moved until morning.

One arm was tucked under him, and as he slid it out, pins and needles cascaded into his fingers. He rolled over onto his back and scrunched up his face as the change in blood flow sent last night's indiscretion thudding across his head. He needed to get himself hydrated. After not having touched a drop in so many years, it had more effect on him than he expected.

He reached his half-paralyzed arm across the bed to the clock to spin it around, swatting it several times with his tingling fingers before succeeding. It was 7:00 a.m. and he had a big day ahead of him. Richard had worked hard to get the funeral organized quickly. It was scheduled for tomorrow, and he still had a mass of paperwork to wade through. Not to mention Andrew's call weighed on him heavily.

He pressed a hand onto his forehead. He forgot to call Bristol. Then he remembered he had. "Oh, shit."

He jumped up and grabbed his phone but was attacked by another onslaught of stabbing pain that had him seeing spots. He dropped onto the bed and pressed his fingers over his eyes then let out a slow breath. Once his focus returned, he brought up her number but then dropped the phone on the bed. She might be sleeping.

He pressed a hand over his eyes. Even though he didn't want to wake her, it was more an excuse than he cared to admit. He had no idea what he could say to her to fix it. He was so tired of there always being a barrier between them, and now he had made it worse.

Little snippets of conversation came back to him, and dread settled in his gut. He was so afraid he had ruined everything between them, he was close to flying back to LA that morning. But she wasn't the only person in his life that needed dealing with, and as much as he needed to get back to LA to fix things with Bristol, if he didn't get her off his mind, he'd never get his father's affairs sorted out.

He cautiously rose off the bed, trying to manage the lashings across his forehead, and headed for the shower.

∞

Bristol woke up and tried to roll off her side but found she couldn't. Her arm that was pressed underneath her body ached terribly. In a panic she threw her free arm out with a timed kicked as she attempted to sit up. By the time she had focused her defense and realized where she was, she had knocked a mug, along with its contents, across the table and onto the floor. She let out a trembling breath and pulled at the blanket that had wrapped up around her legs. She fisted it and threw it aside.

She took a minute to settle her heart rate. The lights were on in the gym, but it was empty. She ran her hands down her face as she stood and walked to the front door. It was locked. She closed her eyes, trying to calibrate her thoughts. For a brief, terrifying second, she was sure she was losing it.

She pushed her fingers into her closed eyes to wipe away the fuzz then looked up at the clock on the wall. 8:00. There were always people in there until well past eight at night.

Taking a deep breath, she turned and went for the door to Eli's apartment. It would most likely be locked as well, but it was worth a shot. When she reached the door, it opened in front of her and nearly caught her on the shoulder.

"Bristol. You're awake."

"Yeah, what's going on? Why is the place locked up? You didn't kick everyone out just because I fell asleep, did you?"

"Well, no. I mean, I did want to give you time to sleep, but I'm also just late getting around to unlocking it. Besides, the customers can wait. Did you sleep well?"

"Wait, I'm … " She put her hands on her head. "What time is it?"

Eli looked around her at the clock on the wall. "Just past 8:00." He saw the confused look on her face and added, "In the morning."

Her hands fell to her side. "I slept here all night?"

"After I finished up with the boys, I brought you a cup of tea and tried to wake you, but you wouldn't budge, so I just put a blanket on you and let you go. After the ordeal you'd been through, I figured you needed it."

"Oh, the tea. I just spread it all over your office. Woke up and didn't know where I was, so I panicked for a fraction of a second."

"Only a fraction? I'll get a towel."

"No, I'll get one. Sorry I didn't do it sooner. I was just so confused." She grabbed what she needed from a nearby locker. When she turned, Eli took the towel from her. "You can sit and rest. Get your head back into order."

"Apparently I've just had a big rest. And I don't mind cleaning up my own messes." She followed Eli into the office.

"Well, rest some more. From what you said, you have a lot of it to catch up on." Eli started wiping. "You heard from Cole?"

"Ugh, don't remind me." She flopped onto the couch.

Eli stopped what he was doing and looked up at her. "What could have possibly happened between yesterday and today to change your mood so drastically?"

"So much you just wouldn't believe me."

"That seems to be the running theme for you at the moment. Why don't you try me?"

"Well, for one thing, it looks like Silas might go free after all."

"The guy who kidnapped you? The one who just got arrested for the child-trafficking ring?"

"Yeah, his lawyers are getting that recording thrown out."

"There isn't other evidence against him?"

"No."

"How is that possible?"

"It just is. He's a very smart man."

"That's bad."

"Yeah."

"Really bad."

"I know. It might be the only evidence they have to convict him."

"But that's not what's bothering you."

She groaned. It was irritating how Eli could always see straight through her. "Yes, it is." She tried to throw him off anyway. "That's the worst possible thing that could be happening right now."

"I agree, but talking about that doesn't give you the same anguished look you had just a moment ago."

"How can you possibly know me that well? I used to be so good at hiding everything."

"You are good, but I'm better."

Bristol let out a sharp breath. "Cole called."

"I gathered."

"He was drunk, and he's not a nice drunk."

"I wouldn't have picked him for a drinker."

"He's not. Or at least he wasn't. Not since he was younger."

"When did he start drinking again?"

"I just told you."

Eli looked at her sideways. "Last night?"

"Yes."

"Last night was the first time he'd had a drink since he was younger?"

"Yes."

"You're sure?"

"Yes," Bristol nearly shouted.

"How can you be so sure?"

Her voice remained raised. "Because he told me all about it, and he's not the type of guy to make up stuff like that."

"So you trust him." He wasn't asking a question and Bristol saw, too late, the trap he had led her into.

She sank into the couch. "Why are you on his side?"

"I'm not on anyone's side. I'm just trying to help you see through your hurt."

Bristol shook her head. "He can't afford to make a mistake. Not right now."

"I see."

"What?"

"Nothing. I'm going to go throw this towel in the wash."

Bristol didn't have the energy to pursue him so let him go, forcing her mind to go blank while he was gone.

When Eli returned, he had a bowl of cereal. He set it on the coffee table. "Eat that."

"I don't eat cereal. Or breakfast for that matter."

"I don't care. I'd bet this gym that you haven't eaten in a while and it's muesli, so it will give you energy."

Bristol sighed but obeyed. She put a spoonful in her mouth. "This tastes like cardboard."

"Sorry, I didn't have any Lucky Charms."

She hated to admit that Eli was right, but she really was starving. On the matter of Cole, however, she would hold out.

By the time she finished, Eli had opened up the gym and a few people were already working out.

Bristol brought her bowl through to Eli's apartment and washed up, then found him again before she left.

"I'm gonna head home and freshen up. Thanks again."

"You don't have to thank me."

"Yes, I do. I had a better sleep here than I could have gotten at home, and it's only because you're so good to me and I know I'm safe here." She smiled and squeezed his arm, her hand barely curving around his bicep. "Oh, you've been working out. Beth must be enjoying it." She laughed and slapped him on the arm before leaving.

"You look after yourself. And let me know if there is anything you need."

"I will."

As she walked out the door, Eli added. "And think about giving Cole a break."

She fumbled for her keys in her bag, pretending she didn't hear him and kept walking, but when her keys continued to elude her, she stopped.

"Dammit." She tucked her hair behind her ear and

shifted things around in her bag. The keys moved into view at the same time she caught movement out of the corner of her eye. She started moving toward her car and let go of her car keys in favor of her sunglasses. She slipped them on in order to take in her periphery without being obvious. A woman, about her own age, in a dark suit and mirrored sunglasses with her hair pulled back into a tight ponytail, approached slowly.

Chapter 6

JUDGING THE DISTANCE, Bristol could see she wouldn't make it to her car before the woman intercepted, so she stopped walking and pushed her sunglasses up on her head to take in her full surroundings. No point hiding it anymore.

A man in a slightly darker suit with the same mirrored sunglasses approached her from the opposite direction.

She considered running back into the gym. She would have made it, but the last thing she wanted to do was involve Eli or his gym. Instead, she hoisted her bag onto her shoulder and held her arms out with her wrists together. She called out to the woman who was still a good twenty feet away. "Did you remember your handcuffs?"

The woman didn't miss a beat, just kept moving toward her. She walked like she wasn't in a hurry but her body was rigid and suggested she expected Bristol to run. Bristol saved her the trouble and just put her hands on her hips while she waited.

"Bristol Kelley?" the woman asked when she got close.

"The one and only."

"My name is Agent Bailey." She showed Bristol her badge and tipped her head toward the man. "This is my partner, Agent Tellis."

"I can get one of those off eBay," Bristol said, tipping her head toward the badge. "How do I know it's real?"

"I guess you'll just have to trust us," said the agent named Tellis.

Bristol ran her tongue along her teeth. "Or I could smash your face in," she said, before turning slowly to look at him.

Tellis laughed then leaned in toward Bristol. "You could try."

Bailey spread her arms between the two then took off her sunglasses. "That's enough. Bristol, we can do this the hard way or the easy way. But when the dust settles, the outcome will be the same." Bailey's eyes lifted over Bristol's shoulder back toward the gym. Bristol turned, already knowing what she would see.

Eli stood in the door with his arms crossed. She could tell from his stance, that if she indicated she was in trouble, he'd be ready to pound some heads for her. She ground her teeth. No matter what, she would not let her problems affect him. He didn't need to get caught up in whatever this was.

She forced a smile and waved to him. It took Eli a

couple second to reciprocate a flick of the wrist. He wasn't buying it, but he stayed put.

"All right, let's go." She looked at Agent Bailey. "Lead the way."

Agent Tellis put a hand on her elbow, and Bristol yanked it away. "That's unnecessary. If I had planned on running, I would have done it already. And you'd probably have lost me by now."

Agent Tells smirked but said nothing. He also didn't touch her again.

They approached an SUV with tinted windows. Bailey opened the door and Bristol turned back again to Eli, who had taken a couple of steps out the door. She smiled and waved again before getting into the vehicle. "I sure as hell hope you really are the FBI. I've already been kidnapped once already, and I'd rather not have to go through the ordeal again."

"We know about that ma'am, and I can assure you, we are real-life FBI agents."

"Well, thanks, lady. That sure makes me feel all warm and fuzzy on the insides now."

"The smart comments won't help your situation."

"Will they make it worse?"

"That depends."

"Until you tell me more about what's going on here, I will continue being a smart-ass because it's the only thing keeping me from losing my cool, which I imagine would definitely make my situation worse."

Tellis was driving. He turned back after starting the car. "You ladies finished?"

Bristol squinted at the woman next to her. "You put

up with his crap?"

Bailey crossed her arms. "You get used to it. Let's go."

Bristol's phone rang in her bag. She looked at Bailey and raised her eyebrows in question. Bailey shook her head and looked forward. Bristol wondered if it was Cole and was relieved she didn't have permission to answer the call. The thought of talking to him again made her stomach tighten, but the thought of talking to him in front of the two agents had her skin crawling.

Brian knocked on the office door, and Cole looked up from a pile of papers. "I brought you a sandwich, sir."

"Cole."

Brian smiled and shook his head. "That takes some getting used to."

"Is it lunchtime already?"

"It's just past 1:00."

Cole stretched his neck and back. "Thanks for the sandwich. I completely lost track of time. If you'll excuse me, I need to make a phone call."

Brian bowed and left the room.

With the phone in his hand, he stared down at another invoice he had found for Lincoln Enterprises. After his mom's confession about Silas, it surprised him that, according to the paperwork, his father continued to work with Silas over the years. Even up until recently there were correspondences between the two. The first thought that came to him was that his father may have been involved with the child-trafficking ring, but he immediately dismissed the idea. His dad was a hard man who had made Cole's life hell at times, but he wasn't a sick bastard.

More likely, he and Silas were involved in a semi-legitimate business scheme. But that still didn't explain why his dad kicked his wife out of the house but continued to do business with the man she had slept with. Silas must have been worth a lot of money to him.

He pushed the invoice aside and called Bristol. He had called her around 9:30 that morning, but the phone had gone through to voice mail. He wasn't relieved. He wanted to clear the air, but at the same time, he had gone through a hundred different things he could say to her. None of them was right.

The phone rang through to voice mail again. "Bristol, it's me again. Look. I'm sorry about last night. That was crazy of me. I'd really like to talk to you about it. Please call me back."

Cole gathered the paperwork scattered around him. His dad had retired years ago, and any paperwork relating to the business should have been at the office. Besides Lincoln Enterprises, there were correspondences with other businesses as well as military and government officials around the country, and he still had a couple more drawers to go through.

He picked up his phone and called his dad's lawyer.

"Cole, I'm glad you called. Everything is ready for the funeral, but I still hope you'll reconsider saying a few words."

"It's not going to happen, Richard. You know how I

feel about my father. But I do really appreciate all you are doing here. It takes an enormous weight off."

"That's what he paid me for."

Cole couldn't manage a laugh. "I have a question I'm hoping you can answer."

"I'll do my best."

"My dad has a lot of paperwork, invoices and correspondence, relating to his time running his business. I don't understand what it's all here for. Shouldn't it be at the office?"

Richard sighed. "The best thing you can do, Cole, is to destroy it."

"That's a concerning response."

"I know. I don't mean for it to be." The lawyer paused before continuing. "Your father had some questionable associates, but he also became paranoid at the end. He was gathering information regarding those he had worked with over the years. He mentioned blackmail once, but I don't think that's what it was for. I think it was for protection."

"He thought he was in danger from these guys?"

"He and you. He talked to me a few times about getting in touch with you to make sure you were protecting yourself. I was able to talk him out of it."

"I hate to sound paranoid myself, but you don't think there is a chance his death wasn't by natural causes? I happen to know some of those he was involved with and how dangerous they can be."

"It's unlikely. I don't think he was as big a threat as he thought he was. I don't like to say it, but I think you'd prefer me to speak plainly."

"Yes, thank you."

"He had a heart condition, and when he had the heart attack, his doctor wasn't surprised. I'm confident he died of natural causes."

"Thanks for being straight with me. This stuff is probably not worth sifting through too thoroughly then?"

"I wouldn't put much time into it if I were you, no."

"Great, because I'd like to get home sooner than later."

"If you'd like, I can send someone around to collect and go through the paperwork for you."

"I'll do what I can while I'm here because it keeps me busy, but I may take you up on that."

"Try to get some rest. I'll see you tomorrow."

"See you then."

Cole retrieved the ledger from the desk and flipped through it again. He couldn't make sense of it still, but if his dad was compiling evidence against different people, that's probably what this was for. Now, with his father gone, it would be useless. The ramblings of an irrational man.

He didn't like to think of his father like that, so he sat down with the ledger to see if he could make sense of anything, but after going through what seemed like reams of paper, he realized it was an impossible task without knowing specifically what he was looking for.

It felt like only minutes before Brian knocked on the door again. "Dinner is prepared and waiting for you in the kitchen. Would you like to have it brought in?"

Cole looked at him, then at the window. It was dark

outside. "Time flies when you're having fun. You can leave it in the kitchen. I'll get it later. Why don't you head home?"

"Thank you … Cole. And as before, please call if you need anything."

"I will, thanks."

When Brian left, Cole called Bristol again and got her voice mail. A shrill of panic arced through him. Bristol didn't seem like the type to avoid a fight completely. It had been a full day now and he may have been a prick, but she couldn't be giving him the cold shoulder this long. The dread began to settle in.

She can look after herself, he tried to tell himself, but that didn't help.

He brought up Andrew's number and bit his lip. If Bristol knew he had Andrew checking up on her, that would only make things worse. It could be she just wanted space from him, and he'd learned enough about her to know you had to pick your battles carefully.

His phone rang while he was trying to decide what his next move should be. He didn't know the number and answered it immediately.

"Hello, Cole. It's Eli."

"Eli." He let out the breath he was holding. "Hello." But the relief he felt at hearing Eli's voice gave way to something sharper. "Is everything okay?"

"I'm sorry for calling you at a time like this. Bristol told me about your father. I'm very sorry."

Cole grimaced at the courtesy, but Eli taking the time to offer his condolences gave him hope that there was nothing wrong. "Thanks, yeah, everything is going fine here, but I'd like to get home. You, uh, you've seen Bristol then? I don't know if she told you, but I said some stuff I shouldn't have."

"Yeah, I heard about your phone call."

"You have my full permission to give me a touch-up when I get home."

"You've been through a lot in the past twenty-four hours, and we all need to give people room to make their mistakes."

"Yeah, well, it would serve me right if Bristol never spoke to me again."

"No, it wouldn't. I stuck up for you. Don't worry."

"Really? Why?"

"Why not?"

"Well, you're *her* friend first, right?"

"She's like a daughter to me, and that's why I don't give in to her overreactions, and from what I heard, it sounded to me like she overreacted."

"I don't know. I said some stupid stuff."

"She'll get over it. She slept here last night, but I'm calling because I'm a little concerned for her well-being."

Cole's skin prickled. "Why? Has something happened?"

"When she left this morning, she was approached by a couple of people, a man and a woman, in suits. She left with them. Bristol smiled and waved to me, and I gave her the benefit of the doubt because she told me about the other night with that guy Silas. I assumed it was law enforcement bringing her in to talk to her again."

"That could make sense."

"But I also know that if they were bad news, she'd do something like smile and wave to keep me out of it."

"That's sounds exactly like something she would do. What kind of suits were they?"

"Dark and important looking. What I would expect to see on the FBI, maybe? Or have I seen too many movies?"

"You've seen too many movies. But that doesn't mean it's not them, and FBI is one group I was thinking of."

"What was the other group?"

"I'd rather not go there if I don't have to."

"Silas."

"Yeah."

"He'd kill her right?"

Cole rubbed a hand across his mouth. "I'm not going to lie to you, Eli. If it's the FBI that could be bad, but if it's not … I thought with Silas being in jail we would get some breathing space. I might have been wrong."

"That's what I was afraid of. I called you hoping you had heard from her. But if not, I hoped you might be able to find her."

"I can try my friend Andrew in the LAPD. He might have a contact with the FBI."

"I'd appreciate it."

"If you do hear from her, can you let me know?"

"Yeah, I will."

When Cole hung up the phone, he didn't hesitate to call Andrew.

"How you holding up?" Andrew asked when he answered.

"Bristol's gone missing."

"What?"

"Eli saw her leave with a couple of suits this morning and hasn't been able to get a hold of her. I was wondering if you had any contacts in the FBI and could check to see if she's with them?"

"You sure it's the FBI?"

"Nope. I'm hoping. Strange how her being arrested by the Bureau would be the best option."

"You think they've arrested her?"

Cole groaned. "I don't trust anything I'm thinking right now. I just need to get some facts so I know what to do next."

"Hmm … I don't know anyone, but I could check around, see what I can come up with. I don't expect to get very far. I'm surprised you don't know someone."

"That's actually an excellent point." Cole frowned and ran faces through his mind, discouraged.

"Look, I'll do the best I can, but if you have any better ideas … "

"Yeah." Cole growled. "Dammit, I never should have left."

"Yes, Cole, you should have. It's important for you to be there."

"More important than Bristol's life?"

"We don't know what's going on yet. And you're not her guardian. You can only do what you can do."

"Just see what you can find out. I'll get back to LA as soon as I can."

Chapter 7

BRISTOL FELT like pacing the sterile room, but she needed them to think she wasn't agitated. She yawned, sucking in too much of the stale air, then put the back of her hand up to her mouth and stretched back. The yawn was genuine, even if her attitude wasn't.

She avoided looking at the mirror that was on the wall across from her but smiled at the urge she had to flip them off.

Pressing the heels of her hands into her eyes, she went back through their arrival to the nondescript building. She was confident now that it was, in fact, the FBI.

They had left her in a holding cell overnight, which she wasn't sure was legal, but she couldn't get anyone to talk to her. And when someone finally came to get her in the morning and she asked for her phone call, the response was "that will be dealt with shortly."

Now she sat, after being given a weak tea with sugar and no milk, the opposite of what she asked for, and she was sure another hour had passed. She wrapped her fingers around the cup to check. It was now cold.

Desperately tired, she yawned again. At most, she had gotten a couple hours of sleep and now felt like she could sleep for a week straight, so she folded her arms on the table and decided she may as well close her eyes.

She lay her head down, and as soon as she drifted, the door opened. Her head shot up out of reflex, and Agents Bailey and Tellis walked in. This time Tellis led.

He had a thick folder that he dropped onto the metal table with a bang that echoed in the compact room. "Sorry, did we wake you?" he said, raising an eyebrow.

Bristol tittered and took a sip of her tea like she enjoyed it. "I give you an A for effort, but I'm a little offended."

"Why is that?" he asked, scraping a chair away from the table.

Bailey pulled her chair back quietly, and Bristol noticed she listened to the exchange with a look of genuine concern. *Nice try*, Bristol mocked in her head.

She turned back to Tellis. "Making me wait, coming into the room just as I got comfortable, and — " She lifted her cup. "Putting sugar in my tea? Come on, that's just obscene." She waved a finger between the two agents, "And this. You think I'm falling for any of it? This isn't my first rodeo. You don't think I know what this is?"

"I don't know what you know, Ms. Kelley." Tellis leaned back in his chair and crossed his arms. "But what

I know is that you've been a very busy little girl over the last few years."

Bristol sighed heavily. "I want my phone call."

"You haven't been arrested."

"So then why have I been held captive all night?"

"I wouldn't call it that."

"Oh, I see. So this is all one big misunderstanding. Someone just accidentally locked me in a cage."

"Oh yeah. Sorry about that. We had a little mix up. I apologize. It won't happen again. But if you'd like to report us to the authorities, I'd happily hand this file over to someone else, someone less willing to have an exchange of ideas." He smiled, and Bristol gripped the seat. When she was overtired, she got testy, but more determined to call a bluff.

"So I can leave then?" She stood.

"You don't want to hear what we have to say?"

"Nope. I've actually been through a lot recently, and I'd like to go home and have a nap."

"I think you should sit down."

Bristol figured it would be less irritating to deal with Bailey, so she leaned forward aggressively to bring her in. "I don't care what you think."

"I think you should sit." Tellis said, louder this time.

Bailey stood and spread her hands between them.

There we go. Bristol leaned back an inch.

Bailey dropped her arms. "Bristol, please, we'd really appreciate your cooperation on this. Just ignore Tellis. He's got a big ego."

Bristol laughed and shook her head. "There's only

one way I'll stop being belligerent. If you can't agree to my terms, then I'll throw a tantrum."

The two agents looked at each other and Bailey spoke. "We'll see what we can do. What is it you want?"

"First, I want a proper cup of tea. Second, I want all of this to stop."

"All of what?" Tellis asked. A smirk on his face.

Bristol cocked her head at him as she put a hand on the back of her chair and pushed it over. The clang of metal on concrete reverberated through the room. "If you can't show me respect and stop trying to manipulate me, I won't show you any respect."

Bailey nodded at Tellis, who stood and walked around the table. It was as Bristol thought. Bailey was senior. She called the shots. And she would have arranged for this little tête-à-tête.

Tellis picked up the chair, then held it out for Bristol. "Your highness, would you like to have a seat?"

Bristol just looked at Bailey. She let her weariness show. She had had enough of the charade.

Bailey quickly moved around the table and put a hand on Tellis. "Maybe you should give us a minute. Why don't you go get that cup of tea? Strong, no sugar, right?"

Bristol shook her head. "I changed my mind. I'm not thirsty anymore."

"Tellis?" Bailey looked at her partner.

"Fine, but I'll be right there," Tellis said, pointing at the mirror and walking out.

Bailey moved back around the table and sat down. "Sorry about that."

"No, you're not." Bristol sighed and pinched the bridge of her nose as she sat. "You're still playing games." She dropped her hand on the table. "I get it that your psychological profile on me and probably your experience, says that the good-cop/bad-cop routine works on a woman like me."

"What kind of woman is that?"

"Now we're going the confidante route? Just cut the crap. I'm not your friend, and I'm pretty sure you don't have any fondness for me, so why don't you tell me why I'm here so we can all go home?"

"Fine. But you're wrong about what I think of you. I've seen your file. You would have been quite the asset if you worked for the right side."

"Oh, I'm sorry. So you're saying I worked against you when I stopped a child-trafficking ring? My apologies, next time I'll stay out of it."

"Well, you should. There are procedures in place, and when you don't follow those procedures, the bad guys go free."

"You're talking about Silas."

"Maybe."

"There you go again." Bristol reached out and pulled her file over. "May I?"

Bailey nodded.

Bristol opened the folder and saw her picture on the top of the pile. It was a black-and-white copy and showed her coming out of her apartment building.

"You've got me under surveillance?" She could have kicked herself. She was usually very self-aware, especially at home. She didn't want her privacy intruded upon.

"Only recently."

Bristol flipped through a couple of documents. Parts had been blacked out. The page she was on mentioned New York, and she was sure it was the guy she killed who was connected to the trafficking. A job she did for Silas unknowingly. "If you've only started watching me recently, why is the file so thick?"

"We've been given information."

"By who?"

"I'm not at liberty to say."

Bristol closed the file and pushed it back across the table. "Doesn't matter. I already know the answer to that. So I only have one question."

"Yes?"

"Why haven't you arrested me?"

"We'd like to wipe the slate clean."

"That's very generous of you."

"It's not out of generosity."

Bristol rolled her eyes. "No kidding."

"It appears Silas Lincoln will not be charged for his role in the trafficking. The DA has decided they don't have enough evidence to continue with the trial."

"Yes, I heard."

Bailey showed a flicker of surprise but hid it quickly. That put a smile on Bristol's face. Bailey misread it. "You're pleased?"

"If you asked me to go kill him right now, I wouldn't hesitate."

"I'm glad to hear that."

"You want me to kill him? Great. When do I get started?"

Bailey ignored her sarcasm. "Mr. Lincoln has details of certain individuals and their crimes, but the only way we can get him to talk is by dangling a long prison term over his head. We no longer have that leverage, and we need to get it back."

"How?"

"We need you to testify. Or at least agree to. We don't expect it to go to trial. What we want is a solid case so we can offer Silas a deal in exchange for information."

Bristol's heart skipped a beat. "So, what you're saying is, if I don't agree to testify, he goes free."

"That's correct."

"But if I do agree to testify, he still goes free."

"In a manner of speaking. But *we* will get the information *we're* after, and *you'll* get your record expunged. You can start fresh."

"I can't start fresh if Silas is free. What if I don't accept your offer?"

"Then we arrest you for everything that's in that file."

"I'd like my phone call."

"I told you, you haven't been arrested, yet."

"Okay then, I don't agree to your terms. Now arrest me and let me have my phone call."

Chapter 8

AGENT BAILEY LED Bristol to a phone down the hall where she called Deb's cell. When Deb's lawyer voice answered giving instructions about leaving a message after the tone, Bristol swore under her breath and tried Deb's office number. Deb had a thing about making people who called her office wait. She said it adds to her air of importance and gives people a confidence in her abilities as an attorney. Bristol never bothered to try to understand. Hopefully, because Bristol had been nice to Deb's PA last time she visited, she'd be able to convince her that the rules didn't apply in her case.

"Hello, this is Deborah VanHousen's office. How can I help you?"

"I need to speak to Deb. It's urgent."

"I'm sorry, Deborah is unavailable at the moment. Can I take a message?"

"Is this Margaret?"

"No, I'm sorry, Margaret doesn't work here anymore."

Bristol dropped the phone away from her face. "God dammit." She mouthed up to the ceiling then spoke back into the phone. "I see. Is Deb in the office?"

"She's unavailable."

"That's not what I asked."

"I'm sorry, but she's asked not to be disturbed." The pitch of her voice rose with each word.

Bristol slowed hers down. "You need to put the phone down and go into her office and tell her that Bristol Kelley has been arrested by the FBI."

The woman sighed just so Bristol knew what a pain she was being but then said. "I'm sorry ma'am, but Ms. VanHousen will not be disturbed. I can leave a message if you like."

"That's fine, just understand that when I do speak to Deb, I will explain to her how you left her best friend to rot in an illegal FBI prison facility and you will no longer have a job." *Best* friend might have pushed it too far.

"Are you threatening me?"

"I'll do whatever I need to do in order to get Deb on the phone immediately." Bristol heard Deb's voice in the background. "That's her! Just tell her who's on the phone."

The woman tsked then huffed out a long breath. "Just a moment."

Bristol heard the scratchy sound of a hand covering the mouthpiece. She eyeballed Bailey, who stood still and straight, while she waited. When the woman came back on the line, she was panicked. "My apologies, Ms. Kelley. I'll put you right through."

There was a click, then, "Oh my god, Bristol! What

is going on? Where are you? Illegal FBI prison? I'm on my way."

Deb had a way of gushing and carrying on unnecessarily when things were casual, but when it really mattered, the woman was brutally abrupt.

Bristol gave her the address, and then Bailey led her back to the interview room to wait. Deb's office wasn't far. After all the waiting she'd been doing, it was a relief to think she'd have some backup soon.

An hour later, Bristol stood in the corner of the room, leaning back against the wall with her arms crossed. She looked menacingly at the mirror. Finally, she pushed off the wall and knocked on the one-way glass. "You're doing it again."

She sat down at the table, tapping a fingernail on it like a leaky faucet. It was another fifteen minutes before the door opened, and Deb was ushered through by a man Bristol didn't recognize.

Deb wasn't done with him yet. "These stalling tactics are appalling. If things don't go well for my client, you can expect charges to be made. I have everything documented, and I have the ear of every judge in this town." There was nothing she loved more than a good bluff. "You are not above the law." She slammed the door shut, and the anger on her face turned to concern as she rushed over to Bristol, wrapping her arms around her and squeezing too tight.

"I didn't think they'd get you, Bristol. I really didn't think they would."

"Okay, Deb, it's okay. Stop, I can't breathe."

"Sorry, I just can't believe it," she said, pulling a chair around from the other side of the table, not noticing the screech it made as she dragged. Angling it slightly, she dropped her ample bottom onto the seat and took Bristol's hands. "Now, tell me everything."

Bristol looked up at the mirror and the camera in the corner.

"They're not listening. They might be a little high-handed in their tactics, but this is attorney-client privilege, and they can't get through that wall."

Bristol nodded at the file laying on the table. "You better have a look."

Deb pulled the file over and plopped it on her lap. She opened it. "Shit." She flipped a few pages. Read one of the files. "Shit, shit." She grabbed a chunk and flipped it over, reading through another section then closed it and looked up at Bristol. "Well, shit."

"Yeah, it is a bit."

"How'd they get all this? And why haven't they done anything with it until now?"

"Remember when I was in touch last?"

"Don't tell me that hottie Cole has something to do with this. I thought he was a winner."

"How could you think he was a winner? All you know about him is from his driver's license."

"I can't believe you'd ask me a question like that? Don't you know me at all?"

"It wasn't Cole. In fact, he kind of saved my life."

"Kind of?" Deb pointed a finger in the air. "Told ya."

Bristol shook her head. "Remember when I stopped by your client's house the other day and he said his neighbor was Silas Lincoln?"

"Yeah. Crazy. That would be a shithole where Silas is concerned. He should be holed up in some razzle dazzle of a place with gleaming chandeliers and fifty rooms."

"Yeah, well, that's a conversation for another time. He's been arrested over child-trafficking allegations."

"No way." Deb scooted forward. "Why isn't this all over the news?"

"Because Silas's people are very good."

"I take it you had a role in taking him down?"

"Yes, and Cole. So much has happened since I last saw you." Bristol put her face in her hands. "God, that phrase is a running commentary in my life right now."

"You going to fill me in?"

Bristol squared her shoulders and gave Deb a basic recap of the last couple days. As she spoke, it seemed as though Deb's hair grew wilder with each fact, though the cause of the increasing unruliness was probably that she didn't sit still through the whole thing. She'd jump up and pace then sit back down and fidget.

When Bristol finished by telling her about Cole's recording being thrown out, Deb pulled her chair around to face the table and laid the folder in front of her, resting her hands on top. She stared at it for a moment. To Bristol, it looked like she was trying to divine something through osmosis.

Deb pressed a finger to her chin. "What's the catch?"

"The catch?"

"Yeah, they've got this file on you that goes back a ways. And like I said, they've never acted on it. So they've either only just gotten this information, or they've been holding it for a long time. Either way, there's a catch. I can smell it."

"They want me to testify against Silas."

"So they'd rather he go to prison than you? That's a start, but it's crazy. You'll never make it on the stand. No offense, but Silas's lawyers will rip you to shreds."

"They don't expect it to go to trial."

Deb's fingers curled into a fist. "Of course they don't. They want something from him."

"Yeah, they want me to testify so they have leverage to get him to tell them what he knows."

"Sonofabitch. You're bait."

"Pretty much."

"He will eat you alive."

"Thanks for the vote of confidence, but he's already tried." Bristol rested her forehead on her fingertips. "Here I was thinking it was all over with Silas, that I could move on."

"You could always say no, but if they press charges," she tapped the file, "they have a solid case. I would defend you. You know I would. To the death, if that's what it took."

"I know."

"But if it were anyone else, I'd recommend taking

whatever deal they offer. It's just that your deal is bullshit. You lose no matter what."

"I know."

"What's your gut reaction?"

"I don't want to go to prison. I'd rather die out of it than live in it."

"Yeah."

The air was quiet and still, so when Deb jumped out of her seat, the room seemed to jump with her. She clicked across the room in her pointy heals and banged on the door with the side of her fist.

There was no response at first, and Deb looked at Bristol, rolling her eyes. "I don't know why they think this will work in their favor."

The door finally opened, and Bailey and Tellis entered.

The four sat down at the table, and Deb did her thing where she commanded the space. Bristol didn't know if it was the look on her face or the way she sat forward with her hands on the table, but everyone knew to wait for her to speak, even Tellis.

"My client is willing to testify against Silas on two conditions."

"We're listening," said Bailey.

"Her entire record is expunged."

"We've already offered her that." Tellis snorted and Bailey held in a sigh.

"And you will cease all further investigation and surveillance of my client."

Bristol held on tight to the smile that wanted to

creep onto her face. She hadn't even thought of asking for that.

Tellis leaned forward, glaring at Bristol. "We can't give you that."

"You can," Deb answered, leaning into Bristol just enough to get Tellis to look her way. "And don't address my client. You've done enough to her. It's me you have to deal with now."

Tellis licked his bottom lip and leaned back with an exaggerated turn toward Deb. "What if she kills someone? We're just supposed to ignore that?"

"She's not going to kill anyone." The look of disdain on Deb's face almost had Bristol laughing. "And I'm not saying if a dead body presents itself with her fingerprints all over it that it can't be investigated." Deb stood now, her knuckles pressing into the table. "But if I find out you're harassing my client and pointing the finger unnecessarily, there will be hell to pay. And I want it in writing." She took a quick breath and then finished with, "And you will let her go while you're preparing everything for the DA."

Tellis cracked his knuckles, his face hard. "That's out of the question."

Deb slammed her hand on the table. Even Bristol jumped a little. "Then go ahead and charge my client and watch me bring a lawsuit down on your ass so fast you won't know your feet from your head."

Bailey reached up and put a hand on Tellis, pulling him back. He didn't want to be pulled back, but he finally assented. "Fine, but if you do a runner," he pointed a finger at Bristol, and Deb looked like she would bite it off, "we'll find you, and I will personally see to it that you go away for life."

Deb laughed cheerfully. It struck an odd chord in the hostile room. "Good luck. You've got no jurisdiction when it comes to sentencing. Come on Bristol, let's get out of this hellhole." She grabbed Bristol's wrist and pulled. Bristol was always surprised at the woman's strength. It seemed almost superhuman.

Bailey held a hand up to stop the women. "We'll need to take a full statement."

"The police have her full statement," Deb said, walking around Bailey and pulling Bristol with her. "You can use that. Once you've typed up the formalities, Bristol can come back and sign whatever it is you need her to sign. With my supervision, of course. But right now, we're leaving."

"What about protection?"

"Bristol will be fine until Silas knows what you guys are planning. So don't tell him until you give us plenty of warning and we can make arrangements."

Deb led the way down the corridor, but Bristol put a hand on her arm, stopping her. "I don't think I can do a safe house situation. It will be just as bad as prison."

"Let's worry about that later. Right now, I just want to get you out of here." Deb looked at the walls and floors in disgust. "Honestly," she said to herself, then looked at Bristol. "Come on. Let's get your things."

. . .

Bristol checked her phone first. It had run out of battery. "Didn't even have the curtesy to turn my phone off."

"The bastards."

Bristol snickered as they walked out into the sun.

Deb shook her head, sweeping her mass of curls back away from her face and started a rapid-fire commentary. "God, that was fun, wasn't it? They tell *you* you're not above the law, Bristol, but look at them. A bunch of animals. One of these days, I will get the chance to do some real damage to them. That will be the best day of my life. Come with me. I'm taking you to lunch. You need it."

"I just want to go home and sleep."

"After lunch. I know you, Bristol. I'm sure you've barely eaten."

At the thought of food, her stomach rumbled. "Okay, you win. Feed me. Then I'm going home and sleeping for a week."

◯◯

Cole straightened his tie in the mirror. The day would have been hard enough if a funeral were all he had to deal with, but he was no stranger to difficult situations, and he'd face this like he had faced the rest.

He rubbed a hand across his newly shaven face. Even with the dark circles under his eyes, he looked presentable. Taking a deep breath, he straightened his back, until the phone rang to indicate someone was at the gate. Then his shoulders hunched and his teeth clenched.

He went to see who it was, and at the sight of the taxi, he closed his eyes and pinched the bridge of his nose. He didn't have time for her, but he opened the gate anyway. When the doorbell rang, he left it for Brian, whose now familiar shoe-fall echoed through the entryway as he headed for the door.

Several seconds later he heard the added clack of high heels, then after another delay there was a knock at his door.

"Yes, Brian?"

The door pushed open. "It's your uh, Samantha. I've asked her to wait in the sitting room. I hope that's acceptable."

Cole's flinch was perceptible only to himself. Pushing it aside, he pulled his suit coat off the back of the chair. "Can I ask you something?"

Brian hurried over to help him put the jacket on. "Of course."

"Did you have a good relationship with your mom?"

Brian's hands swept down Cole's back to brush off what couldn't be seen. "Yes, actually I did. She always encouraged me while she was still alive." He moved around Cole for a once-over. "You look very nice, sir."

Cole didn't bother correcting the "sir." Maybe it was too late to change old habits. He had plenty of his own that he was sure were set in stone. "Thank you. I guess that's where you got it."

"Got what?"

"You've always been an encouragement to me." He

rested a hand on Brian's shoulder. "I really appreciate your being here. It would have been harder without you. Too many ghosts in this big old place."

"It's my pleasure."

"I hope you have somewhere to go after this."

"I was thinking of retiring. I enjoy fishing, and I haven't had nearly enough time over the years."

"That sounds like an excellent idea. I'll see to it that your retirement package is substantial."

"That's not necessary."

"Yes, it is. Don't argue."

Brian smiled. "Is there anything else you require?"

Cole took a deep breath. "No, thank you."

After Brian left the room, Cole took one last look in the mirror. He rubbed a finger between his eyes to try and smooth out the wrinkle between them, but it wouldn't budge. There was no point causing a scene. He'd go find out what she wanted and then ask her to leave.

Chapter 9

WHEN COLE ENTERED THE ROOM, his mother was looking out the window, her arms wrapped tightly around her. She had on a plain black dress and a black veil to match. Silas may have forced her here under threat, but Cole could feel his temper simmering just under the surface. He wasn't impressed by her pretense. She had nothing to mourn but her own poor choices.

"Samantha."

She spun around and started toward him, but then recoiled. "You're looking very handsome," she said, guarded.

"Why'd you come back?"

"I thought we could go to the funeral together. I didn't want you to be alone." She had such an earnest look of concern on her face, Cole was thrown off balance. Part of him wanted to pick her up and toss her out the door, but there was something injured about her that made him pause. The problem was, injured animals could also be dangerous.

He checked his watch. He would already be late, and he just wanted the whole thing over with so he could get back to LA. "You didn't drive yourself, obviously."

"No."

"That was very presumptuous of you. Just like yesterday." He walked over to the fireplace and ran a hand across the mantle, picking up a bit of dust that he rolled into a ball between his fingers, then flicked it away. "You were prepared to give me terrible news with no way for you to escape."

"I know you're a good person, but I was afraid if I had a way to leave, it would be too easy for you to get rid of me."

"What makes you think I'm such a good person?"

"You're — " Her voice broke. "It doesn't matter."

"And you wear black like you're actually in mourning."

"I am." Her voice was raised in defense. "In my own way. I mourn a lot of things these days." Cole crossed his arms, so she threw her hands up in the air. "Call me a taxi if you want. I'm just trying to do the right thing. After all these years, I just wanted the chance to do the right thing for once."

"Was that what you were doing when you told me about Silas?"

"Yes, actually it was." Her chin lifted in defiance.

"And how exactly is that the right thing?"

"Because — Forget it."

Cole laughed sardonically. There was too much running through his head to try to untangle his mother's motives, and it wouldn't be worth the effort. "Fine. We're already late. Let's go."

She nodded eagerly and reached for him, but he turned as though he hadn't seen the gesture and hurried to the front door, calling out as he moved through, "I'm leaving now Brian. I'll see you there."

"Yes, sir," Brian called out from wherever he was. Cole pictured him polishing the silver and smiled. He was glad Brian had decided to retire. He had served others long enough.

It was a quiet drive to the church. Cole noticed the spires first as they approached the street. It was a beautiful old church he had been inside a few times as a boy. Back then, the vaulted ceilings and archways had awed him. It gave his imagination something to feed off of. Now, as a man, he could appreciate the intricacy of the architecture and artwork that went into a building like that. With his father's opulent taste, Cole wouldn't have expected him to choose any differently.

A parking space was reserved for him only because he had his father's name. His refusal to take part in the formalities would give the masses something to gaggle and gossip about. But that wasn't his concern. Most of the people attending, and there were plenty, would be there only for the networking possibilities. People like his father, who never let an opportunity pass to grow their businesses.

When Cole got out of the car, he paused only long

enough to button his jacket. At a quick pace, he walked to the front door, faster than his mother could keep up in her heels. He wanted to avoid her entering the church at his side. There were only so many concessions he was willing to make.

Richard was at the door, an imposing figure as he greeted the crowd still making their way inside. Cole had always found Richard and his father a strange combination. Richard was a good friend to his father, and Cole had always found him cold, but in a different way from the man he grew up with. Where his dad was ruthless, Richard was precise. His father let emotion get the better of him, but Richard seemed to be a master of control. Cole found comfort in the lawyer's formality, today. Cole's ability to compartmentalize was on the edge of breaking. And now, with no idea what was happening to Bristol, he needed the ability to do so more than ever.

"Richard." Cole took his hand when he reached the top of the stairs. "Sorry I'm late. You are a lifesaver."

Richard responded louder than he had to. "It's your grief, Cole. We can't expect you to be perfect under the circumstances." He placed a heavy hand on Cole's shoulder. "At this time more than ever we can afford you some latitude." His smile was conspiratorial.

Cole lifted the corner of his own mouth in a smile that was only for Richard. "Thanks."

Samantha was now at Cole's side. He moved out of the way so she could enter first. She offered a grimace to Richard and walked through the door.

Cole paused and gave Richard a final glance before

he crossed the threshold into a foyer full of people he didn't know, although many of them seemed to know who he was.

He recognized the questioning peeks they gave to either the boy they used to know, or the son of a man they had admired or hated.

Cole made a point of keeping himself separated from Samantha so he didn't have to endure the added wonder as to who the woman in black was.

A round man, near fifty, locked his sad, sloppy eyes on Cole and headed toward him from across the room. Cole didn't know him but recognized the look of someone ready to add his condolences to a long line of monotonous drawl about pleasant memories he had of Mr. Sullivan.

As Cole was considering how to avoid the encounter, a hand clamped on his shoulder from behind. In Cole's distracted state, the power of the hand's grip engaged a fighting response, and he reached up and twisted it around, preparing to punch whatever throat presented itself. Halfway through the motion he realized what he was doing, and he quickly released the hand and prepared for an apology, cringing at the audience he had. Then he saw who it was.

He stepped back a fraction. "Michael Carter, what the hell are you doing here?"

Michael was a few inches taller and broader in the shoulders than Cole. His face was dark and unreadable. "Master Sullivan. It's been a long time."

"You always were a prick."

The two men stared each other down, but Michael

broke first and hooked Cole around the neck into a steely hug. "It's good to see you, buddy."

Cole slapped his friend on the back. "What were you thinking, grabbing me like that? I could have broken your arm."

"We both know that's not true."

Cole shook his head. Michael had a way of claiming the last word. "So what are you doing here?"

"I heard about your dad."

"You came all this way for my dad?"

"Well, more for you. I moved to Chicago a few years ago and when I heard about the funeral, I thought I'd see how my old friend was doing."

"It has been a long time. I appreciate your coming. It means a lot to have a friend in the place. I don't know many people here and couldn't count any of them as friends.

"So you're in Chicago these days. What brought you here?"

"I'm with the feds now. Seems my particular skill set works well with them."

"All I remember is your lack of skill."

"All I remember is a skinny kid with pockets full of money."

"Wait, you're with the FBI?"

"Yeah. Why? Should I be arresting you?"

"Look, let me know if I'm crossing the line here, but I think a friend of mine might have been arrested, or at least taken in for questioning, by the FBI. Problem is, I don't know for sure."

"I would think if your friend's been arrested, you'd

know. I mean, we don't tend to abduct people off the street."

"No one was with her when she got into a van and was taken away. And unfortunately, there are people who wouldn't hesitate to kill her."

"Ah. Her."

"I'd be lying if I said she didn't mean something to me, but I need to find out where she is, so I know if I need to do something about it."

"Yeah, sure. I'll make a phone call."

"Thank you. I don't mean to push, but as soon as possible would be good. It would have happened in LA."

"I'll do it now. You know I wasn't fond of your dad. I'd be happy to miss the service."

"Lucky. I wouldn't mind missing it myself."

Michael nodded. "The things we have to do for family, eh? I'm glad I can help you out at least."

"Thanks, man. I appreciate it."

They exchanged numbers before Michael left.

The time ticked by slowly as Cole sat silently through the service, trying not to be frustrated by the kind words everyone was saying about his dad. But knowing Michael was looking into Bristol's situation meant he could endure it a bit easier. He knew his friend would do everything he could for Cole, just like Cole would do for him.

He slipped his phone out of his pocket and texted

Eli: *I've got someone looking into it with the FBI. I'll let you know when I hear.*

By the time they got to the cemetery, a light drizzle had settled in. He stared with blank eyes at the coffin as it was lowered into the ground and attempted to gain some sort of closure with the burial, but he couldn't make himself feel anything, not with his mind continually drifting back to Bristol.

After the required rituals were finished, Cole stood by a tree with his umbrella. He dipped his hand in his pocket and checked his phone to make sure he hadn't missed a call then scanned for anyone approaching the cemetery in case Michael came by that way.

Out of the corner of his eye, he saw someone approach. He looked up to see a slim, dark-haired woman. She wore a nicely tailored skirt suit that was getting wet. She was the last woman he'd expect to see unprepared.

"Elly?"

"Hi, Cole. It's been a long time."

"It has. Seems to be the way of funerals, bringing people back together who wouldn't normally meet again. Here," he said, offering his umbrella.

Elly smiled shyly. "Thanks." She took it but stood close to him in order to share. "Not great weather for a funeral."

"Oh, I don't know. I think the dreariness adds to the effect. We're all supposed to be sad after all." Cole stuffed his hands in his pockets. "I didn't see you at the church."

"Well, you are distracted with everything that's going on and I didn't want to bother you. This must be hard for you. I remember how difficult it was for you to be under his roof."

"That was a long time ago."

"Mmm." She sniffed and looked around the cemetery then turned back. "Cole, I actually wanted to come over here to apologize."

"For what?"

"Walking out on you."

Cole let out a sharp breath. "That was a long time ago too."

"I know, but don't you ever wonder what would have happened if we had stayed together?"

Cole's phone vibrated in his pocket. He pulled it out and saw Michael's name. "I'm so sorry. I need to take this call." He moved away from her into the drizzle, unsure of what had just transpired. Or what it was that Elly was trying to say.

"Michael. I hope you found something."

"Straight to business then?"

"Yeah, I know, I'm sorry. I'm just really worried about her."

"I would have called you sooner, but I didn't want to interrupt."

"You should have."

"Yeah, well, you're probably not in a position to make the best judgments at the moment, so I'm trying to help you out as a friend."

Cole shifted his feet. "Sorry. I appreciate your help. All of it."

"Happy to do it. I also found your girl. She was taken in by us. As far as I can tell she hasn't been charged, but the agent I spoke to mentioned that there was a file on her."

"Doesn't the FBI have a file on everyone?"

"I mean an active file." Michael cleared his throat. "Unfortunately I can't really help you with more than that except to say that it's ongoing."

"No, that's a tremendous help. It's better than anyone else having her."

"What are you going to do now?"

"Besides catch a plane back to LA? I have no idea."

"Good luck. If I hear anything else, I'll let you know."

"Thanks. And listen. It was really good to see you after all these years. I wish we had time to catch up properly. If you ever find yourself in LA, give me a call."

"I'll do that."

Cole tucked the phone back into his pocket to keep it dry, then lifted his face to the rain. The timing of everything couldn't be worse.

Elly still stood at the tree, waiting for him. "Everything okay?" she asked when he returned.

"Uh, yeah, yeah, it's fine." Cole wondered what flight he'd be able to catch.

"I got a new job," Elly said, trying to turn his attention her way.

"Oh yeah? That's great."

"It's in Los Angeles. I'm flying out tonight."

"Wow, that's really great."

"You think so?"

"Yeah, of course. Don't you think it's great?"

"I definitely do."

"Listen, I'm sorry, but there's a bit of an emergency back home I need to sort out, and I need to get going."

"In the middle of your dad's funeral?"

"It's finished. They don't need me. No one here will miss me."

Elly moved closer. "I know it's been a while, but I still know you Cole. Everything's not okay."

He put a hand on her shoulder. "It's fine. I'll talk to you later."

"Yeah, I'd like that. See you soon."

Cole left the umbrella with her and waved as he walked off. Before walking out of the cemetery, he turned again and saw that Elly was still watching him go. She waved when she saw him look. He frowned but lifted a hand in response. He tried to make sense of the oddness of the exchange, but his mind was too crowded with what he had to do, and he didn't have time to work out the issues surrounding another woman connected to his life.

He paused before getting into his car, texting Eli to update him, but when he opened the car door, his mother came into view. He squared his shoulders.

"Cole, you aren't leaving?"

"I have to. It's an emergency. I've done everything I need to do here. I can come back later to clean up what- ever is left."

"But we're not finished. You're just walking out on your father?"

He thought of a hundred things he could say, but what was the point in saying them to the woman who walked out of his life over twenty years ago after sleeping with the worst person in the world. He shook his head in the end and got into the car, shutting her out.

"Can I visit?" She called through the window.

"No." He emptied her out of his mind and focused on how to help Bristol. If the feds had an active file on her, that couldn't be a good thing. But going up against the FBI would be tricky. It was a good thing impossible tasks were his specialty.

Chapter 10

"IF YOU CAN SAFELY REACH your phone, you may switch it on now. Otherwise, remain seated until the seatbelt sign is turned off."

Cole already had his phone to his ear as they taxied down the runway. He had turned it on while they were landing and was now listening to the message Michael had left advising him that the FBI was no longer holding Bristol.

He called Eli first.

"Cole, have you heard anything more?"

"I just landed at LAX. She's been released, but you haven't heard from her yet?"

"Maybe they confiscated her phone?"

Cole's stomach knotted. "Maybe, but you don't think she would call you to tell you what happened?"

"Bristol rarely involves me in the intricacies of her line of work. I think she thinks she's keeping me safe."

"She probably is. No point your being an accessory to anything. I'll head to her place from here and let you know what I find. Keep trying her and see if you can get through."

It was 7:00 p.m. by the time Cole got on the road. Traffic wasn't bad, but it was never really good in the city, so it was nearly 8:00 by the time he reached Bristol's apartment. He tried calling first, but the phone went straight to voice mail. At the front door of the apartment building, he buzzed her and waited. When there was no response, he walked around to where he could see her window. There was a light. He noticed, too, the light was on at the neighbor's.

Cole returned to the door, scanning the list of names and found M. Deacon. He had liked the woman even after meeting her only briefly, and the fact that he saved her cat should give him some extra credit with her. He pushed the button.

"Who is it?" the woman sing-songed through the speaker.

"Mrs. Deacon, it's Cole. I uh, I saved your cat the other day."

"Oh, yes, the very handsome friend of Bristol's. What can I do for you?"

"Would you mind buzzing me through?"

"I'm sorry, but I don't let people in for other people."

"Right, no, of course, I wouldn't dream of it. I actually wanted to stop by and see how your cat is doing. She really made an impression on me."

"Oh my." He could hear her clear her throat through the static. "Well, in that case."

The door buzzed and Cole pushed through, taking the stairs two at a time.

When he reached Mrs. Deacon's apartment, she was standing halfway in the hall, holding Sheba up like a trophy.

Cole glanced at Bristol's door, then turned his full attention to the old woman. "Aren't you looking radiant tonight."

"You sure know how to make an old lady blush." She handed the cat to Cole, who carried her inside and sat on the edge of the couch. He held Sheba up, twisting her around and inspecting her like he knew what he was doing. The cat squirmed in his hands, so he put her down. "She's looking well. Any more forays out the window?"

"No, she's been good lately."

"I'm glad to hear it." Cole picked cat hair off his pants.

"Can I get you something to drink? Would you like a tea?"

"No, thank you." He slapped his hands on his lap and stood. "Well, I won't keep you. Thank you for letting me visit."

The cat jumped up into Mrs. Deacon's lap and she stroked it. Her gnarled knuckles soaking into the deep fur. "I don't suppose you could do something for me?" she asked with a twinkle in her eye.

"Anything."

"Would you mind paying a visit to Bristol? I think

that young lady is lonely and needs company more than I do. I do well on my own, but Bristol? She's not as tough as she looks."

Cole smirked. "You don't think so?"

"I know so. I let her come help me because I can tell it makes her feel good, but she thinks she fools me with her confidence. I can see right through it. I've been around long enough to know what prolonged sadness looks like."

"I bet you have."

"It's in the eyes. I can see it in yours too. But it's not as pronounced."

"You're very perceptive. I lost my father recently."

"I'm sorry to hear it, but it's not that. It goes deeper. You and she are a lot alike. Both pretending. You think you have something to prove. But you need each other. Oh, that reminds me." Mrs. Deacon pointed at the TV remote on the coffee table. "Would you mind? I don't want to bother Sheba," she said, patting the cat. Cole handed the remote to Mrs. Deacon. "Golden Girls," she said, turning on the TV and wriggling herself into a more comfortable viewing position.

"I'll leave you to your Girls and head over to Bristol's and see if she's home for a chat."

"Oh, yes, she's home," she said, keeping her eyes on the opening credits. "She came in a few hours ago."

"Do you think she might have gone back out?"

"Maybe. But these walls are very thin, and the hallway outside creaks." She turned to him then and waved a hand to draw Cole closer. He leaned in obligingly. "I'm also a bit of a Nosey Nellie. I like to know what's going on in the building."

"Really?" Mrs. Deacon nodded. "I would never have guessed. It has certainly come in handy tonight. I'll go pay Bristol a visit."

Mrs. Deacon patted Cole on the cheek and smiled as though they were sharing a secret. "I used to be quite the matchmaker back in my day."

"Now that doesn't surprise me."

"Let me know how you two get on."

"I will. Thank you for letting me see Sheba. She really is a lovely cat."

The smile Cole held on his face for Mrs. Deacon vanished to concern as soon as he turned his back and went out the door.

He noticed the creaking of the floor that Mrs. Deacon had mentioned, even as he stepped lightly.

Knocking softly on Bristol's door, he waited a moment, trying to be patient, but then decided this whole thing had gone on long enough. If she was there, he had to know, even if just for Eli's sake. She couldn't deny him that.

He banged hard, waited a few seconds, then banged again.

"Hold on!" Bristol yelled from inside the apartment. He closed his eyes and let out a breath in relief until Bristol continued. "I've got a gun, so if you touch my door again I'm shooting. Be warned."

He stood to the side. Just in case.

Several locks clicked before the door opened.

"Cole?" She rubbed sleep out of her eyes but held

herself expressionless. Cole couldn't have been happier. He wanted to pull her into his arms, but her lack of enthusiasm kept him rooted. "I thought you were in Chicago?"

"What?"

"Your dad's funeral?" She looked confused but not concerned.

Cole was incredulous. "Can I come in?" His voice was colder than he meant it to sound, but her indifference was irritating.

She didn't move. "You're not drunk, are you?"

He wanted to be angry, but he deserved it. His head dropped as he exhaled. "No, I'm not."

She stepped aside to let him in.

His gaze swept the apartment like he expected to find a clue. "Have you spoken to Eli recently?"

"Yeah, I saw him yesterday." She stiffened. "Why, did something happen?"

Cole shifted from one foot to the other. "Nothing has happened to Eli, no."

Bristol tightened the belt around her robe in response to his unfriendly reply. "I don't understand. Is something wrong?"

"Did you lose your phone?"

"No, it ran out of — "

"Eli and I couldn't get ahold of you. We were worried."

"You left your dad's funeral because you couldn't get in touch with me? After the last phone conversation we had, I would think you'd expect not to hear from me right away."

"I didn't leave his funeral. It was over. And it wasn't just your phone. It was because you were taken by the FBI, and I came back to help you." Cole rubbed his hands down his face. "Jesus, Bristol, it could have been Silas that had you. I had to find out."

She put her hands on her hips. "How do you know about the FBI?"

"Why did you go with them in the first place? You weren't under arrest."

"What difference does it make to you?"

"What did they want?"

"Hang on. How do you know all of that?"

"I've got connections. You know that. Why won't you answer my question?"

Bristol let out an exasperated breath and went to sit on the couch. "This is ridiculous," she said under her breath.

"Is there a reason you're being evasive? Hang on." Cole pulled out his phone. "I'll let Eli know I found you and that you're okay." After the message was sent, he turned his phone off. He didn't need any more interruptions.

"What is it with you and Eli? I'm a grown woman. I can take care of myself."

"We just want to make sure you're safe. Eli saw you leave with a couple of suits. My first thought was law enforcement. Which I wasn't happy about either, but my second thought was Silas, which was worse."

Bristol frowned and tucked her fingers into her hair. "I'm sorry. You're right."

Cole sat down next to her, but not too close. "Can you please tell me what they wanted?"

"They just wanted me to testify against Silas."

Cole jumped up. "What? Are you kidding? Did you tell them to shove it somewhere uncomfortable?"

She lifted her face to him. "They have a file on me."

"I know."

Bristol scoffed. "You seem to know a lot."

"So you said yes?"

"Yes."

"You shouldn't have done that."

Now it was Bristol's turn to stand. "Then what should I have done?"

"You could fight the charges."

"But they're right. They've got a file on me breaking the law, which I have done. How am I supposed to get out of that?"

"How'd they get the evidence?"

"I don't know. Silas?"

"You could fight the evidence. Same thing Silas is doing."

"Cole, I don't need a lecture."

"If you get up on that stand, you don't think Silas's lawyer will pull you to pieces? That's assuming you live long enough to make it to the trial."

Bristol's voice went quiet. "I won't be getting on the stand."

"What do you mean, you just — "

" — It's not supposed to go to trial. They just want the threat to hold over him so that he'll give them information they want in exchange for a deal." Cole shook his head and walked over to the window. "It's the least I can do after the work I've unwillingly done for Silas over the years. I've got a lot to make up for."

"*You've* got a lot to make up for?" He remembered what Mrs. Deacon said about thin walls and dropped his voice. "I think you served your time growing up. There is nothing you have to answer for."

"Oh, stop it, Cole. Plenty of people have horrible childhoods and grow up to be law-abiding citizens."

"You've got more conscience than plenty of law-abiding citizens I know."

"Stop trying to stick up for me. I've made my decision."

"Then Silas will come after you again. He's not going to let you hold that power over his head."

"Maybe."

Cole exploded. "Maybe? Are you crazy? He will kill you. What is wrong with you!"

"Right now? You. You need to go. Right now." She grabbed him and tried pulling him toward the door, but he wouldn't budge.

"I'm not going anywhere. Not now that I know your life is in danger."

"God, Cole." She dropped her hands to her side. "Always trying to be my savior. I'm beginning to think you have a god complex."

"I'm beginning to think you have a death wish."

At Cole's stony glare, Bristol's stomach twisted. She hated that she was like this. Every time Cole tried to help her, she pulled away. She couldn't stand relying on him for anything. Looking at him standing there, not willing to give in, she wanted more than anything to go to him. But she didn't know how to be weak.

"I'm not in danger. When the FBI are ready to present their new evidence, we will discuss how to keep me out of harm's way." She cringed at the thought of having to allow the FBI to protect her. It would be worse than giving in to Cole. "Right now, Silas doesn't know anything." She watched Cole clench and unclench his fists as he stared out the window. She decided to give him a small concession. She walked close to him and put a hand on his arm, softening her voice. "If you don't believe me, you can speak to my lawyer, Deb VanHousen." She laughed lightly. "Tell her who you are. She'd love to meet you, I'm sure."

Cole's emotions were raw and as much as he had craved Bristol's touch, now, with her hand on him, it was hard not to grab hold of her and refuse to let her go until she gave in to him. He suddenly realized that if he didn't get out of there, he would do something stupid. He wasn't sure if he trusted what Bristol said, but the fact that she had a lawyer and had given him her name surprised him enough for him to give her space. No matter how hard it was.

He left her apartment without another word and camped out in his car outside her place. He wouldn't be able to stop worrying until he knew for sure.

Chapter 11

COLE'S EYES sprang open as soon as his mind awakened. He was sitting with his arms still folded against his chest and had to blink a few times to remember where he was. His intention had been to stay awake through the night. Now, he was staring at a foggy window that he quickly wiped to peer through at a quiet street. Oddly, he was relaxed, not fearful.

He unfolded his arms and stretched, then got out of his car. Jogging in place, he twisted left then right and moved his arms in wide circles. He wanted to check on her but knew he couldn't. After stretching toward his toes, he got back in his car just as Bristol came out the door. He slid down in his seat, but it didn't matter. She knew his car. It would take her a simple scan of her surroundings and he'd be exposed.

Although she didn't look his way, he was sure she had seen him. If their places were swapped, he wouldn't have missed her.

She looked dressed for the gym, and Cole was sure

she'd be headed to see Eli. She might act like she was bothered by the big guy's concern for her, but he knew Eli meant a lot to her.

Cole started his car as she pulled away. If she was going to spend some time with Eli, it would give him a chance to go home and have a shower, and then catch up with Bristol's lawyer.

When Bristol entered the gym, she had every intention of keeping things casual and act like it was no big deal, like she usually did. But it was only moments before she found herself cocooned in a hug.

"Ughph. Eli, stop. I'm fine."

"I was worried," he said, loosening his arms, but not letting go.

"I know, and I'm sorry. I thought I threw you off when I smiled and waved. Then my phone went dead and I didn't know everyone was looking for me."

Eli pushed her back then and swatted her lightly across the head, scattering her hair across her face. "You must think I'm an idiot."

"A girl can dream." Bristol's face distorted as she pushed the hair back.

"You going to tell me what happened?"

"Which part? The part where I finally got my act together and decided to help the FBI? Or the part where Cole ambushed me."

Eli jutted his chin out at her. "First of all, I know you're not helping the FBI out of the goodness of your heart. Don't ask me how I know, I just know. And second, Cole risked his life to save yours and then flew across the country because he was terrified that something had happened to you. I'm disappointed in you, Bristol. I've put up with you a long time and I love you, but sometimes you try so hard to keep people at arm's length that you act like a little shit."

Bristol pulled her chin back. "I don't think I've ever heard you swear before." She nearly laughed.

"That's because I don't. But right now, I don't have any other language for the way you're acting."

Bristol's shoulders dropped, and she pushed past Eli to drop her bag on the bench. She leaned her weight on the seat. "I don't know what's happened to me. I used to have everything under control, but lately I don't seem to be able to handle anything." She spun around to face him. "You're right." Somehow tears had found their way into her eyes and they burned like fire. She brushed one away stubbornly. "I just don't know how to do it."

"Don't know how to do what?"

"Let people get close."

"You let me get close."

"Yeah, but that's different. You're neutral. Cole's … " Her voice lost strength. "I think when he called me drunk, it affected me more than I realized. I don't want to make a mistake like my mom did."

"Cole is not like your mom's boyfriends."

"Of course he isn't. And I know that, but that doesn't change how I feel."

"How do you feel?"

"I don't know," she erupted. "Alone?"

Eli nodded. "He saved you and then he left."

"What? No, he had to go. It was his dad's funeral."

"But you didn't want him to go. You wanted him to stay. Then when he was gone, and he called and upset you, you had a good reason for pushing him away so you didn't have to miss him anymore."

"What, are you my psychologist now?"

"Am I wrong?"

"You really drive me crazy, do you know that?" She leaned down to retie her sneaker.

"I think you should talk to him. Tell him all that."

She spun up. "What? Are you crazy?"

"Why not?"

"'Cause we're not … like that. We aren't at that place where we talk about that stuff."

"You two haven't talked about serious stuff?"

She closed her eyes and sighed. "We're not … "

"I've got you cornered."

She blew out an aggressive breath. "The one place I know I am definitely at, is the place where I need to punch the stuffing out of that bag over there and stop talking so much."

"You want me to hold it?"

"Yes, please."

"I'm glad to hear you haven't lost your manners."

By 9:00 a.m. Cole was at the office of "Deborah VanHousen, Attorney," as the large sign on the window read. He had considered calling her, but he could take

someon's measure better in person, and he wanted to make sure this one was up for the job of looking after Bristol.

While he waited to cross the road, he saw a short woman trucking it into the office. She was walking head first. Her curly hair seemed to scatter out of her way as she went. If the door had been locked, he was sure she would have plowed right through it.

When he entered the office, he analyzed the waiting room. The chairs looked expensive and formal. Magazines in orderly stacks. On top of one pile sat an issue of *Time* from the previous month. The other pile started with a yachting magazine. Behind a stylish reception desk sat an older, sour-looking woman. She watched Cole with a frown that sat deep in her face.

When he approached the desk, he offered a casual warm smile that never failed, until today. It only seemed to make her suspicious. He was impressed.

"Can I help you?" she asked with the gravelly voice of a chain smoker, although her fingers, perched on the computer keyboard, didn't look stained.

"Yes, good morning. I was wondering if I could see Ms. VanHousen?"

"Do you have an appointment?"

"No, I'm a friend of a friend."

"I'm sorry, but she is a very busy woman and doesn't have time to see every Tom, Dick, and Harry that walks in off the street."

Sarcasm. Interesting. She didn't seem the type. "I see. Could you at least tell her Cole Sullivan is here? I'm a friend of Bristol Kelley."

At the mention of Bristol's name, the woman's eyes narrowed. Her lips puckered further than he thought they could go and she finally said, "One moment." She picked up the phone and pushed a button, not taking her eyes off of Cole. "There is a gentleman here by the name of Cole…" She lifted her eyebrows at Cole.

"Sullivan."

"Sullivan. He says he's a friend of Br — "

There was a squeal from behind a door toward the back and out came the same short woman he had seen before. When she reached him, she grabbed his hand with both of hers and shook it hard. Her grip was a vice. "Cole Sullivan, it is an absolute pleasure. Come on back. Helen. Coffee." She turned and pointed at Cole. "Anything for you?"

"Uh, no, thanks."

"Water? Tea? You know Bristol loves tea."

"Yes, I do know that."

"Of course you do," she said with the flip of her hand. "Follow me."

When they entered her office, she pushed Cole into a chair then walked around her desk and sat in her own, leaning forward on her elbows, red nails clacking on each other. Her voice was like butter. "So, Cole. You're even better looking than your DMV photo."

"You've seen my DMV photo?"

Deb grinned conspiratorially. "Back when you and Bristol first met. She asked me to find out who you were."

"And how did you find me?"

"She had a picture of your license plate. It's easy

from there. If you two end up getting married, then I just want you to know it was all down to me finding out who you were. And if things don't work out, well … " She spread her hands wide. "That's your own fault. I can only do so much."

The woman talked a million miles a minute. He wondered if that was a strategy she used in the courtroom, spin them around until they didn't know which way was up.

There was a knock at the door.

"Come in!" Deb bellowed.

Helen came in with the coffee. "Anything else?"

"No," Deb said, swishing her off with her hand without looking at her.

Cole glanced at the woman who, instead of looking defeated by her boss's dismissive attitude, looked esteemed. It wasn't the type of environment he could see Bristol comfortable in. This was not what he expected.

"Sorry, was there a specific reason you are here? Or just popped by to say hello?"

"Uh … no." He turned back to Deb and settle himself into the chair. "Actually, I'm curious how you and Bristol know each other."

"Oh, we go way back. Known each other since we were kids. She found me getting picked on by these bullies and punched one of the girls right in the nose. I'm pretty sure she broke it. That woman has always gone at things full speed. Maybe that's why we get on so well together." She smiled and waited for Cole to speak again.

"Interesting. What I really came here for was I wanted to talk to you about Bristol's visit with the FBI."

"Sorry, attorney-client privilege." Deb's boisterous face was now a locked vault. Cole didn't know what to make of it.

"I was just concerned about Bristol and I wanted to make sure — "

"Sorry, you're not going to budge me. I like you already, but I don't mess around when it comes to that stuff."

Deb's phone rang, and she clicked her tongue and pushed the phone up to her ear. "What!" She yelled into the phone. "Oh, put him through." She put her hand over the mouthpiece and looked at Cole. "Sorry, I have to take this. It will only be a second." She spoke back into the phone. "Phillip, what the hell?" She listened. "You little shit. I'll do whatever the hell I want. You told me yourself you changed the outcomes." She listened again. "Attorney-client privilege my ass. You think I can't find out something else, you little dipshit? You are so full of it. I won't have to turn over too many stones to find out what I want, you son of a bitch. What? ... Go to hell." She slammed down the phone then looked up and smiled sweetly at Cole. She laced her fingers together. "Now, where were we?"

Cole smiled. She was something else. "Bristol and the FBI."

"Yeah, not giving you shit. Oh! Sorry, I don't like to talk to my friends like that. I've got plenty of enemies to save it for. If Phillip Ryder thinks I will go quietly after the way he treated me." She shook her head. "But anyway, no, I'm not going to give you anything."

Cole blinked a couple of times, trying to find his footing. There weren't many people that could have him fighting to stay upright. Bristol's friends were an unusual bunch, but it was obvious she had the best on her side. He had no doubt this woman would stand in front of a bullet for Bristol — literally or figuratively — if she could.

He tried a different tactic. "How about I give you what I've got. Bristol told me she agreed to testify against Silas, so naturally I was concerned for her safety."

"Naturally."

"She said I had nothing to worry about because Silas wouldn't know yet. I just wanted to make sure she gave me the facts."

"You think she was lying to you?" The arc in Deb's lifted eyebrow spoke louder than any words.

Cole laughed lightly and leaned back. "Bristol isn't above lying when it comes to protecting those she cares about. In this case though, no, I don't think she's lying. But I'm here to give myself some amount of reassuring."

"Fascinating." She smirked.

"What?"

"You've got her worked out pretty well. But she's right. They wouldn't have approached Silas yet. Not until they were rock solid and had informed me. Although ... " She stood and walked over to the window, separating the blinds and looking up and down the sidewalk where she spotted a black van that had been there since she came in this morning, then she turned back to Cole and crossed her arms. "Once he does know, we will have to find a way to keep her safe."

Cole's mouth twitched and Deb leaned forward, her eyes narrowing. "The FBI have offered, but I trust them about as much as I trust Bristol to always tell the truth."

"I'd rather not leave the protection to the FBI either. I'd expect Silas to find his way in there. Also — " He grinned. "It's not in my nature to stay out of it. I'm confident I can keep her safe, but you know how she feels about people helping her. I might need a hand persuading her to agree to my protection."

Deb's smile was wicked. "I'm very good at convincing people of things. Let me help."

Cole laughed. "I was unsure about you at the start, Deb — "

"Uht." Deb pointed a crimson finger at him like a dart. "Deb*oh*rah. Only Bristol gets to call me Deb."

"Right, Deb*oh*rah. I'm glad she has you."

"It's a mutually beneficial relationship for both friendship and business."

"Okay, well then. I won't take up any more of your time. But I'll be in touch."

"Yes, please do that. And stop by anytime." She winked.

Cole shoved his hands in his pockets when he stepped out into the late morning sun. Deb would be an excellent asset to have.

His phone vibrated against his hand, and he pulled it out. He didn't recognize the number.

"Yeah, Cole here."

"Cole, hi," said a vaguely familiar woman's voice.

"Sorry, who's this?"

"It's Elly."

"Oh, Elly … hi."

Chapter 12

COLE PINCHED the bridge of his nose. He wasn't expecting to hear from Elly again. "What can I do for you?"

"So formal," she said, almost to herself. "I was wondering what you were doing."

"Right now?"

"Yeah."

"Uh, standing on a sidewalk in the city, why?"

"I thought we could have coffee."

"I'm not in Chicago anymore, remember?"

"I know, neither am I, remember?" There was a glint in her voice.

Cole paused. "You're in LA?"

"Yeah, I told you. You really don't remember?"

"No, I'm sorry, I don't. I had a lot on my mind when we spoke."

"Of course. Well, to refresh your memory — at your dad's funeral, I told you I got a new job in Los Angeles."

"Oh … right."

"I'm in the city too. Can I see you?"

"Uh." Cole looked around him and saw a busy café across the road. "I'll text you a place if you can meet me here?"

"Yeah, sure. See you soon."

Cole hung up and swallowed hard. He texted through the address and stared at the screen.

Someone bumped into him as he stood in the middle of the flow of pedestrians and he nearly dropped the phone. He moved out of the traffic on the sidewalk then called Andrew.

"Hey Cole, how'd everything go with your dad? I haven't heard anything further on Silas."

"Yeah, no, I'm fine. Listen. I just got a call from Elly."

"*The* Elly?"

"Yeah, that one."

"What did she want?"

"I bumped into her at my dad's funeral."

"Uh-huh."

"She just moved to LA."

"Uh-oh."

"Yeah, well, that's what I'm afraid of. But a girl wouldn't just do that, would she? With no idea how the other person would respond? She wouldn't have any expectations? God, this has totally thrown me. If it's not one thing, it's another right now."

"No, I'm sure it's unrelated. She's just looking up an old friend. One she walked out on years ago."

"You don't sound convinced."

"I'm not, but my wife could probably translate the

situation better than I would, and unfortunately, I'm not at home to ask. Do you want me to call her and see what she thinks?"

"I'm not that desperate."

"Yet."

"I'm about to meet up with her for a coffee."

"Make sure there's a crowd, and you know where the exits are."

Cole laughed. "Don't I always?"

"Call me if you need backup."

"I will, and wish me luck."

"You won't need it 'cause there's nothing to worry about."

"Yeah, right."

◯◯

Bristol felt energized after her workout and nearly gave Deb's a miss, but she was feeling so good she thought she'd pay a visit to her friend and at least check in.

Out of habit, she walked fast enough to make good time, but slow enough that she could scan her surroundings. Anyone, or anything suspicious looking, she'd spot it.

A young man, tall and gangly with a cap pulled low over his eyes, stepped out of a convenient store. His hands restless in his pockets. He'd swiped something. Judging by the bulge, it was a drink. Judging by his age, it was probably Mountain Dew.

She grinned. She'd done it before when she was

young. Usually it was a box of mac and cheese because her mom had nothing in the house for dinner.

She passed a café with a large window. Her eyes moved quickly from face to face. There were a few suits. One girl sat in the corner in black clothes and black hair. Her fingers moved across her phone expertly. Maybe it was a text. Maybe she'd been inspired to write the great American novel.

Her eyes shifted again. She froze, her feet anchored to the ground. A man in a suit with his phone to his ear slammed into her and his cell flew out of his hand. Bristol thrust forward and caught it. He looked at her for a moment, his face contorting from anger to surprise like he couldn't decide whether to thank her or swear at her for getting in his way. When she handed the phone back to him, he mumbled a quick thanks and shoved the phone back to his ear as he continued on his way.

Bristol went back to the window. Cole. He was frowning and picking at something on the table. The way her stomach knotted irritated her. She was tired of being a coward about him. She was a big enough woman to apologize and now seemed as good an opportunity as any.

The place was full, and from the door, she could no longer see Cole.

Curving her way around people and tables, she wondered what would have happened if Cole's dad hadn't passed away, and they had stayed in that café the other night.

A woman, standing at a table, gestured widely with her hands, taking up a lot of space in the crowded room. It reminded her of Deb.

She focused on the woman's arms as she attempted to skirt around behind her. She dodged a hand that Bristol assumed was being used to describe the fish that got away.

When she was finally out of danger, she turned her attention back to where she judged Cole had been seated then stopped.

He had been alone when she saw him through the window. Now he was with a woman. A very good-looking, sophisticated one.

Bristol knew it could be anyone, but she still held her breath in a ridiculous attempt to become invisible. She decided to execute a hasty exit and began to turn, but Cole spotted her. She couldn't read the surprise on his face, but he lifted his arm in greeting. The smile that followed was warm. Her stomach twisted again, but she ignored it and smiled.

Cole leaned in to say something to the woman and stood, walking toward Bristol. The woman's gaze followed his movement, with the corners of her mouth turning down not long after.

Bristol walked forward to meet him, and the woman stood to join them.

Cole spoke first. "You headed to see Deb? I mean Deborah."

The quickness of Cole's correction had Bristol laughing. "You've met her, I take it?"

"Yes, just this morning. I like her."

"Yeah. She's good value. I was just on my way to see her, but then I saw you … Sorry for interrupting." She looked at Elly.

"No, you're not interrupting anything. Elly's an old friend. She's just moved into town."

Elly put her hand out. "It's nice to meet you."

Cole jerked. "Uh, Elly, this is Bristol. Bristol, this is Elly."

Cole rubbed a hand down Bristol's arm. "You're looking better. Get a good rest last night?"

Bristol saw Elly's eyes twitch down at the gesture, and Bristol resisted the urge to put a possessive arm around Cole. This whole — liking a guy — was horrible. "Actually, I didn't sleep well, but I had a good training session at the gym."

Elly leaned forward slightly. "Oh, do you do aerobics?" The tone held a hint of sickly sweet condescension.

"Kickboxing." Bristol responded flatly. The last thing she wanted was a girl fight over Cole, but she would not allow herself to be put down.

Elly smiled like she tasted something awful but was pretending it was good. "Cole and I used to be engaged."

"Right hook," Bristol said under her breath.

"Pardon?"

"That was a long time ago, Elly," Cole said.

"I know." She turned her attention back to Bristol. "I left him heartbroken and went to New York. It was the biggest mistake of my life."

Bristol looked at Cole, who was looking at Elly with

his mouth partly open. "Cole, I just came in to apologize for the way I acted the other night. I know you were just concerned for me, and I wasn't very appreciative of your concern. So, I'm sorry. In case I don't see you again."

Cole seemed to finally find his tongue. "No, it's fine. It's been a crazy couple of weeks. Wait, why wouldn't I see you again?"

"Have you two known each other long?" Elly interrupted.

"Nope," Bristol said before Cole could respond. "We barely know each other. Well, I'll leave you two now. Sorry again for interrupting."

Cole followed her toward the door. "Bristol, this is not what it looks like."

"What do you think it looks like?" She said over her shoulder as she avoided patrons.

"Well, I don't know. I just don't want you to think it's something it's not."

"Look, Cole." She stopped and turned. "It's really none of my business."

Elly appeared. "Cole, coffee's here." She said it more to Bristol than to Cole, but as he turned to her, Bristol took the opportunity to escape. This was way out of her area of expertise. She practically ran to Deb's.

Cole turned back to Bristol after acknowledging Elly and watched her disappear through the crowd. He wanted to go after her, but with Elly's hand on his arm, he thought he had better be a grownup about it and take care of this first.

When they sat back down, Elly said, "Bristol seems nice."

"Elly, I'm not sure what your expectation was moving here … "

"I don't have any expectation except that I would have the opportunity to hang out with an old friend and maybe get to know him again."

"So this isn't about getting back together?"

She laughed delicately and touched her fingers to her lips. "You always did get straight to the point. I can't expect you to fall into my arms after the way I treated you, can I? Look, there's no pressure from me. We can just see what happens."

Cole dropped his head and took a sip of coffee. He didn't want to tell Elly that he had fallen so hard for Bristol that all he wanted to do was jump out of his seat and go after her. That would be cruel. But how could he make her understand that even if they regained a friendship, that's as far as it would go?

Cole took another sip of his coffee while Elly told him all about her new job. She even dropped in a detail about a house she was looking at buying that was just like the one they had always talked about getting together one day. Cole didn't bother mentioning that it was the house she had always wanted, not he.

He waited what he thought was a polite amount of time after finishing his coffee and then excused himself. Elly stood and kissed him lingeringly on the cheek. Cole grimaced a smile and left, quickly calling Andrew as he walked to his car. He had originally started toward Deb's but changed his mind. He'd give Bristol some space and then get in touch.

"Hey, Cole. How'd it go?"

"Well, she met Bristol accidentally."

"How does that happen?"

"Bad luck? I told you, you should wish me luck."

"Did it go as badly as I think it did?"

"I don't know. I've got to talk to Bristol. You don't know of any buildings I could break into?"

"Uh … No, why?"

"I find it calming."

"Did you tell Elly you're with someone else?"

"But I'm not really with Bristol."

"Yet."

"And I didn't want to be mean by telling her that I would rather be sitting there with Bristol."

"Why not? If there were no Bristol would you be interested in Elly?" Cole didn't respond. "You can't be serious. You wouldn't seriously consider it?"

"No, I wouldn't, but we have all this history and there was a time when I was in love with her, and I don't want to hurt her now."

"Even though she hurt you?"

"I'm not after revenge if that's what you're thinking."

"Maybe not, but I called Jenny, and she said you'll have to be clear, otherwise you'll lead her on and that will just make things worse."

"God, I know. I just … I don't know why Elly would move here."

"You did just inherit your father's fortune."

"I don't — I don't think she'd go through the trouble. Maybe. She'd be disappointed. I'm not interested in living the same lifestyle as my father. That was one reason we never would have worked."

"There you go. Next time she gets in touch, you're going to have to tell her. And if you're interested in keeping Bristol, I'd recommend cutting ties with your ex."

"She did say we could just be friends."

"If Bristol had an old boyfriend who she was suddenly friends with again, how would you feel about that?"

"Ah."

"Exactly."

"You are so wise, my friend."

"I'll tell my wife you said so."

"By the way, just for your ears only — Bristol is cutting a deal with the FBI to testify against Silas to get him to hand over information to the feds."

"What?"

"I know. If you have any ideas about how we can keep her safe, let me know."

"A life with Bristol would never be dull, that's for sure. You think you're up for it?"

"Don't think I have a choice."

"The feds could put her in witness protection?"

Cole shook his head even though Andrew couldn't see it. "I'm sure they've offered. But he'd find her."

"I don't know. It's a good program."

"Yeah, but Silas seems to have contacts everywhere. I'd prefer it if no one knew where she was."

"Except you?"

"Well, naturally me." Cole grinned. "I know I can keep her safer than the FBI can."

"I know you're definitely motivated too. But Cole, there's really only one way I can think for her to be safe."

"Don't worry. If I get the opportunity to kill Silas, I'll take it without hesitation."

Chapter 13

BRISTOL WALKED through Deb's front door. A man in a suit sat looking at his phone. His legs were crossed casually, but when he lifted his eyes to her, she recognized the sober attention he paid her. It was the same look she had gotten while in the custody of the FBI.

She nodded to him as she approached the reception desk. His eyes dropped back to his phone.

She turned to Deb's new personal assistant with eyes narrowed and slapped her hand down on the desk when she reached it. She couldn't see the agent, but she could feel his eyes on her again.

With Cole and Elly forgotten, a concern for Deb bubbled away, frothing into edginess. "I believe we spoke on the phone. I'm Bristol Kelley and I'm going through to see Deb, now." She stepped around the desk.

"No, Wait … Ms. Kelley … you can't … " The woman's shirt had somehow tangled in the chair, and she pulled it along behind her as she worked to yank herself free. It slowed her enough for Bristol to slip by easily.

"No use arguing," Bristol added as the woman caught up. "You know she'll let me through."

She rapped a knuckle lightly on the door as she opened it. It only took Bristol a moment to scan and interpret the scene.

Three men in suits had been riffling through Deb's drawers and cabinets, but now, all eyes were on the door. Deb's red stiletto had paused its tap and Bristol could see that she was nervous. Her arms were crossed against her body, but if she had felt in control of the situation, her hands would have been set firmly on her hips.

Bristol still had her hand on the knob when Deb lifted her chin into the air and walked toward Bristol, grabbing her by the arm.

The lead man in the room stepped forward. "Excuse me, but who's your friend."

"You should already know that," she fired back. "Your mob harassed her only … what … a few hours ago? You can grill her later. Right now, we're going to go have a private conversation."

"Don't leave the building."

"Imbecile," Deb stated under her breath as she pulled Bristol out the door. Then she spotted Helen, who was opening and closing her mouth like a fish, trying to decide what to say.

Deb spoke first. "I told you to keep an eye on the spook at the front. I don't want him getting into anything that I don't know about."

Deb clicked her tongue as she pulled Bristol the

other way down the hall. "It's hard to find good help. Especially when the FBI decides to turn your place upside down."

She yanked Bristol to a stop in front of a closed door after a couple of thundering steps. Her eyes darted back and forth as if she were casing the place, then she opened the door and pulled Bristol in, shutting them into the dark.

"There's got to be a light switch in here somewhere." Bristol could hear a faint swooshing as Deb groped for the switch. "Gotcha."

The lights went on and Deb went rigid. "I always wondered what was in here." She shrugged and lifted her hands. "Welcome to my new office."

Bristol scrutinized a mop, bucket, and shelves full of various items. "This is a cleaning closet."

"Yeah. Who knew?"

"You didn't know what it was?"

"Didn't seem important."

Bristol watched her friend for a second, then asked, "What's going on out there?"

"They've got a warrant."

"That's the feds?"

"Yup."

"What's the warrant for?"

"Apparently, they think I'm breaking the law." She scoffed. "I mean, my job is to get my clients what they believe to be justice. That's my job."

Bristol ground her teeth. "They're doing this because you're my lawyer."

"Ever think that maybe not everything is your

fault?"

Bristol huffed. "How long have they been here?"

"Less than an hour. But I will give them this — they don't waste time."

"Have you covered your tracks?"

"Of course I have."

"Then why do you look scared."

"I don't like people going through my stuff."

Bristol put a hand on her friend's shoulder. "You shouldn't worry about prison. You'll do great. You'll own that place within six months."

Deb's eyes narrowed. "Did you just make a joke, Bristol Kelley?"

"Desperate times."

"OH!" Deb's hand clamped down on Bristol's. "I met Cole today. Wow, he is even better looking in person. Please tell me you are all over him like a rash."

Bristol shook Deb off. "You're so vulgar. And no, I'm not, but that's what I wanted to talk to you about."

Deb sucked all the air from the room as an open-mouthed smile took over her face. Bristol winced at what she knew was coming. "This is the best day of my life. You coming to me for advice about love. You've just made me the happiest woman in the world." She finished with a squeal that, to Bristol, was like fingernails down a chalkboard.

"Hey, I never said anything about love."

"Didn't need to. I can see it in the little crease between your eyes."

Bristol rubbed at the crease. "That's the product of

letting myself slip up. And if you don't settle down, I'm out of here."

Deb grinned seductively then said, "Sorry, I'll settle down." She pulled a bucket over and tipped it upside down, sitting and crossing her legs demurely. "So tell me. What can I do for you today?"

Bristol glared, but then leaned against the wall and slid down. "I want to know how to make it stop."

"Make what stop?"

"This horrible tingling I get in my stomach every time I think of him." Bristol put a finger up when Deb's smile turned sultry. "That's your first warning."

"You're no fun," Deb pouted

"This isn't supposed to be fun. And it isn't fun. I ran into him with his ex-fiancée and I wanted to rip her face off."

"That's a completely normal response to an ex. But more importantly, what was he doing with her?"

"I don't know. He said it wasn't what it looked like, but I would say his ex didn't agree."

Deb's eyes widened. "Ooh, I love a good love triangle."

"Well, I don't. I want nothing to do with it."

"Then you'll have to make sure he knows that you're the one for him."

"Stop. I'm not the one for him. We haven't known each other that long."

"When's the last time you liked a guy?"

"I don't know. Never? I've certainly never been so twisted up over one. Is this normal?"

"Honey, that is multiple shades of normal. What

isn't normal is never liking a guy. Geez Bristol, whatever happened to you, it must have been tragic." Deb never knew what was going on in Bristol's life growing up, and Bristol wasn't going to start telling her now. She was relieved when Deb continued. "You know what your problem is?"

"Please enlighten me."

"You're scared."

"Of course I am. That part I already knew. But what I don't know is why I can't get rid of it. It has totally messed up my head. Life was so much simpler when all I did was screw around with crime scenes. Blood and gore I can handle. Guns and fighting make sense."

Deb tipped her head sideways. "My little girl is growing up."

"Just tell me how to get rid of it."

"You don't," she said matter-of-factly. "You just go for it scared."

"Is that what you do?"

"Honestly? No, I think the guys are more afraid of me." She tittered.

"Well, it doesn't matter. Doing it scared is not an option. You need to tell me how to get over him."

Deb leveled her eyes at Bristol and reached out to grab her hands. "Bristol, you are one of my oldest and dearest friends, and I say this in all seriousness. You don't want to get over him. You don't want to go back to the way things were. Trust me. Let this guy in. Yeah, it's scary, but if you stay closed off your whole life…" Deb shook her head. "Trust me, you'll feel better if you go for it. Even if it hurts a little. It's better than being numb."

"Damn you." Bristol ripped her hands out of Deb's. "I think I like it better when you're crazy. When you go all serious, you're harder to dismiss." Bristol huffed and leaned her head back against the wall. "Maybe I'm just not the sort of person who has long-term commitments."

"First of all, I'm going to forgive you for that crazy comment, not because you might be right, but because I love you. Second, you're definitely the long-term commitment type."

Bristol looked at her friend, waiting for the punchline. When she didn't continue, Bristol shook her head with a cockeyed smile on her face. "What makes you so sure I'm *definitely* the commitment type. You know enough about me to know that commitment is not my thing."

"No? Then why are you one of the most loyal people I know. You were made for marriage and babies and all the other family stuff. You just had some shit happen to you that screwed all of that up. Trust me. If you had had a normal upbringing, you'd already be happily married by now with at least one baby."

"How can you say that?"

"Because I see how you are with the people you care about. You'd give your life for any of your friends. You don't get offended easily, at least not when it comes to real stuff — "

"Hey, I get offended plenty."

"Yeah, if I told you you were gorgeous, you'd be

offended, but if I told you I hate your guts or something, you'd shrug it off."

"That's just because some stuff's not important enough to fight over. Besides, if you told me you hated me, I'd know there was something else going on. So why would I get offended when it's not personal?"

"Exactly. You'd make a brilliant wife and mom if you gave it a chance."

"Ugh, I can't believe the words that are coming out of your mouth. I thought you knew me better than that."

"Apparently I know you better than you know yourself. Which is unsurprising." Deb picked invisible lint from her pants.

"If you knew me that well, you'd know kids aren't my thing."

"Oh really? So that whole thing where you were willing to sacrifice your life to save that little girl — Lila, was it? You can't stand her?"

"She's different."

"Of course she is, and so would your own kids be."

Bristol grunted her annoyance. She knew she wasn't going to win this argument.

Luckily, there was a rapid knock at the door, and it opened. One of the agents was standing there. He looked back and forth between the women.

"What are you two doing in here?" he asked.

"Hatching an evil plan," Deb said.

"I'll have to search your friend here before she leaves."

"Well then, I should introduce you two. Bristol, this is Secret Agent 007. Secret Agent 007, this is Bristol."

"Pleasure," Bristol said, standing.

The agent didn't look amused. "Make sure you see me before you go."

Deb saluted the agent, then nudged him out of the way and closed the door again, then started giggling. "I think I'm having too much fun with this."

Bristol raised her eyebrow. "You think maybe that's your defense mechanism?"

"Oh, listen to you. Yes, of course it is. Just like shutting everyone out is yours. I'll tell you what, I'll stop mine if you stop yours."

Bristol frowned. "You've been absolutely no help to me. So let's talk about what we can do to help you."

Deb tapped her lip. "You know that tech friend of yours?"

"Who, Mick?"

"Yeah, has he ever hacked into the FBI?"

"Uh, I don't think he'd go that far. There must be something else we can do. I'll go talk to him and see. He might have some good ideas.

"Okay, then before you leave, there's just one last thing, and this might help you with your problem."

"I'm all ears."

"When Silas finds out about you, he'll come for you. Forget about the FBI's help. You need to let Cole keep you safe."

"I don't need Cole to keep me safe." Bristol felt the blood rush to her face and was relieved Deb was kind enough to ignore it.

"Yes, you do. You'll have to put your misgivings aside and let him help you because otherwise you'll end up dead, and I can't have that."

"And how exactly does that help me with my problem?"

"I'd tell you, but you'd probably hit me."

Bristol growled. "I'll think about it."

"That's not good enough."

"Well, it will have to be because you know I need time to get used to the idea."

"As long as you're used to it by the time the FBI gets their shit together."

Bristol moved to go out the door, and Deb grabbed her arm. "Promise me. Right now, or I'll make a scene."

"Fine, I'll let Cole help. Happy?"

"I'll be happy once all of this mess is over and you're happily married."

Bristol slapped her friend lightly on the shoulder. "I gotta go. I'll stop by Mick's and see what he has to say."

"Stay safe." Deb pulled Bristol into an uncharacteristic hug, then let her go with a tight smile.

Bristol sighed several times as she was frisked on her way out. Every time she caught Deb's eye, Bristol lifted her eyebrows suggestively. It was the least she could do to lift Deb's spirits. When she left, she gave her friend a wink the agent didn't see.

Chapter 14

BRISTOL REACHED the main door of Mick's apartment complex just as a tiny woman with a green vest came out the door with a tiny dog wearing a green vest.

Bristol grabbed the edge of the door for the woman and smiled, then let herself in.

At Mick's apartment she lifted her hand to knock but stopped when she heard an "Oof" followed by a muffled bang, like something soft and heavy had hit the ground. She pressed her ear up to the door

"I … told you … I don't — "

There was another sound that Bristol recognized as fist on flesh.

She glanced down at her bag and swore under her breath when she realized she didn't have her gun with her. She dropped the useless bag against the wall and stood back, locked her eyes just below where she knew the lock was, and did a front kick, focusing her momentum into her heel. It cracked. She kicked it again and then a third time.

As the door ripped open, she jumped to the side in case a weapon was fired and skimmed the scene before her, blocking out all emotion and taking in only the facts of the situation.

There were two men in the room besides Mick, who she observed only long enough to confirm what she already suspected — he was tied to a chair and had a swollen and bleeding face.

There were no guns that she could see, but the man that was closest to her was built like a bulldozer. His eyebrows and chin even stuck out like a shovel.

She judged him to be about the same height as Eli, but he didn't move the same as her friend.

As he waded toward her through his overabundance of muscle, she could see that he wasn't coordinated enough to manage his own bulk. He did his job by intimidating his victim into submission, not by fighting.

The other man was much more agile. He was the real threat and probably the leader. His muscles moved in a synchronized twitch. Every movement he made was fluid and controlled. The dozer was window dressing. This guy could have managed on his own. He also had brass knuckles on his right hand.

This wouldn't be pretty.

She focused on the big man first. He needed to be removed from the equation and would be the easiest to take down. A big guy like that had only a couple of weak spots. Trying to get him in his thick neck or punch through to a kidney would be pointless. It helped that he led the attack.

Bristol made eye contact and grinned. "That's a lot of muscle you've got there."

He grunted and came at her.

"Must be hard on the knees," she said, and she lunged forward and kicked out at his leg. It bent in an ugly way and he howled as he went down. *That's one.*

The other man hadn't moved yet and looked slightly offended. "You'll pay for that."

"Doubt it." She lifted her arms lightly, keeping them loose and ready for his attack. He wasn't the type to waste time.

He hopped from one foot to the other and fisted his hand into his palm. His head dropped almost imperceptibly as he went straight in with a jab with his hand that didn't have the knuckles. Bristol fell back slightly, taking his fist to the shoulder.

He underestimated her, beginning with his weaker arm. He'd soon learn his mistake.

She spun around and kicked, but he was a quick learner, and he moved fast. When she missed, she kept spinning and lifted another leg that caught him on his side. He grabbed her foot, but she already knew which way he would twist, so she went with it, bringing her other foot around to follow, hitting him in the head. It meant she fell hard on her side, but she got him enough to stun him a little.

She jumped to her feet, and he shook himself out. His movement triggered something in her memory. He reminded her of someone, but she couldn't place him.

She shouldn't have let herself get distracted. That second of pause was all he needed. He kicked her in the stomach, throwing her backward against a table. She was winded but not dazed, and she saw a book. A pinpoint of attention told her it was a dictionary, and a thought splashed through her mind of why Mick would have a huge dictionary sitting out. She could have smiled, but she was still trying to get air into her lungs when she twisted around as the guy rushed to her. He grabbed her by her hair to lift her off the table, intending to smash his knuckles into her face, but she had the book in her hands and swung around with it smashing it into the side of his head, sending him sprawling. If she were a different person, she would have come up with some pithy remark about using words as a weapon. Instead, she sucked more oxygen into her lungs as her mind raced to come up with a plan of attack. He was as good at reading her as she was him.

She slid across the room and grabbed a chair to break over his head as he rose, wiping a hand across his bloody mouth and curling his lip up to suck on a gold tooth. Bristol froze with the chair lifted. Her eyes wide. He changed his stance, ready to rush her, but she didn't move. "Jimmy?"

The smile dropped off his face, and he pushed his head forward, squinting. "Holy shit. Bristol?"

"What the hell?"

"Bristol, what are you doing here?"

"I should ask you the same question. I haven't seen you since we were practically kids." With the threat of attack over, the rest of the room came back into focus. The big man was groaning on the floor. "This is who you're running around with now?"

"Oh, Bernie's all right. He's just a bit slow."

She glanced at Mick, who looked baffled, trying to follow the exchange through a blur of pain. "Can we call a truce so I can look after my friend?"

Jimmy looked at Mick. "I don't know Bristol. I'm just doing what I'm told."

"Who told you to mess up Mick?"

"My boss, Mr. Tesco."

"You're working for Tesco? I didn't even know he was still around."

"Yeah, he's all over the place now. Big business. He's even gone across the border."

"Wow, I'm really out of the loop. But what's he want from Mick?"

"Apparently, your friend double-crossed him."

Bristol walked over to Mick and squatted. She looked him over then in the eyes. "Is this true?"

He shook his head lightly.

She stood and walked back to Jimmy. "It's not true."

"You just take his word for it?"

"There are only a few people in this world whose word I trust. He's one of them. What does your boss think he did?"

"Mick did a job for Mr. Tesco last year and then handed that information over to the FBI."

She looked at Mick. That was one thing she knew he'd never do. She pushed her lips together and looked back at Jimmy. Her voice was quiet but annoyed. "Would anyone else have had that information?"

Jimmy shrugged. "How should I know?"

"Did Tesco do any time?"

"No, there wasn't enough to press charges, but Mr. Tesco doesn't enjoy being double-crossed."

"I don't blame him, but Mick isn't the one that handed the information over."

"That's not my problem. I told you, I'm just doing my job."

"Well, guess what? It's your problem now."

Jimmy crossed his arms. "How's that?"

"You remember that jam I got you out of? You know what would have happened to you if I hadn't stepped in? You had no money and no friends. If I didn't fix that place up, we wouldn't be having this conversation right now."

Jimmy's shoulders dropped. "That was a long time ago, Bristol. I can't believe you're holding that over me."

She clenched her fists. He was right. It was a pretty lousy thing to do. "I do what I have to," she finally said.

"Do you know what will happen if I walk out now? You know what Mr. Tesco will do to me?"

"Ring him up and let me talk to him."

"What, you're my mom now?"

"You're telling me your mom would talk to Tesco?"

Jimmy grimaced and looked at the floor. "She died last year." He toed the carpet.

"I'm sorry. Listen. I don't want to get you into trouble. Just tell Tesco I have information for him that he'd be way more interested in than what he can do to Mick. But he's got to give Mick a break until he hears me out."

Jimmy licked at the blood that had gathered on his lip again. "I can try, but I won't promise nothin'."

"That's all I ask."

Jimmy walked to the other side of the room to make the call and Bristol rushed over to Mick.

Bernie had pushed himself up against the couch. His eyes were closed and his breathing shallow. Every now and then he moaned. He wasn't much of a sidekick for Jimmy. Although, with Jimmy's fighting skills, it didn't really matter. Jimmy hadn't been much of a fighter when she'd met him, but he'd obviously been trained in the years since, and he was a natural.

Bristol turned her attention back to Mick and touched his face gently. "You okay? Looks like your cheek is fractured." She ran a hand down each arm and leg. Noticing that he had at least one broken finger.

"Bristol." She could tell it hurt him to talk. He might have internal bleeding.

"I'll get you to the hospital. We can tell them you were mugged."

He nodded lightly then said, "Can you pick Lila up from school. It was her first day back today. Take her to your place. I can't let her see me like this. Especially after what happened to her."

"Uh, Mick, I don't think that's a good idea."

"Please. She'll be terrified to see me like this."

She knew he was right, but she had things to take care of. She had to clean the mess up, and she certainly couldn't do it with a six-year-old tagging along.

Mick coughed and brought up blood.

"I gotta get you out of here. Okay. I'll get her. I'll figure something out."

Jimmy came back in the room. "He said he's willing

to put things on hold. He remembers you. Said you did some work for him."

"I did. A long time ago. I found him to be very professional."

"He'll meet with you tonight at 9:00. Make sure you're in the Long Beach area by 8:30, and we'll send you details when you get there."

"Thanks."

He looked down at Bernie and rested his hands on his hips. "You sure made a mess here, Bristol."

"Please tell me what I should have done instead. I'm all ears," she said as she untied Mick.

"I don't know how Mr. Tesco will take it."

"You can tell him to thank me later. You'd do better on your own and it would save him money."

"Don't listen to her, Bernie. She's just jealous of your muscle bulk." He leaned down to grab hold of the big guy, pulling hard. "Jesus, Bristol. You messed his knee up bad."

"Then we're even," she said, pointing at Mick. "By the way, Jimmy. Your sidekick might be useless, but you're looking good. Your skills have improved over the years."

Jimmy looked suddenly shy and reminded Bristol of the kid she used to know. "You too."

Bristol got Mick loose and his hand grabbed at his opposite shoulder. Bristol went to his other side to pull him up. "Broken collarbone?"

"I think it's just dislocated," Mick rasped.

Once he was standing, Bristol went around to the

front of him and looked at it. "Yeah, I think you're right. You want me to try to fix it?"

"No! That's okay. Just get me to the hospital, and I'll be fine." He limped toward Lila's room.

"Where are you going?"

"To get some of Lila's things."

"Wait, I'll get them." She leaned him against a wall and headed for the girl's room.

She grabbed a bit of everything, including a stuffed rabbit Lila had shown her last time she was there.

When she got back to the living room, Jimmy was finally pulling Bernie off the floor.

Bristol pushed the broken door out of the way and called back to Jimmy, "Make sure you lock it on your way out." Then she looked at Mick. "Have you got someone who doesn't ask questions that you can call to come fix this?"

"Yeah, I'll get it sorted out."

∞

On the way to the emergency room, they agreed that Bristol should drop him off so she wouldn't be stuck answering questions. Bristol watched him limp through the doors. He was in a lot of pain, but she was impressed. You can never tell how well someone can handle pain until they're in it. She knew Mick could handle emotional pain but didn't expect him to hold up under possible internal injuries.

Bristol also hesitated to leave because her next stop was the primary school to pick up Lila, and there was something terrifying about walking into a place with so much innocence. Or maybe it was that everything from toilets to drinking fountains was miniaturized. Either way, it was a foreign environment, and she was suddenly too aware of herself.

She called Deb as soon as she left the hospital. "The FBI are screwing me over," she said as soon as Deb answered.

"You know they're probably listening in right now."

"Good. Not only are they suddenly after you, but they've told a crime boss that my friend Mick double-crossed them, so the boss sent his guys after him. It's not a very smart way to get me to cooperate."

"What are you going to do?"

"I haven't decided yet, but to whoever is listening in on this conversation, if things don't change soon, the deal is off the table."

Chapter 15

BRISTOL WALKED to the front of the school and read the banner that hung limply in the still, afternoon air.

INTEGRITY. COMPASSION. RESPECT. TRUST.

With its fading colors, it didn't garner much emotional response.

She pushed, grunted, then pulled on one of the large double doors.

She hadn't expected to feel small walking into a primary school, but under the ominous stare of the portraits hanging on the wall and the flickering fluorescent light at the entrance, she had a strong desire to back out. Because no one was around to see, she shook herself out and remembered why she was there.

Advancing into the school, she turned the corner into a hall where kids' drawings took the place of the portraits, and streamers hung from the ceiling. This was better.

She scanned the hall and spotted what she was looking for.

The door to the administration office had a beveled window that reminded her of an old private detective movie. It made her smile.

The smell of stationery greeted her when she entered the room, and a faded beige carpet led to a wood laminate reception desk that was empty.

A woman with long fingernails clicked away on an ancient keyboard at a desk a few feet behind.

The woman looked up at Bristol and smiled while she continued to type. "Won't be a moment." She beamed.

Bristol rested an arm on the reception desk and tapped her other hand on her leg while she waited, trying to keep her nerves in check.

"Is everything okay?" the woman asked as she stood and swooshed nearer to Bristol.

Bristol's muscles tightened. "Yes. Why wouldn't it be?"

The woman smiled reassuringly. "It's just that when parents visit in the middle of the day, there is usually a problem."

"Oh right. I'm not a parent." She cleared her throat. "I'm the friend of a parent. I'm here to pick up Lila Collins. Her dad called earlier to say I'd be coming?"

"Oh, yes. Lovely girl." She pulled a binder across the desk. "Paperwork." She rolled her eyes. "I just need you to fill this out."

Bristol balked, but at the woman's quizzical look she pulled it toward her. It had a list of names on it, each with an explanation for the early pickup. Some said sick, others had appointments. Bristol reminded herself again where she was and she wrote her name and Lila's, but paused over the reason for leaving.

"Just write 'family reasons.'" The woman whispered like it was their little secret.

"Thanks. I'd hate to get it wrong and end up in detention."

"Did you have a problem with that in your day?" She glanced appreciatively at Bristol's leather jacket.

"Maybe a little." Bristol signed her name and laid down the pen.

"Why don't you have a seat and I'll call Lila's class-room and let her know you're here. She won't be long."

"Thanks."

Bristol sat down on a skinny wooden chair with arms that lifted her shoulders up to her ears. She crossed her legs, pulled her elbows in, and linked her fingers around her knee.

The office door opened and a bald man dragged a boy, who looked about eight, past Bristol.

"I didn't do it," the kid said as he was escorted past her.

The kid looked at Bristol as he went past, and she lifted her eyebrows. He stuck his tongue out at her.

She snickered and said under her breath, "I bet you did do it." No one who's innocent makes a face like that.

Bristol watched the minutes tick by. It was another ten before the door opened again.

"Bishy!" Lila ran over and gave Bristol a big hug.

A woman in her sixties with her hair pulled back in a soft bun and a pink scarf wrapped around her neck joined them. "You must be Bristol," she said, reaching out to shake Bristol's hand.

"Yes, hi. I'm a friend of the family."

The teacher handed Bristol Lila's backpack and leaned in over the girl, dropping her voice. "Can I ask, is this related to what happened to Lila?"

It took Bristol a concerted effort not to take a step back. "You know what happened?"

"We were debriefed. I have to say, Lila is handling it all very well."

"She is an astonishing girl."

"She said you're the one that saved her?"

"One of the ones. It was a team effort."

"Are you a police officer?"

"No, just a friend. I was lucky. I was in the right place at the right time."

"Well, thank you for your part. Lila is a special girl."

"Yes, she is." Bristol felt awkward with the attention but surprised at the warm reception. "Well, we have to get going, but it was nice meeting you."

"You too."

Bristol put a hand on Lila's back and ushered her through the door.

"Oh, one other thing." The teacher stepped forward with her hand raised. Bristol pulled Lila to her, wrapping her arms around her in reflex. "We do special presentations with students and their parents or other important people in their lives. I would love it if you could come in one day and share. Not the specifics obviously, but … something."

Bristol loosened her grip on Lila who turned and

grabbed Bristol's hand, shaking it violently. "Will you Bristol? That would be so awesome!"

"Uh, yeah. I um … Maybe once this has all … you know. Settled." She pushed Lila forward again. This time more urgently. "I'll … uh … get back to you."

When they made it to the parking lot with no more incidences, Bristol took a deep breath. "She seems like a nice teacher."

"Yeah, I like her." Lila was skipping, a wide grin spilling over her face. "Am I having a sleepover at your place tonight?"

"Actually, I've got some things to do today, so I'm going to take you to see a friend of mine. He looked after me when I was a kid. He and his wife are two of my favorite people. But I'll come back later and check up on you."

"But I want to stay with you," she whined.

"Let's just go meet my friend Eli, who is a doctor and also runs a gym. Then we'll see how things go from there. How about that?"

"He's a doctor? Is he looking after Daddy?"

"They told you he's hurt?"

"Yeah. They said he got a bump on the head and that he's fine, but the hospital just needs to check him."

"So you're okay?"

"Mm-hmm. Is Daddy with your friend?"

"No, not this one. But he is with someone very good at making sure your daddy gets better fast. The doctor you're going to see has punching bags and exercise equipment you can play with."

Lila's mouth screwed up to the side in thought. "Maybe."

"What? Don't you want to be tough like me?"

"Daddy says it's because you're so tough that you don't see us more often. I don't want to be so tough that I can't be with anyone I want."

Bristol stopped mid-stride, jerking Lila to a stop.

Lila tipped her head at Bristol. "What?"

Bristol shook her head and laughed. "I think you are wise beyond your years."

At the gym, Bristol kept Lila out of sight at the side of the door before going in. She didn't need the little girl to see people punching the crap out of each other in the ring. That couldn't be good for her mental health. She didn't know how much Lila had seen while she was kidnapped and tried not to think about it.

It was quiet inside, and Bristol spotted Eli across the room in his office, which was unusual. He was never in there unless he was talking with someone, usually her. His forehead was resting on his hand. She couldn't tell if he was reading something on his desk or staring at nothing. Either way, the slope to his shoulders wasn't a good sign.

She walked Lila to his door and knocked as she pushed it open. Eli looked up, then saw it was her and looked back down, but he quickly lifted his head again when he noticed Bristol had brought a friend.

"Everything okay?" she asked, dropping Lila's bag on the couch and pointing for her to sit down.

He leaned back in his chair and focused on Lila. "Hi there."

"This is Lila. My friend Mick's daughter."

Eli stood and walked over to Lila. As he towered over her, the girl's mouth dropped open. "You're huge."

"Out of the mouths of babes," Eli said and held out his hand. She put her hand in his, spreading her fingers across his palm. He lifted her hand to his mouth and kissed it. "It's a pleasure to meet you, Lila."

"Bishy said you're a doctor. Do you cut people open?"

"No, but I do stitch them up." He glanced briefly at Bristol then back at Lila. "I do other things too. Help people get stronger, for example."

A smile spread across Lila's face, followed by a significant intake of breath. "Can you make me strong like you?"

Bristol shoved her hands onto her hips. "Hey! So you can be strong like him but not like me?"

"If I were as big as him, I could do anything I wanted."

Eli chuckled. "Well, let's see." He pulled Lila up off the couch and spread her arms away from her sides, looking her over. He opened her mouth and Lila poked her tongue out. Then he tipped her head and looked in her ears. "Looks to me like you've got a good start on you. You're healthy, and judging by the way you walked in here, without fear, you've got a strong mind. And what you need to be strong, more than anything, is a strong mind."

"My brain is super strong. I got all my spelling words right this week."

"Well then, I suppose you're an excellent candidate." He looked at Bristol then and frowned. "Which reminds me, there might not be a gym here for her to train in soon."

"What? Why, what's happened?"

Eli went back to his desk and picked up a piece of paper, handing it to her. "This came to my door today. I had to sign for it."

Bristol read through the paper with First Union Bank letterhead that basically said the building was in the process of being purchased, and Eli was receiving advance notice that he would be evicted from the premises. She stared at it. "Is this a joke?"

"No. I thought it was strange that the bank would send a letter like that, before a sale was finalized, so I called them. They confirmed that the buyer had asked for a letter to be delivered in order to give me time to get my stuff together. The bank manager felt the buyer was being generous."

"Generous my ass. I thought your landlord would never sell."

"He's the next person I called. He said he got an offer he couldn't refuse."

"From who?"

Eli opened his mouth but then closed it again. He winced before finally saying, "Lincoln Enterprises."

The paper crinkled in Bristol's fist. "Son of a — "

She turned and looked at Lila then back at Eli. "The letter was for me. He wanted me to know. Eli, I need you to look after Lila."

"Wait, Bristol — "

Bristol put her hand up to stop him from continuing and nodded a head toward Lila, who watched them with her mouth slightly open, not really following what was going on and she was starting to fidget.

"Hey Lila, see that bag out there hanging from the ceiling?"

"Yeah."

"You ready to get stronger?"

Her eyes widened. "Right now?"

"Yeah. Go punch it as many times as you can."

"Really?"

"Yeah."

"Cool."

Bristol opened the door, and the girl ran straight at the bag. She jumped up, wrapping her skinny legs around it, and slid to the ground, then scrambled up and started punching and pushing into it with her little body.

Eli watched her for a minute, nodding lightly. "Impressive." Then he turned to Bristol. "It's Silas Lincoln, isn't it? Lincoln Enterprises. I did a bit of research after I saw you last."

Bristol nodded. "Remember I said he kidnapped a friend's daughter?" She nodded toward Lila.

Eli's muscles spasmed in unison, and his face darkened. "He kidnapped that little girl." He pointed a thick finger toward Lila.

"Yeah."

"Is she okay? Of course she's not okay." He ran his hands over his head. "But how is she doing so well?"

"I don't know. She's talking to people … Or maybe it's like you said, she's got a strong mind. She's come out of this somehow feeling safe. He didn't do anything to her. He just wanted to get to me, so he took her." She pushed her fingers into her temple. "I thought it was the FBI."

"You thought what was the FBI?"

"Everything." She walked over to the couch and collapsed. "I should have known. I took too much for granted with Silas being in custody, but looking back at it now … " She shook her head. "Silas either found out I agreed to testify, which I can't put past him, or he's just being vindictive for my involvement in his arrest. Either way, he's the one who's going after all my friends."

"*All* your friends? You mean there's more happening than this? He pointed at the paper."

"Like I said, I thought it was the FBI threatening me, making my life hell to put on the pressure."

"What else is going on?"

"They're investigating a lawyer friend of mine, and I just found Lila's dad being beaten for apparently leaking information to the FBI. That's why she's here with me. I found him in time, he'll be okay, but he's at the hospital. And after everything she's been through, we couldn't let her see him hurt. I can't believe I didn't see it before."

"So what do we do about it?"

"Right now, you can watch Lila. I need to make a phone call."

"You really drive me crazy, you know that?"

"I drive everyone crazy."

"Bristol, you need to let people help you."

"I will, but the way you can help now is to look after Lila so I can do what I need to."

Eli's mouth screwed up, and his eyes were like daggers. Bristol let out a sigh and walked over to him. "She's been through so much. I'm not pushing you out of things, but you're the only one I trust her with and I need to know she's safe, or else I won't be able to function."

His face softened, but his eyes stayed hard. "Fine, but you're going to get Cole's help."

"This is a conspiracy."

Eli managed a smile.

Chapter 16

BRISTOL TOLD Lila she had a few errands to run and watched for a minute as Eli worked his magic and wrapped the girl snugly around his little finger, which wasn't that little.

He put one hand on her hip and the other on her shoulder. "When you punch the bag, make sure your hip moves with it," he said, pushing her forward, light and quick. "That gives you more power."

Lila practiced, and Bristol's chest tightened at the memory of herself as a girl and the interest Eli had taken. "Hey Lil'."

Lila spun around with her fists up by her chin like Eli showed her.

Bristol pointed a finger at Eli. "Call him Bear."

"No, no, no, don't call me Bear."

"Bear!" Lila squealed. Then punched him in the leg.

"Sucker," Bristol called over her shoulder as she walked out the door.

She sent a text to Deb: *Call me on my landline.* Then

she walked to a phone booth a block down from Eli's and waited.

It wasn't long before the phone rang. "Deb."

"Bristol."

"You're on a secure line?"

"Yup."

"Something's come up."

"Uh-huh."

Bristol looked at the handset then put it back to her ear. "You're very short all the sudden."

"They took my car."

"Oh no. Deb, I'm so sorry."

"I love that car. If there is one scratch on my little beauty, I swear to god — "

"Listen, I know what's going on. I know who tipped the feds off."

"I thought it *was* the feds."

"That's what it looked like, then I turned up at my friend's gym and found out his building has been bought by none other than Lincoln Enterprises, and my friend's getting kicked out."

"Shit. So Silas knows. Damn those feds. They have a leak."

"They might. Or he's doing it because I helped get him arrested."

"Doesn't matter. We have to assume he knows. That means you're in danger."

"If he's going after my friends, he's not coming after me."

"Are you kidding me? I know guys like Silas. They're the kind of guy who doesn't *just* go after you. They go after you, your friends, family, and any other connections they can get their hands on. Like *The Godfather* … I think … I've never actually seen it, but I remember hearing something about a horse's head."

"Deb."

"My point is, you need protection. Have you spoken to Cole?"

"Deb."

"I'm serious Bristol. Silas isn't messing around. You need to call Cole and tell him what's happening. At the very least you have to warn him that Silas may be after him too. If he hasn't gone after him already. No scratch that, you need to get his help too. Period."

At Deb's words, Bristol's stomach twisted. Everything within her was constantly resisting Cole. She knew he was the best person to help her figure out what to do, but the thing that kept her away was that, unfortunately, she couldn't deny that she had feelings for him. She lifted her eyes up to the ominous-looking sky as those words *feelings for him* formed in her mind. She felt so foolish.

"Bristol. You hear me?"

"I'll speak to him."

"Good. I've gotta go. I'm trying to find a way to sue the feds, so I'm a busy little beaver, but let me know if you need anything. Or if there is anything I can do."

"I will. Keep in touch. And you let me know if there is anything I can do from my area of expertise."

"I definitely will."

Bristol sat in her car as rain pattered on the windshield. The sound made her eyes droop, and her mind began to float.

A loud bang sent her body flailing. The panic had her rifling blindly through her stuff, trying to find her gun, but as the fear subsided and her mind began to stitch back together, she was able to decipher the sound as something harmless, like a car door slamming.

She breathed in through her nose and out through her mouth till her breathing was under control even though her heart rate was still up. Then she picked up her phone and texted Cole asking to meet at his place since it was closer to Long Beach than hers, and she still had that meeting with Tesco in a few hours.

Cole responded almost immediately and said he'd be home by five.

Deb's words about warning Cole that he could be a target had her driving over early and keeping a watch on his house till he got home.

If Silas went after Cole, he'd probably be more clever about it than attacking him at home, but it gave her something to focus on.

Just before five, she spotted Cole's car in her rearview mirror. She pinched her leg in response to the flutter that tickled her stomach and got out of the car.

Cole waved as he drove past, and she smiled weakly.

She waited by the door.

"Hey," he said as he walked up.

"Hey."

He stuck his key in the door and then pulled back. "Look, I'm sorry about earlier today."

"No, forget about it. It's fine."

He opened his mouth to say more, but when he saw Bristol wouldn't meet his eye, he unlocked the door and stood back to let her go in first.

When they got to the top of the stairs, he watched her grab a lock of hair and start twisting it around her finger, then quickly drop her hand and wipe it along her jeans.

She stood stiffly in the middle of the room while Cole went into his bedroom for something. When he came back out, his phone dinged. He lifted it and winced. "Sorry," he said as he texted back a reply.

"Everything okay?"

"Yeah. Elly's trying to make dinner plans."

Bristol took a step toward the door before she got ahold of herself. "I won't be long. This is just business."

"You can be as long as you like."

"I mean, I don't want to interrupt anything. It's cool. I hope everything goes really well for you two. I'm happy for you." Bristol grabbed the hem of her shirt to keep from touching her hair. Every instinct for fight or flight was taking hold. Currently, flight was winning, which was unusual for her.

Cole tilted his head one way, and a grin went up the other.

Bristol frowned. "What?"

"You said you're happy for us?"

"I am."

"You don't sound happy."

Bristol scoffed. "How do I sound then?"

"Jealous."

Bristol scoffed again. "Whatever, I've got more important things to do than think about my love life." She turned and went to his kitchen to get a drink even though she wasn't thirsty. "God, I hate myself right now," she muttered into the fridge.

She grabbed two mineral waters and pulled them out, holding one up to Cole, who was leaning on the counter with the same grin. He nodded and Bristol set it down in front of him with a loud clunk. She unscrewed the cap from her own and sat in a chair in the living room. The same chair Cole sat in after she saved his life. That time, there was a dead guy on the floor.

Cole came over and sat on the couch. "There's nothing going on between Elly and me."

"It's none of my business."

"I disagree. When she called to say she was in town, I had convinced myself that her interest in me was strictly platonic."

Bristol choked on the bubbles she was swallowing.

Cole laughed. "I know. I'm an idiot. I only agreed to dinner tomorrow so I can set her straight."

"Well, whatever, it doesn't matter. I'm not actually here about any of that. I've got actual important things to discuss."

"Aww, you mean you don't want to talk about you and me?" he joked.

"No, definitely not. Not when you hear what's happening."

Cole sat forward, suddenly serious. "Why, what's happening?"

"I think Silas knows."

Cole pushed himself to the edge of his seat. "What's happened?"

"What hasn't happened? After I saw you, I went to see Deb and walked in on an FBI raid of her office."

"That happened today?"

"Yeah. And apparently they've taken her car."

"I take it that's bad?"

"For Deb, that's the worst thing that could have happened."

"Is she going to be in trouble?"

Bristol grimaced. "I'd like to say she'll be fine, but if it's Silas who's feeding them information, then who knows what they have. But that's not all."

Cole took a deep breath. "I'm somehow not surprised."

"Have you heard of Tesco?"

"You mean the crime boss guy."

"I guess you could call him that, yeah. I found his guys beating up Lila's dad because someone told Tesco that Mick had double-crossed him."

"Oh my god! Is Lila all right?"

"Yeah, she wasn't there. Mick's getting fixed up at the hospital. I picked Lila up from school and left her with Eli."

"How bad a number did they do on him."

"Luckily I found him in time."

"I take it you left them a mess."

"A little, but you wouldn't believe it. The guy who

was beating him up is a guy I used to know, so I was able to stop the 'interview.'"

"A guy you used to *know* or a guy you just used to know."

Bristol grabbed the pillow she was leaning against and threw it at him. "Don't be weird. I saved his ass back when we were basically kids. He's a good guy, Jimmy. He's a good fighter too."

"If he's a good fighter, why did you need to save him before."

"He was just a scrawny little weasel back then, but I didn't save him from a fight. I saved him from a mess he made. Or more accurately, from a mess that was made for him. I did what I do best. Took the illusion they made to set him up and turned it on them. But that was quite a few years ago. When I fought him at Mick's, I had my work cut out for me."

"Wait." Cole put his hands up. "I'm confused. I thought you just said you saved Mick because you knew Jimmy?"

"I didn't recognize him at first, but he's got this gold tooth that he always used to suck on. Apparently he still does. He didn't recognize me at first either."

Cole sat back in his seat. "That confirms my suspicions about my mother."

"Uh, I don't see the connection."

"Not with Jimmy. Remember how I said I just found out she was sleeping with Silas? I'm pretty sure Silas put her up to telling me in order to mess with my head."

"Right. Well, hopefully that checks you off his list for now."

"I doubt it."

"You're probably right, but I'm not even done with my day yet."

"There's more?"

"I went to see Eli."

"Oh no, don't tell me. Not Eli."

"Lincoln Enterprises is in the process of purchasing his gym and knocking it down."

Cole crossed his arms. "Damn."

"So now I've got to try and figure out a way to help all of my friends."

"And keep yourself safe."

"I can't worry about that now. I need to clean up the mess I've created."

"Silas."

"What?"

"The mess Silas created," Cole corrected.

"Whatever. I've got a meeting with Tesco tonight to see what I can do for Mick."

"I'm coming with you."

"I don't need you there. It's fine."

"No, it's not. You can't just go meet a guy like Tesco on your own."

"Yes, I can. I know him. I've worked with him before. And what makes you think your tagging along won't make things worse. He's expecting me to be on my own."

"Your excuses are getting pretty weak. What if Silas has guys lurking around, waiting for an opportunity?" Cole leaned forward again. "You're not going home."

Bristol looked at him and chewed on her bottom lip.

She didn't want to be scared, and she didn't want to be pushed out of her own home. "I'll think about it."

Cole blew out a breath. "I guess that's the best I can hope for at the moment. What time are you meeting with Tesco?"

"9:00. Somewhere near Long Beach."

Cole looked at his watch. "Good. Then we can stop at your place and pick up a few things before we head out that way."

"I came out here to meet you so I wouldn't have to go all the way back to my apartment."

"There's time."

"And you really think staying at a hotel will keep him out if he's determined?"

"I wasn't thinking of a hotel."

"Well, I'm not staying here if that's what you think."

"Why not? You afraid you won't be able to control yourself?" He smirked.

Bristol's face felt like a beacon. She jumped out of her seat, hiding her blush as offense, and went to the window. The sun was setting over the ocean. The sky looked bruised.

"You think your place is safe? As I recall — " Her blushing receded enough that she turned back toward him. "This place isn't safe from him either." She tapped a finger on her lip. "And wasn't I the one who saved you? What makes you think I'm not safer on my own?"

He walked over to join her at the window, looking out onto the patio where he had been attacked. He leaned into her. "Okay. You don't need me to protect you, but apparently I need you to protect me." That snarky smirk again. "But you're right. If Silas is serious, this place isn't really set up for serious." He took a deep breath. "But I do know a place that is."

"Where?"

Cole hesitated. "Chicago. My dad's place. It's like a fortress. And I can get us there without anyone knowing we've left."

Bristol stared at Cole for a moment then shook her head. "No. That's out of the question."

"Why?"

"Chicago?"

"Yes. And don't tell me it's extreme. You know Silas will go to any lengths to get what he wants."

Bristol blew out a breath. "We don't know what he wants."

"I beg to differ. We know exactly what he wants. What we don't know is the means he will use to get it."

A tingling raced up Bristol's spine. "I'll think about it."

Cole brooded. She ignored it. Finally, he shrugged. "Great. I'll pack my things now, and then we'll head to your place and get your things." She started to protest, but Cole put a hand up to stop her. "Just in case you choose in favor of Chicago. Then we can go see Tesco."

"Fine." Bristol turned back to look out the window. Silas might be dangerous, but staying with Cole had its own hazards.

Chapter 17

BRISTOL TWISTED her finger around her hair as they drove to her apartment.

"It's not just my safety," she said after she and Cole had driven a while in silence, each processing in their own way how to prepare for what was ahead. "I could use your help."

"I'm listening."

"Hopefully, I'll sort out Mick's mess with Tesco tonight, but I have no idea how I'm going to help Deb and Eli." Cole glanced at her and smiled. She glared at him. "I'm serious. My friends need help."

"I know they do. That's not why I was smiling."

She was afraid to ask but did anyway. "Then why are you smiling?"

"Forget it."

"You can't say something like that and then not tell me."

"You don't want to know."

She lifted her eyebrows. "I don't want to know?"

"You don't want to know."

"Well, now you're definitely going to have to tell me."

"Okay, but don't say I didn't warn you."

"Consider me warned."

"I think you're beautiful." She pinched her lips together and Cole laughed. "I told you you didn't want to know. What did you *think* made me smile?"

"I thought you were giving me a hard time," she growled. "Why would you say something like that?"

"Because it's true, and you asked. You're beautiful inside and out." Bristol groaned. "I'm serious. One of the reasons I like you so much is your loyalty to those you care about."

"Uh-huh."

Cole tapped a finger on the steering wheel. "You know, it's funny. I'm not usually into all this honesty with feelings, but with you, it's like I just don't care." He shrugged his shoulders obnoxiously.

Bristol tucked a foot up under her, leaning her knee on the door. "I know why you don't care."

"Why?"

"Because you know it drives me crazy." She looked at him then, because she thought she was onto something. "That's what it is. You know I won't be able to handle it. It's not about your being honest about how you feel. It's only because you know I won't be able to take it seriously. Wait … " She twisted her body toward him then. "I bet it freaks you out as much as it freaks me out."

Cole processed that thought. "You might be right. Let's test it."

"I can't tell whether or not you're serious."

"I am serious. You might be right."

"Fine. How do we test it?"

"I'll compliment you, and you respond like a normal woman."

She narrowed her eyes at him. "This is a trap."

"You don't trust me?"

"I trust you with a lot of things, but not with this."

Cole coughed. "You trust me with a — Talk about not being honest about your feelings. I don't think you trust me at all sometimes." His comment started out in jest, but the tension that now filled the car made Bristol squirm.

She scratched at a jagged edge on her nail. "It's not *you* I don't trust."

"Well, who the hell is it then?" He winced at the anger he was struggling to suppress. She brought out the best and the worst in him. "Sorry, I just. I'm tired of fighting with you about it. I have to push you about everything. I'm tired of pushing."

Her insides twisted, and her face puckered, but she finally answered. "It's me."

"What's you?"

"It's me I don't trust. Not you."

"You don't trust yourself?" He was incredulous. "I'm pretty sure you've been trusting yourself just fine for most of your life."

"No," she groaned. If there weren't still an edge to his voice, she would have let it go. She grunted then said, "I don't trust myself with you, okay?" Her voice was loud in the car, but she wouldn't have gotten it out if she hadn't pushed so hard.

The silence that followed seemed louder.

Finally, Bristol couldn't handle it anymore. "I trust you, Cole. I know you'd do everything in your power to keep me safe."

"I *can* keep you safe."

"You can't say that, you don't — " Cole's glare shut her up.

The car was silent again. Cole drummed his fingers on the steering wheel, then looked over at Bristol. "So you trust me?"

"Yes."

"So we'll go to Chicago?"

She suppressed a sigh. "Yes."

"And you'll do everything I say?" A grin played at the side of his mouth.

"Don't push it." The return of his teasing relaxed her as they pulled up outside her place. "Right. Can we get back to business now?"

Cole lifted an eyebrow. "For now. So what is it you plan on telling Tesco?"

"I don't know. He trusts me right now, and I don't want to taint that trust. I was considering telling him the truth of what I think about Silas."

"You think that will work?"

"Don't know. Maybe if I can promise to find him proof."

"It's dangerous to make promises to a guy like that."

Bristol rolled her eyes at Cole. "Thanks."

Cole shrugged. "Sorry, can't help myself." He got out of the car and leaned on the roof while scanning the area. "Anything look unusual to you?"

"Nope." Bristol shoved her bag onto her shoulder and walked toward the building with Cole bringing up the rear, his eyes on every shadow. Nothing stood out, but he kept alert just the same.

Bristol turned her key in the lock and pulled the door open, but Cole put a hand on her shoulder. "I know you can look after yourself, but as a favor to me, will you let me go first?"

Bristol sighed, but she didn't mean it. She stepped back and ushered him inside.

He went up the stairs slowly, one firmly planted foot after the other. He was ready. She could see it in the way he carried himself up the stairs. At the top, he leaned back against the wall and patted himself down, then looked at Bristol with his fingers splayed. "I'm an idiot," he whispered.

"You're only just figuring this out?"

"You pick some odd times to be sarcastic."

"Who said I'm being sarcastic?"

He grinned. "Did you bring a gun?"

"It's in my apartment."

"So we're both idiots." Cole took a deep breath and held it. She watched him coil himself then quickly push his head around the corner and pull it back like a spring.

"It's clear." His body was still tightly wound as he shifted into the hall. Bristol was ready right behind him. She put a hand on his shoulder. "You don't think we're going a little overboard with the kung fu?"

"Not where Silas is concerned." He pointed at Mrs. Deacon's door. "Maybe we should check on her. She's one of your friends."

"I don't think Silas would think of my neighbor." But even as she said the words, dread filled her. "But yeah, maybe we should."

She knocked lightly on Mrs. Deacon's door and listened. Cole stepped forward and covered the peephole with his hand, but then heard the old woman shuffling to the door. "Who is it?" And Cole stepped back.

"It's Bristol, Mrs. D."

The locks clicked, and the door opened. She smiled when she saw Bristol, but her face lit up when she saw Cole was with her. "Well, hello you two." She winked at Cole. Cole took her hand and kissed it. "You two headed out?"

"No, we're just coming in," Bristol said, feeling a bit impatient.

Mrs. Deacon's nonexistent eyebrows pushed together in confusion, laying the wrinkles on her forehead on top of one another. She looked down the hall toward Bristol's door, but then she turned coy. "You know, back when I was a young lady, I never would have gotten away with having a gentleman stay at my house."

"He's not staying Mrs. D. Actually, I'm going away for a little while so can you do me a favor and don't open the door for anyone you don't know?"

"Oh no, I never do that. There are too many people waiting to prey on little old ladies. You know, one time I got a phone call from a young man who said he was my grandson."

Bristol started flicking a finger against her thumb. Cole glanced down and saw it, then smiled and asked, "What happened then?"

Bristol paused her flicking and glared stealthily at Cole. She didn't want Mrs. Deacon knowing she wasn't interested in stories, but she could tell by the way Cole cocked his head that he was only asking to annoy her.

"I went along with it, of course." Mrs. Deacon snickered. "He didn't know I didn't have a grandson, and I made him stay on the phone with me for over half an hour. In fact, I missed the beginning of MacGyver, which I never did, but I was having so much fun."

"That's a great story, Mrs. D, but we do need to get going," Bristol said before Cole could pipe up.

"Wait, I want to hear what happened." Cole showed Bristol all his teeth when he smiled at her.

She held back the glare this time as Mrs. Deacon leaned in toward the two of them. "I told him I didn't have any money, but he could come stay with me and my twelve cats for as long as he wanted." She tittered. "He hung up very quickly after that, and I got to watch my show."

Cole laughed jovially. "That is a great story. Well done."

"Very impressive, but we really need to get going or we'll be late." Bristol patted the old woman on the arm and grabbed Cole's, pulling him out the door.

"You two have a good time," Mrs. Deacon called out as she shut the door. Bristol paused long enough to hear the locks engage and then walked down the hall with her key ready.

"You really are a pain, you know that?" Bristol said as she unlocked the door and opened it. "It's almost as if you are on a mission to annoy — "

She dove to the side, pushing on Cole as soon as she saw the gun. She barely felt the bullet tear through her skin.

Cole bounced when he hit the wall as he watched her fall. He knew when she hit the ground that she had been shot. Something inside snapped, and he pushed off the wall toward the gunman, forcing the man's arm up before he could get off another shot. Cole's focus was intense. He knew each move in slow motion before he executed it.

First, he landed a punch on the guy's nose, breaking it. The man grunted and turned his head. Next, Cole lifted his arm and chopped down on the side of his neck. The guy dropped, and Cole jumped on top of him, punching first with one hand then the other. He felt a yank at his arm as he started another punch but ripped it from Bristol's grasp without a thought. Bristol moved back then tackled him off the man.

Cole wrestled with her for a second before he snapped out of it.

"Cole! Come on. He's out."

Cole got up onto his knees, breathless. His hands moved over Bristol's body without seeing. "He got you." He found the spot on her arm, wet with blood.

"Yeah, but it was a clean shot. Just a deep scratch. I'll be fine. Let's just get my stuff and go."

He put a hand on the side of her face and shook his

head. "I thought it was worse. It's a good thing you have quick reflexes."

"The good news is, I'm now fully convinced that if my life is in danger, you will completely nuke whoever is responsible."

"It's about time." Cole stood. "Get your stuff. I'll make a few phone calls. We should be able to leave as soon as we get to the airport."

"Not before we go see Tesco."

Cole threw his arms up in the air. "Did it ever occur to you that Tesco might just hand you over to Silas?"

"He's not the type."

"Oh? And what type is that?"

"He said he'd hear me out. He's one of those honorable bad guys."

"I'm pretty sure that's an oxymoron."

Bristol lost steam. She breathed out a shaky breath and looked at the floor. "Well, whether you like it or not, I'm actually one of the bad guys."

"Bristol — "

"No, I'm serious. I'm not saying it to be hard on myself or anything, but I've worked for Tesco and I've done plenty of other illegal contract work. So if you don't think it's possible for a bad guy to be honorable, then perhaps this is where we should part ways."

"You know that's not what I meant."

"He's not the double-crossing type. And he doesn't let anyone double-cross him. That's why he went after Mick in the first place."

"Okay. But I'm definitely coming with you."

"You can come. You just need to stay back."

"Back where? Just tell him I'm your bodyguard or something. Surely he can understand that you would have a bodyguard."

"You're too skinny to be a bodyguard."

Cole's hand went to his hip, and he huffed. "That was a low blow. What about Jimmy? You said he's a great fighter. Or is he one of those guys who started off scrawny and turned into the Hulk?"

"No, he's about your build, but he's not a bodyguard. It's got nothing to do with strength or fighting skill."

"Who says bodyguards have to be big?"

"When you meet Tesco, you'll understand." Bristol turned on her heel and went to her room to pack.

When she walked back out, Cole pointed at the guy on the floor. "What do we do about him?"

"Just leave him there. If they've gotten in once, they'll just come back in if they want. I'll have to find a new place."

"You're just leaving everything here?"

"I have nothing of value in here. They aren't going to touch my clothes so I can come back for them later."

Cole lifted the guy onto his shoulder. "I'll drop him in the bushes. I don't like the idea of him waking up in here."

Bristol shrugged and walked out the door, hiding the girlish smile that approved of the strength he displayed. She allowed herself that one small concession.

Chapter 18

JIMMY WAS PUNCTUAL. At exactly 8:30, Bristol got the first of several texts telling her to drive from one point to the next. It wasn't far, but she figured Tesco had people lined up making sure there was no one tagging along behind. He'd already know she had a driver with her before she arrived. It could possibly complicate things, but it was better than him being surprised by it when they got to where they were going.

Bristol and Cole ended up at the port area near Long Beach. There was only one exit, and Cole's hands gripped the steering wheel till his knuckles were white.

Bristol tried to keep things light. "You're not nervous, are you?"

He grinned, but Bristol could tell it was forced. "Nothing like a proper challenge. You know, if Tesco doesn't want us to leave, we won't."

"I thought you liked a challenge? Besides, Tesco has no reason to want us dead."

"You don't think there will be a price to pay if he feels we've wasted his time?"

"I think he'll give me a chance."

Cole clicked his tongue and opened the car door.

There were three vehicles facing them. The one in the middle was a Lincoln Continental.

"Sweet ride," Cole said as he and Bristol got out of the car, keeping their hands exposed so that everyone concerned could see they were unarmed.

Two men with semi-automatic rifles approached from either side. One of them was Jimmy. The other man frisked them, then checked the car.

"Jimmy. Good to see you again."

"Tesco told you to come alone," Jimmy said, eyeing Cole.

"Cole's my protection, and I trust him with my life. He actually saved it the other day."

Jimmy nodded and put a hand out to shake Cole's. "I can't speak for Tesco, but any friend of Bristol's is a friend of mine. Tesco seems to be in a good mood today. My guess is he'll be fine with it, but I'm not making any promises."

"Not asking you to."

Jimmy flicked his arm up. "This way."

They followed until Jimmy pointed at the ground. "Stand there."

They stopped and Jimmy moved into position then nodded toward the vehicle. Two doors opened and a couple of guys the size of trucks got out. Bristol whispered to Cole. "The bodyguards."

"Uh, okay, you win. I do feel kinda skinny around those guys."

Tesco slid out from the back passenger door. He wore a red tie with a single-breasted black pinstripe suit that fit tighter than last time Bristol saw him. His hair was slicked back and had streaks of white that weren't there before. He was holding a fedora as he exited the car, but he put it on as he stepped forward. She had always thought he'd be more comfortable in the 1920s.

As he stepped closer, Bristol noted that one of his eyes drooped, and there was a scar in his eyebrow.

Tesco put a hand out toward Bristol. "Sorry for the formalities," he said in the same casual tone she remembered, but she knew he was anything but. She had told Cole he had honor, but he was also impulsive and he had a bad temper. He took another step forward. "You can never be too careful these days."

He gave Bristol a once-over and ignored Cole, who shifted uncomfortably. "You're looking good. Last time we met you were still very youthful. You've grown into quite the woman."

Bristol remained still under his gaze. "It has been a few years."

He scratched the scar over his eye. "Who's your friend?"

"He's my bodyguard."

Tesco kept his eyes focused on Bristol. "A little small to be a bodyguard." She shrugged. "You know, Bristol, I don't normally allow my work to be interrupted, but when I heard it was you, it piqued my curiosity. What important information could Bristol Kelley have that she would risk interfering?"

"Bigger fish."

"How big?"

"Silas Lincoln."

Tesco chuckled and crossed his arms. "You want to give me Silas?"

"With pleasure."

"If you're planning on handing me a fish that big, it had better be on a silver platter. You have one of those?"

While they spoke, Cole analyzed the situation. If they were quick — and they were — they could disarm the men, but not before at least one of them was shot. If they had more time, he would have tried to get Jimmy on their side.

Bristol didn't appear unnerved, but Cole could tell she was ready by the way she stood. One foot was slightly behind the other. Her weight on her back leg. "I don't have a silver platter, but I thought you'd want to know that he's feeding you false information."

Tesco pulled a candy out of his pocket, unwrapped it, and popped it in his mouth. "A word of advice, because I like you. Don't get involved where Silas is concerned."

"Too late. He's going after my friends and he's using you to do his dirty work. Tell me you haven't stooped that low."

Tesco's face darkened, and his eyes narrowed. He pointed a finger at her with the result that the guns that had dropped slightly over the conversation were now lifted straight again. "I don't do anyone's dirty work. So don't expect me to clean up a mess that you've made yourself."

Those words cut right through Bristol. Of course she had made the mess for herself, but she needed Tesco on her side to fix it. He stepped forward and grabbed her by the arm. She saw Cole flinch toward her, and she threw out her other arm toward him. He froze.

Tesco leaned into her. "Silas is a very lucrative business partner of mine. He's also not very forgiving. If you're going to come in here and start pointing fingers, you'd better have proof."

Bristol swallowed. "I can get it for you."

Tesco tightened his grip. "How much do you think you're worth to Silas?"

His head tipped a fraction to the side, and there was a flinch in his cheek. Bristol looked at Cole, who was ready to attack. She screamed at him with her eyes to stay where he was. It appeared for the moment that he read her loud and clear, but she didn't know how long he was willing to listen.

Bristol was one of a select few who had figured out Tesco's tell. She had taken a gamble when she worked for him and it had paid off. He was bluffing — testing her to see if she would cave, or if she believed in what she was saying. All she had to do was show him that her honor was worth more to her than her life.

She ripped her arm out of his grip and slapped him across the face. Not too hard, but it would have stung. Cole was coiled to spring for her, but Tesco put a palm up toward his men. He looked at Cole and waited a breath to see if he would hold. Then he turned back to

Bristol. "You've just earned yourself a few more minutes. Make them count."

"What if I *could* hand Silas to you on a silver platter?"

Tesco shook his head. "It'll never happen. A guy like that has too many people in his pocket."

"But what if I could?"

Tesco rubbed his chin. "If you want to get your friend Mick off the hook, you'll have to show me that his life is worth more to me than Silas's. And it'll take more than bad manners. I already know Silas is a bad guy."

"Aren't we all? But I'm not talking about proving he's a criminal. I'm talking about proving he's more harm to you than good."

Tesco considered her proposal. "I'm definitely intrigued. But what if you can't prove it?"

"I can't have you going after my friend again."

"I'll assume that's not a threat since you're not in the position, so I take it you're open to another offer?"

"I'll consider it." She heard Cole swear under his breath.

"Good. If you recall, when we last worked together, I made you a job offer."

"I remember."

"But at the time you said you don't work for anyone but yourself."

"Yes."

"I'm expanding over the border, and I need someone I can trust. If you can't satisfy the Silas angle and you want your friend to remain unharmed, then you'll come work for me. Permanently."

Bristol ground her teeth but couldn't show any weakness. She kept her eyes fixed on his. "Deal. Give me a couple of weeks and I'll get you the proof."

"You've got seventy-two hours."

Bristol bit down on the inside of her cheeks. She could only imagine what was going through Cole's head. "Fine."

Tesco lifted his chin. "I expect to hear from you in three days."

"Thank you." Bristol put her hand out to shake Tesco's.

He didn't lift his arm. "If you don't come through, it won't be your friend's life at stake. It will be yours. You don't follow the rules then you'll think Silas is a walk in the park compared to what I will do to you."

Bristol almost cracked a smile. There was nothing he could do that would be worse than Silas. "Deal."

Tesco smiled and took her hand, then kissed it lightly. "It's a pleasure working with you again. I trust we will both come out of this satisfied."

Bristol tipped her head slyly. "Either way, you win, right?"

"True. Till we meet again," he said, then turned to go back to his car.

Cole was immediately by Bristol's side with his hand on her back and was carefully turning her toward the car. When they reached it, Tesco called after her, "You know, the only place you'll ever be rid of Silas is the grave."

"Thanks for the heads-up," she yelled back and lifted a finger to wave as she got in the car.

Cole turned the car around and drove out without saying a word.

"You're very quiet," Bristol said, once they were clear of the port.

He glanced over at her then back at the road. "You'll give yourself to Tesco if you can't get what you need on Silas?"

Bristol clicked her tongue. "If I didn't make a deal with him, he wouldn't have let us go. And I'm not letting Tesco hurt Mick anymore."

"And you think *I* have a god complex?"

She turned her body fully toward him. "What's that supposed to mean?"

"You think you have control over everything and responsibility for everyone."

"That's not what this is about."

"Oh, it's not?"

"I wouldn't hesitate one second to sacrifice myself for Mick and Lila." Cole was silent. "The only reason you don't like it is because, if it came down to it, you'd choose my life over theirs."

"That's not true." Except he knew it was.

"I did what I had to in order to get us out of there in one piece. Hopefully, neither one of us will have to choose when the time comes." Bristol looked out her window. She was done arguing.

When they reached the airport turnoff, Cole was trying not to brood, but it was hard work. Keeping Bristol safe from herself was a difficult task. The word *insufferable* kept coming to mind. The fact that she agreed to Chicago would ease things a bit, but only for seventy-two hours. Then Cole had to figure out how to keep her from selling her soul to Tesco.

"So how is it you plan to fly us to Chicago incognito?" Bristol asked, breaking his contemplation. "I don't have any other ID on me to book a flight,"

"We aren't flying commercial."

She waited a beat and when he didn't continue, she said, "So, what, are we being smuggled in by dog carrier?"

Half his face lifted in a smile and it surprised her how relieved it made her feel. "You ever flown in a private jet before?"

She scoffed in jest. "Yeah, sure. All the time."

She couldn't help the peal of excitement that she felt. She'd never wanted much out of life and wasn't impressed by wealth, but she also hated flying economy. Being pressed up against other people in a giant tin can in the sky didn't suit her. But she was stubborn enough not to admit her enthusiasm and pressed a scowl onto her face in place of the smile that was threatening.

"We're flying as Mr. and Mrs. Donaldson. The paperwork is all taken care of."

Bristol's scowl deepened. "Mr. and Mrs.?"

"I knew you'd like that."

Bristol decided the cheeky grin he now wore suited him, so let him keep it. She also couldn't come up with a suitable comeback.

•   •   •

As they walked onto the tarmac, Bristol whistled, pretending it was sarcasm.

"Yeah, she's not a bad way to travel," he said as they reached the plane. He tapped the railing of the stairs. "Would you like to go first, wife?" he added as he swept a hand across the stairs for her to climb.

Bristol patted a hand on the side of his face as she walked past. "In your dreams."

"For now," she heard him murmur as she climbed but chose to ignore it.

When she entered, she was glad she had gone first so she could hide the look on her face while she took in the new surroundings. The interior was cream leather with smooth wood and chrome accents.

"So who owns this piece of scrap metal?" she asked as Cole came up beside her.

"A friend of mine who owed me a favor."

"He's got pretty bad taste. This place is a disgrace." She eyed the couch. The weight of fatigue never seemed to be far from her lately.

"Yeah, we'll be lucky if we make it to Chicago," he said as he watched her lie down on the couch and attempt to put her arms behind her head. She winced and brought them back down. He went to a phone on the wall and spoke quietly, nodding a few times, then sat on the edge of the couch. "Is that the gunshot wound, or the burn on your shoulder?"

"My shoulder's starting to itch, actually. And hurts when I scratch it, so it's mostly annoying."

"What about your other wound?" He knew what the

grimace on her face meant. "Everything's a battle with you. If it hurts, you're allowed to admit it."

"It hurts." Back at the apartment, she had slapped on a bandage and tied a strip of fabric around it to stop the bleeding. She hadn't let Cole look at it at the time because she knew he'd fuss over it.

"I'll get you some painkillers, and when we get to Chicago, you're going to have to let me have a proper look at it." She groaned, but he slapped her lightly on the leg. "Don't give me that. If it gets infected you'll be out of action, and we only have three days to enact whatever plan it is you have. I just hope it's a good one." She looked at him, worried. He was surprised at her vulnerability, and he sighed. "We'll figure something out. There is no way Silas is doing everything he's doing and not leaving a trail. We just have to find it."

Bristol felt tears welling up and pressed her fingers into her eyes. "My life seems to be an endless cycle of trying to fix the chaos I've created for myself."

Cole made a move to sit back down next to her when a man came through a door at the front. He looked at Bristol, blinked, then turned to Cole. "It's time to go."

"Thanks, Steven. We'll get buckled up."

Bristol let Cole pull her up off the couch and they settled into a couple of plush chairs. "You mind if I steal that couch once we're in the air?"

"Be my guest."

Cole watched her sleep for a few minutes. He was constantly surprised at the reaction he had just looking at her. She was crazy and mixed up, and yet he felt more at home with her than he did with anyone else. Everything about her presence seemed right. If things didn't go the way they needed, he would find a way to keep her safe. No matter what it cost.

———————————

Chapter 19

———————————

BRISTOL PINCHED her mouth closed to keep it from falling open when they pulled up to Cole's father's house. She was not accustomed to the wealth that surrounded Cole. He was comfortable in it, but she could tell he didn't strive for it. It was just there.

She was quiet when they walked in but lifted her head to take in the vaulted ceiling in the entryway.

"This is quite a house." She was annoyed by the awe in her voice. For something that was normal for Cole, it was completely foreign to her. A spasm of embarrassment swept through her and she ran a self-conscious hand down her old beat-up jacket that was draped over her arm.

"Mmm." Cole dropped the bags on the floor.

"Did you grow up here?"

"Yeah, I did."

"What was that like?" She pictured him sliding down the railing as a boy while her eyes skimmed up the elegant staircase.

Cole shrugged. "I guess I took it for granted. It was the only thing I knew. Not really my style, though."

Bristol had never felt so out of place. She didn't belong here. "I guess this is what Elly expects if the two of you get together." The words had slipped out and Bristol wished she could take them back.

"God, you know what?" Cole kicked a bag out of the way, and Bristol winced as he stomped toward her. "I'm getting tired of this." He grabbed both her arms. She let out a squeak when his hand inadvertently fastened over her wound. "I'm not interested in Elly. I'm interested in you, and I'm not sure how many more times I have to say it before you'll get it into your head." He glanced down at her lips when they parted and pushed his own together. If she were any other woman, he wouldn't have hesitated to kiss her.

◯◯

The expectation that he was about to kiss her had all but numbed the pain in her arm. She lied to herself that she was unsure of whether or not she wanted him to.

He jerked and let go of her arm, lifting his hand that now had her blood on it. He swallowed to regain control. "I've got a first aid kit around here somewhere. We'll fix this up."

Bristol hesitated for a moment. It took her a second to get her feet moving, but then she followed him into the kitchen. He opened a couple of drawers and then pulled out a box. "Sit there." He pointed at the kitchen counter. Bristol jumped up and pulled her sleeve up.

This was good. A gunshot wound put a nice barrier between them.

Cole focused on the injury. His tongue poked out as he peeled the bandage off. "It's not too bad, but I'm going to clean it. I'd recommend a hospital visit for stitches, but I already know your response so I'll close it up as best as I can."

She didn't flinch when he poured the disinfectant over the cut, but he blew on it anyway, knowing it stung.

She watched him as he dabbed at the blood, taking in the line of his jaw and the angles of his nose and lips. The injury turned out not to be much of a barrier. Everything between them seemed to pull them together instead of pushing them apart. Even when she was mad at him, there was something that wouldn't let go.

Bristol found her breathing had become labored. This was dangerous territory that needed boundaries.

Not one for tact, she said in a small voice, "I'm not going to sleep with you."

Cole stopped what he was doing and looked up at her. "What? I didn't — I mean — what?"

"It's just … if this were a movie or something. The two of us here alone? We'd end up sleeping together. I want to make sure you understand."

"Yeah." He scoffed, focusing on the bandage he was now working hard to wrap around her arm. "Hadn't even crossed my mind."

Bristol snorted and watched him wrap and rewrap in earnest.

Finally he stopped, staring down at the counter. "Okay, so maybe it had crossed my mind, but I —

Wait." He looked at her. "So you're saying this because there *was* the possibility?"

"I didn't say that."

"That's what it sounded like."

She sighed, resigned that she owed him the truth. "I do like you, Cole. I already told you that."

"When?"

"In the car before. When I said I didn't trust myself with you."

"That was your way of saying you liked me?"

"You're really going to make this difficult for me?"

She watched him hold back a smile. "No, you're right. Sorry."

"It's just that people treat sex so casually, like it's not something important, but it is. I had it stolen from me when I was young and I won't go handing it out to whoever seems interesting at the time."

"So you're saying I'm interesting." He smirked.

"You just can't help yourself." She mocked indignation and put a hand out to slap him in the chest, but he caught her hand and held it. He understood how hard it was for her to be honest with him.

"I hear what you're saying. And I respect you more than you probably realize. I'd never do anything that's not right for you. You can trust me."

She bit her lip. "I know I can."

"Listen, it's late. I'm finished with your arm, so why don't we go to bed. And in the morning, we'll see if we can figure something out for Silas."

She nodded and hopped off the counter.

The curtains were slightly parted when Bristol woke up the next morning. She stared out at the blue sky.

The bed was unlike anything she'd ever slept in before. If it weren't for the memory that their hours were slowly dwindling, she probably would have stayed all day. She made a mental note to check what made the bed feel like a cloud and kicked off the covers to let the coolness in the air help to get her moving.

When she padded into the kitchen, looking for a cup of tea, she found Cole leaning over the counter reading something on his tablet with his fingers tapping on a cup of coffee. He looked up and smiled then turned on the stove to heat the kettle. "It's already warm so shouldn't take too long. I was surprised you slept in. I expected you to be an early bird."

She leaned next to him. "I usually am. I think exhaustion finally caught up with me. Not to mention that bed is amazing."

Cole stood up straight. "You tell me you won't sleep with me and then tell me how wonderful your bed is?"

She grinned and pushed off the counter to get her tea. "I slept like a log."

"Yeah, me too," he lied. Knowing she was in the next room had made it difficult to fall asleep. "Did that good sleep get you any ideas?"

"It's pretty simple, I think."

"How's that?"

"Weren't you listening? All we have to do is get Tesco to turn on Silas. Simple."

"Yes, very straightforward. And your brilliant plan to make that happen would be?"

"Don't you know me at all? Smoke and mirrors, naturally."

Cole grinned "Of course, why didn't I think of that."

"Is there a computer in the house? I might do some research and see if I can come up with a little smoke. Silas has to have a weak spot somewhere. If I can find it, Mick might be able to get some intel."

"Yeah, my dad's office. I should probably sift through a bit more paperwork anyway while I'm here. I'll get my dad's lawyer to finish, but I want to make sure there's nothing in there that I should see."

"I hate paperwork. That sounds like a nightmare."

"It is. You want breakfast?"

"I'm not much of a breakfast eater."

"Good, 'cause there isn't much to eat. I'll call Brian and get him to bring something over. I've also contacted a friend of mine to come over later and see if he can help at all."

"You think it's safe to bring people in?"

"Brian's the butler, and he's been here since I was a boy. My friend is from the FBI — " Bristol's chin jutted out and she was about to protest, but Cole cut her off. " — But I trust him with my life."

"You're absolutely sure you can trust him?"

"100 percent."

Bristol pushed her tongue onto the back of her teeth. "If we've got a friend in the FBI, I guess that's an asset we can't pass up."

"That's what I thought."

Hunched over at the computer with her cup of tea, Bristol tapped a pen on a legal pad while Cole emptied a drawer and sat down at another table.

She glanced up at him now and then. Most of the time his forehead was wrinkled in confusion and his head was resting on his hand with his fingers tangled in his hair.

As she read through another news story related to Lincoln Enterprises, she began furiously clicking the pen in her hand until Cole cleared his throat. She did one last slow click then dropped the pen. "Sorry."

Despite the fact that most of the articles she read didn't paint Silas in a good light, there was nothing that gave her much of a lead. Mostly, they were hidden accusations regarding the buying and selling of properties.

By late morning, the only note she had written on her legal pad was that Phillip Ryder, Deb's ex and CEO of Lisco Pharmaceuticals, was listed as a director of one of Silas's businesses related to market research. And there was a news article from an online journal called *Showdown*, no author listed. It suggested, for those reading between the lines, that the market research company was providing misleading research.

It was easy to create misleading generalizations from statistics. She already knew from her line of work that most facts can be used to design whatever truth you wanted, but the article implied that they were manufacturing false statistics. Not something she was personally against, but it was definitely against the law.

There was a knock at the office door and Cole and Bristol both jumped.

"Brian. You startled me. I was so absorbed I forgot you were coming."

"I'm sorry, sir. I got what you requested."

"Thank you. Brian, this is a good friend of mine, Bristol Kelley. Bristol, this is Brian."

Bristol stood and walked over, shaking Brian's hand in two of hers. "It's lovely to meet you."

"You as well Miss Kelley. Mr. Sullivan mentioned that you liked to drink tea, so I took the liberty of bringing over one of my favorites. It's from a specialty grower in India. I think you will find the flavor is quite superb."

"Wow, thanks Brian. It's nice to meet someone who has proper taste." She glanced at Cole. "We can't all have good taste though, can we," she said to Brian under her breath, but loud enough for Cole to hear.

Brian smiled. "Would you like me to make you a cup?"

"That's very generous, but I can make it myself. You don't have to trouble yourself."

"Please, I insist."

"Well, okay. That would be lovely, thank you." Brian left the room. "I like him."

"Me too. I was probably closer to him than to my father, growing up. He's always encouraged me, even when I didn't deserve it." Cole looked at his watch. "We should stop for lunch while you have your tea."

Bristol stretched and yawned. "Yeah, sounds good. I need to clear my head."

As they walked out of the office, there was a knock at the door. "I'll get it." Cole called to Brian. He had left the gate open in expectation of his friend's arrival.

When Cole opened the door, Bristol observed a tall man in a dark suit. She no longer trusted anyone in a dark suit. His face was set in a murderous scowl. Before Cole had time to react, the man grabbed him and twisted him around, putting his own arm around Cole's throat while pulling Cole's up behind him. Bristol was already moving when the man first reached out. She was surprised at Cole's lack of reaction. He usually had faster reflexes.

She punched the man in his side and shoved him sideways. He took Cole with him, but it created enough gap that Bristol was able to come around and kick him in the ribs, at which point Cole jumped up. She didn't want to knock him out like she could have. They would need to question him. If Silas sent him, she might be able to find out the information she needed. Pulling back her leg, she thought one more swift kick should keep him down for a bit, and now that both she and Cole were prepared, the man wouldn't be any more trouble.

Cole grabbed at her. "Bristol, no."

The man on the ground coughed out a laugh and put a hand up toward her. "Uncle!" he yelled, lifting his leg in defense and exposing a yellow and green argyle sock.

"Nice socks." Cole laughed.

"What's going on?" Bristol kept her hands fisted.

The man looked down his pant leg. "They're very comfortable I'll have you know. Also, my wife bought them for me."

"Cole?" Bristol dropped her arms.

"Bristol, this is Michael Carter."

"Who?"

"My FBI friend."

She looked from one man to the other. Michael lifted his arm into an awkward wave. Bristol put her hands on her hips as Michael sat up. "Bristol. It's nice to meet you."

Cole reached a hand down and pulled Michael up.

Bristol shook her head. "So, you're just a couple of jockstraps? What the hell? I could have hurt someone."

Michael held out a hand. "Sorry. Cole and I have only just caught up after a long hiatus. I couldn't help myself."

Bristol shook his hand and made sure she squeezed hard. Michael lifted an eyebrow. "When the FBI had you in custody, did they try to recruit you? Because if they didn't, they should have."

"Not interested."

Cole shut the door. "All right you two. Come on, let's call a truce and go eat some lunch."

Chapter 20

WHEN THEY ENTERED THE KITCHEN, Brian was whistling a clear, lilting tune. He stopped to smile and then continued to lay out plates piled with different ingredients.

"You whistle like an old man," Cole said as he leaned on the counter.

Brian stopped, but his lips stayed puckered.

"I meant that as a compliment." Cole laughed. "Young people these days lack the proper skill to whistle in a way that doesn't pierce the eardrum."

"I agree," Michael added. "Nothing like an old man's melody."

Brian's ears reddened.

"Ignore them," Bristol said and added a slap to Michael's arm because he was the closest.

Cole picked up a plate with sliced tomato, then put it down, letting it clink with a little drop. "You know I can cut my own tomatoes."

Michael leaned forward. "I don't know, Brian. I

think you made the right choice not letting Cole handle a knife."

Cole grunted. "It was the one time, and you still won't let me live it down?"

"Not something *that* good."

Brian grinned at the exchange as he put the teakettle on, then he finished setting everything up to make sandwiches and turned his attention to Bristol.

"Miss Kelley," he said as the kettle whistled. He lifted a finger and turned to pour hot water over a tea strainer and into a gold-rimmed cup with bluebells painted around the outside. He lifted the fancy cup and held it out to her like he was presenting her with a valuable gift.

Bristol took it delicately in her hands, breathing in the fragrance of the steam before taking time to admire the cup. "This is beautiful. I can understand why people drink with a pinky out. I feel like I'll crush it if I'm not careful." She paused. "Maybe you should have given me one of those sturdier mugs."

"Definitely not. Things that are beautiful are often wasted by leaving them on a shelf only to be looked at."

Bristol smiled and took a sip, then closed her eyes and moaned before swallowing the aromatic liquid. Cole dropped the block of cheese he was holding but recovered quickly.

"This is amazing. The flavor is so … clear."

Brian's cheeks tinted. "I'm glad you like it."

"Thank you for sharing this with me."

"I always enjoy sharing things I treasure with those who can appreciate it. Well, I'll leave you all now."

"Sir, if you need anything further, don't hesitate to contact me."

"Thanks for everything, Brian."

Michael and Bristol sat down on stools at the counter while Cole set to work making their lunch.

Bristol eyed the sandwiches that kept growing larger with each addition. She was unsure whether she could fit one in her mouth.

She turned to Michael as Cole continued to work. "So how do you and Cole know each other, and what's the deal with Cole having a knife?"

Michael opened his mouth, but Cole pointed the knife he was holding at Michael and spoke first. "There is nothing wrong with my having a knife." He flicked the knife down, stabbing it into the thick wooden cutting board. "We did some training together. Then I went into the police, and he went into the FBI." Cole added a shrug at the end that he hoped would put an end to the question.

Michael smiled, but put a hand over his mouth as he looked over at Bristol with his eyebrows lifted.

"Okay, Michael, spill."

"There's nothing more to tell," Cole said, shooting daggers at Michael before he turned and went to the fridge.

"It still bothers you?" Michael asked.

"No, it was a long time ago, so it's irrelev — "

"Cole trained with the Navy SEALs," Michael said to Bristol.

"What the hell, Michael?" Cole slammed the fridge door closed with a rattle.

"You said it doesn't bother you." Michael put his hands up in defense.

"You were a SEAL? That explains a few things."

Michael chuckled. "I didn't say he *was* a SEAL, I said he *trained* with them … us."

Cole groaned and leaned over. "I can't believe you're going to do this to me."

"She deserves to know."

"I absolutely do deserve to know. After all I've done for you, Cole," she taunted.

"You shot me in the chest," Cole jousted back.

"Are you going to hold that over my head for the rest of my life?"

"If he's going to hold the knife thing over mine, yes."

"Fine." She turned back to Michael. "Tell me."

"Well, apparently, Cole's dad thought he was a bit of a wimp."

"That's just hurtful," Cole said.

"But true. His dad paid a lot of money to give him the opportunity to train with some real men. He had to sign some sort of waiver, and I think he had help from a government official somewhere high up the ladder as well."

"Yeah, well, I wasn't happy about it. You guys gave me a hard time about it too."

Bristol pressed a fist into her mouth to keep from smiling.

Michael nodded. "Of course we did. You didn't

deserve to be there. Not at the start, anyway. And after the knife thing … "

Bristol put a hand on Michael's arm to stop him. "Okay, wait, you have to tell me about the knife."

"Do you want me to tell her, or are you going to be a man about it?"

Cole glared at Michael. "The story's not that interesting." But he spread his fingers out on the counter in front of Bristol. "See that scar?" he asked, wiggling his pinky. "I was cutting a rope and thought my pinky was part of the rope." Then he made a fist with everything but his pinky and held his hand up to Michael. "You gotta admit. It's a pretty good cut though."

"Yes, Cole, it was a very good cut. Well done. But you forgot to add the part where you had just boasted about your skill with a rope. How you went on and on about your experience handling all kinds of rope. Big rope, small rope. It all gave you a remarkable talent for what you were about to do. Then you almost cut your finger off."

Cole leaned across the counter and slapped Michael lightly on the cheek.

"I hope that wasn't supposed to hurt."

"You'd know if it was supposed to hurt."

Bristol put her arms up. "Hey, can you two stop with the testosterone party and tell me what happened next?"

"We joke about it now, but seriously, Cole worked harder than anyone else to earn his place."

"I had to."

Michael focused on Bristol. "He may have started

out his time with us without deserving it, but by the end, he was as much a SEAL as any of us."

"Fascinating."

Bristol watched Cole focus too hard on the sandwiches until Michael spoke again. "So what about you? Where'd you get your training?"

"Me? The school of hard knocks. And I have a friend who has been good to me for many years."

Cole served up the sandwiches. "How about we eat?"

Michael took his plate greedily. "The first time I tasted one of Cole's creations, he immediately increased in my estimation."

"That doesn't mean much coming from someone who will eat anything."

Michael ignored him. "He's good with ingredients."

Bristol pressed a hand down on the sandwich to flatten it. "I've had an introduction to his cooking previously. Any Halloumi in this sandwich?"

"No, this one is Swiss."

"That I've heard of." She gave one last press before lifting it to her mouth. The effort was worth it. Not much else was said until lunch was finished.

Bristol wiped her mouth, having enjoyed the break from reality. "We should get down to business. The clock is ticking." She got up from the counter and headed toward the office.

They sat down together around the coffee table and Michael crossed his legs and hooked his linked fingers on his knee. "I'm not sure what I can do for the two of you. Cole, I looked into those couple of situations you mentioned. The evidence they have on Deb isn't bullet-proof, but she'd have a better chance if she had something she could offer as a deal."

Bristol drummed her fingers on her leg. "She'd have plenty of stuff. She's been the lawyer for some shady people."

"Not lawyer stuff. That's confidential."

Cole sat up straight. "What about her ex?"

Bristol screwed up her face. "There's a few of those she wouldn't mind screwing over, but I don't know. We need an easy target."

"That's what I mean. When I was at her office, she was talking to this guy on the phone. Sounded like she had information and he was hiding behind the lawyer crap. Something about changing outcomes." Cole rubbed his forehead. "What was his name? I think his last name was Ryder."

"Phillip! Of course." She smacked her hand on her forehead. "Yes. He's the CEO of Lisco Pharmaceuticals, Phillip Ryder. She hates his guts. And for good reason." She jumped up and grabbed her legal pad. "I actually had him written down here. I saw an article about him."

Bristol looked down at her pad. "I need to make a phone call. You two keep chatting. It shouldn't take long. Cole, can I use the house phone?"

"Yeah, sure."

She sat at the desk and dialed the number for *Show-down*. It went to voice mail, and she left a message telling them which article she was calling about and asked them to call back urgently, then sat back down with the guys. "No answer."

"I was just telling Cole that I've looked into Jacob Tesco, but there isn't a lot I can help you with there. He's part of an ongoing investigation, so I can't touch it."

"His name is Jacob? Huh, I never knew that," Bristol said. "All I need is something I can give to Tesco regarding Silas that makes Silas look bad. Very bad."

"I can have another look, but I'm sorry I can't really be much more help."

The phone rang, and Bristol jumped up and raced for it.

Cole watched her as she spoke, standing straight as an arrow with one hand on her hip. All business.

Michael whistled softly. "She's somthin' else."

"I know, but she's a hard nut to crack."

"The best ones always are. You wouldn't want it to be too easy, would you?"

"Yes." Cole laughed. "No, not really, because then she wouldn't be her."

"How far have you fallen?"

"Pretty much all the way."

"Does she know?"

"Maybe, but if she does, she's hiding it from herself. She's got some baggage."

"Don't we all? But I've seen the way she looks at you. Don't give up."

"I don't plan on it."

Cole watched Bristol's demeanor change. She looked at Cole. Her face had gone pale.

"Thank you for your time," she said and set the phone down gently, then walked over and sat down. Her body seemed to vibrate.

She looked down at her open palms. "I found what we're looking for."

She clenched her fists until her knuckles were white, then grabbed a pillow and threw it hard across the room. "Shit." She blew out a breath and dropped her head into her hands. "Not again."

Michael stood and mouthed to Cole, "I'll go."

Cole walked him to the door. "Thanks for your help."

"I'll call you if I can think of anything."

They shook hands and Michael left. Cole wanted to race back to Bristol, but he walked tentatively instead. She was still holding her head in her hands, moaning. He sat down next to her and put an arm across the back of the couch behind her.

"Goddamn Silas!" She jumped up off the couch. "I'm gonna kill him. If it's the last thing I do. He's dead. Everything I've done is for that goddamn son of a bitch." She picked up another pillow and threw it across the room but not as hard as the last one. Defeat took over and her body shook.

Cole stood up and walked over to her, running his hands down her arms and taking her limp hands. "What's happened?"

She didn't hear him. "At least I can give Deb something. But I've got to call Mick. He can get in and get the information she needs." She moved to make the call, but Cole held her in place. She looked up at him with blurry eyes and tried to pull at the anger in the pit of her stomach to keep from crying.

He was always there when she was ready to break. She put her arms around his middle and pulled him close, resting the side of her face on his chest. The darkness didn't threaten her as it had before, but it broke her heart to know she'd been used again — without even knowing it.

Cole wrapped his arms around her. His chest tightened, and he wasn't sure he'd be able to let her go.

"He used me again," she said. "There was an article written last year about Lisco Pharmaceuticals falsifying reports. When I called to get more details, they said the person who wrote that article died soon after. John Stevens." She pulled back and looked at Cole. "I killed him."

Chapter 21

COLE TIPPED his head in confusion. "You killed him? Are you sure?"

Bristol's shoulders dropped. "You don't think I'd know if I killed someone?"

"But you said it was just last year. I thought you stopped killing before then."

"I was. I did." She turned away to pace the room. "He had a drug habit, and they hired me to make sure he got caught. I slipped him a mickey and set it all up. But when the cops arrived, they found him dead."

"Why do you assume you're the one who killed him?"

"I — Well, who else would have killed him? They hired me. I did the job too well."

"You remember physically killing him?"

"Well, no. I put a needle in his arm with enough cocaine to kill him."

"So you didn't kill him."

Bristol looked cynical. "You think someone went in

after me? But then why would they hire me in the first place."

Cole shook his head. "If Silas was involved, then he had his own reasons. He enjoyed watching you work, remember? He would have enjoyed it for the game it was. The control."

Bristol shivered at the thought, and Cole stepped closer, putting a hand on the side of her face and wiped a stray tear away with his thumb. "We'll get him. We'll make it right."

Bristol pushed her cheek into his palm and tipped her face up to his. "I don't — " She took a deep, shuddering breath. "I don't know what I'd do without you."

All the fight had drained out of her and in that moment, all she wanted was something good. Something to make her forget for one second all the mess that was going on around her. She leaned forward, closing her eyes.

Cole watched the calm that settled on her face as she leaned into him, and that was all he needed. He closed the distance and kissed her.

Time was still, and as they pulled each other closer, neither one could tell where one of them stopped and the other began. But as Cole felt an urgency build within him, he pulled gently away.

"Better?" His voice was quiet and coarse.

Bristol nodded and rested her forehead on his chest. "We should probably keep moving. Time's short."

Cole had already decided that Bristol would have to make the first move to separate herself. He wanted to keep her there for a while, even though he knew that the longer he held her, the more complicated things got.

Bristol hadn't moved yet but asked, "Is this phone secure?"

"Yeah."

She slid her arms from around him, wishing they could stay that way for longer, and went for her phone. She sent Mick a text with the house number.

It was only a minute before the phone rang, and Bristol picked it up. "Mick, you're on a secure line?"

"Yeah."

"Good. I need you to do a hack for me."

"Sure thing, as long as it's not the FBI."

"Coward."

"Shut up and tell me what you need."

She looked at Cole, who was looking at something on his phone. "Pharmaceutical company by the name of Lisco."

That perked him up. "Oh, awesome."

"They've been falsifying the results. I need the actual results. Are you somewhere safe where you can do that?"

"Yeah, I've got what I need. Are you safe?"

"I am. And I've got myself a bodyguard. He's a bit skinny, but he'll do." She winked at Cole who looked up from his phone, pretending to be offended. "You can call me on this number if you have to. I'll email you the details. Any info you find you need to pass on to my friend Deb."

"The lawyer? Great. I always love sticking it to the big guys."

Bristol hung up and sat down next to Cole. "That's

Deb taken care of, but we still have nothing for Tesco." Bristol rubbed her face.

"What we need is a break," Cole said, standing and pulling her up behind him.

She pulled back. "We don't have time for a break. Our deadline is approaching way too fast."

"I know it is, but we'll get a lot more thinking done if we have a break. You ever go to the batting cages?"

"No." She frowned. "Come to think of it, I don't think I've ever hit a baseball."

"You're kidding. You need to come with me. Trust me. If we don't stay active, we'll lose our edge."

He had a point. "Fine."

◯◯

It was a forty-five-minute drive, and Bristol looked at her watch every five minutes until Cole had had enough. "Take it off."

"What?"

"Your watch. Take it off and give it to me."

"Why?"

"Because you are driving me crazy."

Bristol's throat buzzed in irritation. "I can just look at the clock on the dash."

"Then do that instead, that way I won't know." He continued to hold out his hand for her watch. She clicked her tongue and tossed it at him, then turned on the radio for a distraction.

The station had a news item that was discussing the diminishing health of a shipping magnate who had given control of his business to his daughter, who had somehow managed to stay out of the media her entire life. No one really knew who this woman was who suddenly had the weight of her father's empire behind her.

"That's it," Bristol said, turning the radio off. "I have an idea for Eli."

"Really? Smoke and mirrors, or are we going to use real evidence like with Lisco?"

She thought for a second. "Smoke and mirrors, actually."

"Oh good. So what's the smoke?"

"Melissa Zimber."

"Who?"

"Weren't you listening?"

"You mean the daughter of that shipping magnate?"

"That's the one."

"Can't say I know much about her. Don't even know what she looks like. All that money, it's a wonder she's remained a mystery."

"It's *because* of the money. All anyone knows is that she's twenty-eight, slim, and has dark hair." Bristol grinned.

"Why do I have the feeling you're going to tell me that you're Melissa Zimber?"

"A magician never reveals her secrets. But I bet Silas's bank would be very interested in meeting this young woman and would do just about anything to get her business. Especially if she were to give them some rather unseemly information about Lincoln Enterprise's relationship with Lisco that could come to light in the near future."

"I think you just gave away your secret."

Bristol shrugged. "It would be unfortunate if the bank pulled the loan on the purchase of Eli's building, wouldn't it?"

"Terrible."

Bristol rubbed her hands together. "Now all we have left is to save Mick from Tesco."

Cole looked at Bristol, his face grave. "Not Mick. You."

"Right. At least we can focus on him now."

They pulled into the half-empty parking lot surrounded by vacant lots and ragged buildings.

"This isn't what I expected," Bristol said as she watched a plastic bag blow across the sea of asphalt.

"What were you expecting?"

"Not sure. A baseball stadium maybe?"

"I grew up hitting here, but it is more run down than I remember."

"Well, let's get in there so you can show me what you've got."

"That sounds like a challenge."

"It is."

"All right then, let's get going."

They hurried from the car to a small building as the cold wind nipped at them, hinting at the freezing months that lay ahead for Chicago.

A blast of warmth and sticky floors greeted them when they pushed through the heavy door. Cole breathed in deeply of the smell of hotdogs and something sweet. "Just like I remember. You hungry? Want a hotdog?"

"The last time I ate a hotdog I threw up."

"Probably for the best. I don't remember them being very good, anyway."

Cole went to the desk where a middle-aged woman with spiky pink hair stared at her phone. Cole had to wave a hand in front of her face to get her attention. She blinked at him, then pulled earbuds from her ears.

"Yeah?"

"I'd like to buy an hour in the cage."

She pointed above her head at the sign with the prices listed, and he pulled out a credit card. She rang him up without making eye contact again and then waved toward a stack of bats before popping the buds back in her ears and proceeding to ignore him again.

Cole led Bristol over to choose a bat. He hefted one in his hand then held it out to her. "Here, how's that feel?"

She took it, but let it drop to her side. "I don't really have a context for this." She lifted it up to the side of his head with a wicked grin. "I could tell you how it feels as a weapon, but is that the same for hitting a ball?"

He pushed it aside. "Probably."

She stepped back and swung it a couple times. "Then it's fine."

They stepped into a cage, and Bristol stood in the middle of the plate. Cole smiled. "Step back a bit."

Bristol pushed her tongue into her cheek. "I realize that. I may not have hit a ball before, but I've seen the game … well, parts anyway. I'm assuming no balls will come flying at me yet? I'm just waiting for you to give me room."

Cole put his hands up in surrender. "Okay, I'll step back. You do your thing."

She glared at him competitively and moved to the side, leaning over like she'd seen. Or thought she had. It occurred to her that she might look like a fool, but that just meant she had more to prove. A challenge she readily accepted.

She eyeballed Cole. "Turn it on." She lifted the bat like she was going to knock someone's head off. The ball flew through the air. She swung and missed, spinning herself around. She got ready for the next and knocked it to the side.

She stepped back, and Cole stopped the balls. "Would you care for any tips? Or should I just keep my mouth shut?"

Her shoulders jerked. "I'm not used to missing."

He walked up and stopped short of tapping her on the head. "Mostly, it's the head space you're in. In kick-boxing, when you're training, there's a space your body occupies. It's not the same as the one your body occupied when you were trying to hit the ball, was it?"

"No."

Cole walked over and put a hand on Bristol's hips from the back, pulling them around. "The other problem is your form." His hands went to her shoulders, and he straightened her there. "Bend your knees a little and lift the bat to here," he said, lifting her arms. He reached around her and readjusted her hands slightly.

She turned her head to him. "If I didn't know you better, I'd say you're coming on to me."

"You must not know me very well then because I'm definitely coming on to you." He stepped away. "But you've got work to do. Now, that place you go to when you're training, go there."

Bristol closed her eyes for a second then looked across the open space at where the ball would come from. She took a deep breath and felt that mix of relaxation and readiness. She focused on the position of her body and how the momentum would move through her body up to the swing of the bat. "Go."

The ball flew across the space again, and she smashed it off to the side. The vibration up into her arms was familiar. Although, perhaps, for different reasons, but it was enough to get her head in the game.

Cole saw the change and knew she had it. She knew her body and how it moved. "Don't be afraid to shift your body to add momentum."

The next ball came, and she was ready for it. She lifted her leg and swung hard. The ball sailed into the nets. Her head was in now and she kept going.

Cole watched her swing. He couldn't take his eyes off her. He leaned against the fence and enjoyed the freedom to look at her. Until he had to stop. This wasn't doing him any good. He paused the machine.

She stood ready for the next ball until she realized the next ball wasn't coming. "Why'd you stop?"

"My turn." He needed to get rid of some tension.

"Oh." She swung at the air before moving to the side.

"You've got good form, but let me show you how us pros do it." He swatted her on the butt with his bat as they passed each other.

She studied how he stood and how he swung. He was good. She picked up a few things she had missed. She imagined him being forced by his dad into the SEALs. A rich kid's daddy paying for his acceptance wouldn't have gone down well. He would have paid for it in more ways than one.

"You ever want to play baseball?" she asked as he took another swing, sending the ball off into the nets.

"It was my childhood dream."

"Did you ever try?"

"It was *my* dream. Not my father's."

"What would he have done if you'd gone for it anyway?"

"Ship me off to the SEALs." He missed the next ball.

Bristol looked at her watch, which she had stolen back when they arrived. It had been an hour. A fast hour. "We should get going. We're running out of time."

Cole leaned the bat against the cage and wiped his arm across his forehead. "Yeah."

The walk back to the car was silent. It wasn't until they pulled out of the parking lot that Bristol said, "You were right."

"About what? No, wait, don't answer that. I'll just savor the moment if you don't mind."

Bristol shook her head. "About the exercise. I feel refreshed and my head is clear. I usually head to Eli's, but without that, I guess I thought I'd just push through."

"You know what else helps me think?"

"What?"

"Pizza. You like pizza? Or did you puke after eating that, too."

"Don't be ridiculous. Pizza doesn't make you puke."

"There's a place on the way home that makes the best pizza. We'll swing by and grab one for dinner."

"Okay, but I only eat cheese pizza."

"What?" He looked like he just found out Andrew's baby had been born with two heads.

Bristol laughed. "I'm kidding. Get one with everything."

"I can do you one better. They've got this chicken one with satay sauce on it. Trust me."

"I do, remember?" She smiled and looked out the window.

———————————————

Chapter 22

———————————————

BRISTOL HAD NEVER BEEN a fan of pineapple on pizza, and when she saw it on the slice he handed her, she balked. But when she bit into the mixture of toppings, she decided she could make an exception.

"This is delicious," she said with her mouth full.

They sat together in a dining room she hadn't seen previously.

A large rectangular chandelier illuminated the table, while the floor-to-ceiling windows let in what was left of the daylight.

The room was chilly and Bristol gazed longingly into the empty fireplace until Cole caught on and flipped a switch on the wall.

Bristol squinted at the fake logs, untouched by the fire. "I thought those were real. When I was a kid, we had a cheap space heater that had lights in it to make it look like fire. I guess this is the expensive version."

"Something like that. Personally, I like the real thing better."

"I think I have to agree," she said as she licked sauce off the side of her hand and took the opportunity to glance at her watch. "We're running out of time."

"You've said that."

"Because it's true. And I'm not sure where else to look."

"I might have an idea. My dad wasn't exactly a clean businessman. Despite my mom's indiscretions, he kept working with Silas. It's a long shot, but there may be something there."

"You sure you don't mind bringing your dad into this?"

"Not if it helps our situation."

"Okay, well, I guess it's worth a shot."

Bristol couldn't help the pout on her face when Cole turned the fire back off before they left the room.

"There's one in the office I can turn on." He couldn't help but grin at the delight that lit up her face. "May as well take advantage while we can. Not much use for fireplaces back in LA."

"LA gets cold."

Cole grunted. "Spend some time in a northern winter and then tell me that."

They settled on the couch with the new fire, and Cole dropped a pile of papers on the coffee table, handing a few sheets to Bristol.

She spread them out in front of her and pursed her lips. "Right." She let out a long, slow breath. "Is it too early to admit defeat?"

Cole looked across at her papers. He pulled a sheet that was shoved off to the side and put it in front of her. "You know what this is?"

She turned her head slowly. "Yeah. I've seen an invoice before."

"Good, then this should be easy for you. All you have to do is piece the puzzle together."

"Numbers were never really my strong suit in school."

"Forget about the numbers. At least in an accounting sense. Look here," he said, tapping one side of the paper. "It says here that the invoice is for work done on a property my dad owned. That's mostly what he did. He bought a business, land and all, and sold it off bit by bit. We're looking for a connection to Silas that proves … anything. The numbers are important, but they're not necessarily the answer to the puzzle."

She tapped a finger on her lip, then flipped through the rest of the pile. "Is there more?"

"Yeah, in the filing cabinet."

"I might have an idea," she said, walking over to the cabinet. "May I?"

"By all means. I must be the world's best teacher if you've picked that up in a matter of seconds."

With her fingers poised over the drawer, she turned to Cole. "Like you said, it's a puzzle. One of the reasons I'm so good at my job is because I know how to find short cuts to solve puzzles. Your father ever do business in LA?"

"Yeah."

"Tesco's got a *legitimate* business he uses to launder

money. Or at least he used to. Maybe your father worked with him and maybe," she closed one drawer and opened another. "If we're lucky, we can find a connection from there. It's easy to sift through a lot of paperwork when all you're looking for is a name."

After about half an hour, when she was considering that her idea was a flop, she found an invoice. "Bingo."

"You're kidding."

She pulled out the folder and flipped through it. "It's a file from Tesco's business for demolition work. This will be for money laundering, I'm certain." She stopped and looked up at Cole. "I don't mean … "

"No, it's fine, I told you, I knew my dad wasn't an honest businessman. But do you think you'll be able to prove anything?"

"We don't need to prove anything. We just need enough to convince Tesco. This isn't a court of law. It doesn't even matter how we come about our evidence as long as it's what we need."

Cole took the folder from Bristol and looked it over. "This invoice is high, but there's nothing wrong with overpricing a job. People do it lawfully all the time. Doesn't surprise me that my dad was involved." He handed the papers back to Bristol.

She looked over the next sheet as she paced the room and stopped mid-stride. "Hang on. Mocrossen Street. I know this block. It's near where I used to live."

"Yeah, my dad probably bought property all over the city over the years."

"But this block is vacant."

"Isn't that the point of demolition?"

"Look at the date." She passed the piece of paper over to Cole. "This was less than ten years ago. It's been vacant since I was a kid. There was a building there originally, but it burned down. They knocked down what was left, and it never got rebuilt. I went past there enough over the years to know there was never anything else there to knock down."

Cole sighed and ran his hands through his hair as he leaned back on the couch and stretched his arms up. "That connects Tesco and my father, but it doesn't give us Silas. Or a way to make Silas look bad."

"But your father worked with Silas." Bristol sat down and licked her finger, thumbing through the rest of the paperwork. She stopped and swatted at a page triumphantly. "Lincoln Enterprises." She held the paper up for Cole.

"Silas bought the land off your dad, and it looks like he paid a lot more than it was worth. That must have been your dad's cut." She read through the figures, shaking her head. "I don't understand most of what I'm looking at here, but it feels like something is missing."

Cole scooted over to her and looked at the papers. Several figures were circled.

"Hang on." He went to the desk to retrieve the ledger from the drawer. "It's probably nothing, but … what was the date on that invoice?" he asked, flipping through the pages.

"September 22. Eight years ago."

Cole found the page and laid it down next to the invoice. He found the circled numbers listed in the book with an 'SL' next to them, then a dash and another number was listed. "Nice one, dad."

"Your dad's got all the real figures listed?"

"I don't know exactly what he planned on doing with it, but I wouldn't be surprised if he was looking for a way to screw Silas."

"Really?" Bristol chewed on her lip. "But wouldn't Silas be able to just screw him right back? There's no way Silas didn't have stuff on your dad."

"You didn't know my dad. He would have done it just for spite. Just so he could say he had the information." Cole tapped the ledger on his leg. "But judging by the numbers, I bet they were screwing Tesc — What?" Cole stopped because Bristol had that look he had learned to dread.

"You don't think Silas had your dad killed? Made it look like a heart attack?"

Cole blew out a breath and dropped his head. "I guess it's possible."

"You don't seem overly concerned."

"Honestly? It doesn't really change anything. I had the same suspicion, but he had a heart problem and his doctor wasn't surprised." He shrugged.

She put a hand on his knee. "He's your dad. It's okay to care." She watched the muscle in his jaw clench. The phone rang, breaking the stare. Cole got up quickly to get it.

"Hello?"

"Hi, it's Mick."

"I'll put Bristol on." Cole handed her the phone. "Mick."

She nodded. "Hey, it's a bit late for you isn't it?"

"Is it? Oh! Sorry, I forgot about the time difference. I didn't even look at the time. Did I wake you?"

"It's not that late for me. Just tell me you've got good news."

"Good and bad. How are you at breaking and entering?"

"Not my best feature, why?"

"I didn't find the information you wanted, but what I did find is correspondence saying that the documents exist and where."

"Where is it?"

"At the Lisco headquarters."

"Where's that?"

"LA. They've only got the hard copy. Someone was paranoid."

"For good reason, obviously."

"If you can get in there, you'll find it in the archives, file 155-3756 BNC."

"The question is, can we get in there?" She rubbed a hand across her forehead. "Thanks for the information. I guess we'll have to take it from here."

"You staying safe?"

"As always."

"That's what I was afraid of."

"I'll call you soon." She glanced at her watch after she hung up and put her hands on her hips as she considered Cole, who looked uncharacteristically disheveled on the couch. "You don't happen to be any good at breaking into highly secure buildings?"

Cole's demeanor changed instantly. "Is it my birthday?"

"Is that a yes?"

"It's what I do best."

"Good. Because it isn't my forte. Mick couldn't get the information because they only have it in hard copy at Lisco. We'll need to go in and get it."

"It *is* my birthday. Except that means we'll have to head back to LA tomorrow morning. Which means no more time to spend sifting through this stuff. Do you think we have enough to convince Tesco?"

Bristol pinched her lip. "He might not be as smart as Silas, but he's not an idiot. What we have is pretty circumstantial at best. We can suggest that Silas was shortchanging him, but it will be Silas's word against ours in the end."

"We'll lose a lot of hours breaking into Lisco that could be spent solidifying our lead."

"Or we could spend all our time sifting through this paperwork and find nothing, leaving Deb to hang out to dry. I need to get this for her." She sat down next to Cole. "There's no point saving myself if Deb isn't going to be okay."

Cole knew it was futile to argue. He'd do this for her, but only because he knew she'd try to do it on her own if he didn't help. He rested a hand over hers and nodded lightly.

Bristol took a deep breath. "We should probably get some rest. We'll head back tomorrow and face whatever we face."

"You don't want to spend any more time looking through the paperwork?"

She knew they should probably keep looking, but her focus was now trained on helping Deb. It would be useless for her to continue. "We should get some sleep. Get an early start."

Cole walked her to her room. She turned around before walking in.

"Thank you for everything. Again. I couldn't have done any of this if you weren't with me. I'd have been dead a few times by now."

"Well, we still have two more days to get through." He reached up and put a hand on her arm, smiled grimly, then dropped his head. When he looked up, he took his hand off her arm and put it on the door frame. "Bristol, I really don't want to lose you."

She swallowed hard but didn't say anything. Instead, she leaned forward and kissed him. It was meant to be a small kiss goodnight, but as soon as they touched it sparked and set something on fire. The air around them turned frantic and deadly. She saw it waiting for them. Saw death ready to take them both, so she pulled him in toward her and fell a step backward into the room.

Cole let go of the door frame and fisted the back of her shirt and kept stepping her backward until her legs bumped against the bed.

Somehow, he managed to lift his consciousness above the rush of need and pulled away.

He had trouble finding his voice in the cloud of desire. "Is this what you want?"

Her brows creased. She did want it. Everything in her wanted it. But she also didn't. That small part of her hung on.

Cole stepped away. His body screamed at him, but he was a man who had control when it mattered. "Get some sleep," he said with his eyes on the floor. If he were to look at her, he wasn't sure he'd make it out the door.

◯◯

Back in his room, he rested his forehead on the wall. "Cole Sullivan, you idiot. Why do you have to be such a good guy?"

He turned and headed for a cold shower.

◯◯

Bristol pulled the blanket up tight around her neck. She couldn't believe Cole had walked out. A strange part of her wanted to be offended that he had left, but she didn't know why. She also couldn't figure out why he did it. Next to the feeling of offense, it made her ache for him deeper, but there were still things she needed to protect.

It took her a long time to fall asleep.

◯◯

In the morning, Bristol found Cole in the same position as the previous morning, looking at the news on his tablet with a coffee next to him. When he saw her, a smile lit up his face. The awkwardness Bristol felt as she entered the kitchen disappeared.

He turned the kettle on. "Did you sleep well?"

She paused before answering. "Nope."

"Me either."

She kept looking at him until it was awkward again, but she didn't care.

Cole tipped his head to the side. "You okay?"

"Why'd you do it?"

"What?"

"Walk away. I would have gone to bed with you."

He ran a hand through his hair and lifted his head to the ceiling, letting out a deep breath. "I know. But it wasn't what you wanted."

"That can't be the only reason."

"I guess not."

"So why'd you stop?"

He walked over to her, close enough that she had to look up at him, but he didn't touch her. "Because, as it turns out, I've fallen in love with you. And I work really hard not to hurt the ones I love."

"Shit," she whispered.

"Yeah." He laughed and ran his fingers down her cheek. "I thought we should be honest with each other."

She crossed her arms, creating a barrier between them. His words made her skin tingle, but also terrified her. "What do we do now?"

"Get ready to go."

"Thank goodness. Business I can do. I just need to make a phone call."

"Wow, you are amazing at compartmentalizing when you want to."

"It's my happy place."

Bristol had her phone in her hand, but she set it on the counter.

"Look. You were honest with me. I can be honest with you. I might not be able to … you know, say … you know. But despite all my efforts to the contrary, I've fallen for you. I want to give this a chance, assuming we make it out of this."

She squirmed, and he opened his mouth to say something, but she put her hand up. "But right now we still have work to do."

The last thing she saw before she turned and stalked out of the room to make her phone call was his sideways grin.

Chapter 23

BRISTOL EXPECTED to enjoy the flight back to LA more because she was awake for it, but the closer they got, the more she dreaded the reality of what she would face with Tesco. Knowing her friends were safe was a comfort, but dedicating herself to Tesco was a life sentence that brought bile to her throat.

She watched Cole as he poured over the blueprints of the Lisco building that one of his contacts had sent through before they took off.

To take her mind off her problems, she joined him. "You have a plan yet?"

"Maybe. How are your acting skills?"

"Oscar worthy. I've already made an appointment to visit Silas's bank as Melissa Zimber."

"When's that happening?"

"Tomorrow morning."

Cole brooded for a moment. "I take it you're trying to fit it in before your meeting with Tesco."

"I don't want to face Tesco without knowing my friends are safe."

"Fine," he said to let the matter drop before pointing at his blueprint. "If Melissa has an appointment at the bank tomorrow, then how about we make her an appointment for Lisco today."

"You need Melissa to break into Lisco tonight? You think she's better at B and E than me? I'm a little offended."

"Sorry, but she'll serve our purposes better than you."

"I'm not following. How does my pretending to be someone else when we break into a building help our situation?"

"We won't be going at night."

"Umm, I know I'm not the expert at this, but I thought breaking in at night was pretty standard. Fewer people around and all of that."

"Fewer people, yes, but more security. At night they want to keep people out, but during the day, they invite people in. People like Melissa. Not to mention it's a Sunday so there will be minimal staff."

"Ah. Now I see. Funny, Miss Zimber has always wanted to have a tour of Lisco. And who will you be?"

"I'll be your personal assistant, since I'm too skinny to be a bodyguard."

"Terrance Nightingale."

"Who?"

"My PA. You'll be Terrance Nightingale." She kept her face deadpan.

"Are you trying to hurt me?"

"What? It's a great name."

"Fine. Terrance." They sat quietly for a moment. "We should maybe talk about the fact that Tesco might not take the bait."

"It doesn't matter."

Cole slammed his hand on the table, and Bristol jumped. "Dammit Bristol, that's not an option. I'd kill him first."

She laid her hand over his but didn't speak because she had no answers. Eventually he pulled his hand away and focused on the blueprints again.

They were back in LA by noon and stopped at a mall to buy Bristol a change of clothes for her meeting at Lisco. She had something suitable in her closet and would have liked to have checked in on Mrs. Deacon, but going back to her apartment was too risky, and they didn't have much time.

Bristol walked out of the change room and spun around for Cole. She wore a charcoal dress with a keyhole neck and a pencil skirt. With the capped sleeved and stilettos, she was dressed like power. The CEO look suited her.

Cole nodded. "Yup. That works."

"Good." She gave Cole a once-over. "I was going to suggest we get something for you as well, but you seem to be dressed nicely all the time."

Cole slapped his hand to his chest. "Hang on, did you just give me a compliment?"

"Oh shut up and let's go."

◯◯

Bristol's heels clicked on the marble floor. A noise that boosted her confidence. Cole walked dutifully behind, and they both turned their heads away from the security cameras that Cole had confirmed the location of in advance.

"Good afternoon," she said to the woman behind the counter as she approached. "I'm here to see Dr. Ross. My name is Melissa Zimber. He's expecting me."

"Certainly, Miss Zimber."

They didn't have to wait long. Apparently, Lisco Pharmaceuticals was very interested to hear Melissa's ideas about how they could work together.

A short man in a white lab coat came buzzing through the door. "Miss Zimber," he said a little too loudly.

Cole would have called the smile that filled Bristol's face effervescent. He didn't know she had it in her.

Bristol's height with the high heels meant she was tall enough to admire Dr. Ross's impressive comb-over. "Dr. Ross, it's lovely to meet you. And thank you for agreeing to see us on the weekend," she purred as they shook hands. "This is my personal, assistant Terrance Nightingale." She glanced at Cole who pressed his lips together to stifle a laugh.

Dr. Ross reached out to shake Cole's hand. "Terrance. Nice to meet you."

Bristol smoothed her skirt with her hand. "I've heard wonderful things about your company."

"Well … it's … it's not my company." He clasped his hands together. "I have to admit, I'm a little unclear about what it is we can do for you."

"I'm particularly interested in the market research side of your business. Statistics are only as useful as the person who wields them, and I understand Lisco has excellent swordsmanship."

Dr. Ross was completely charmed. "You have a way with words. You make what we do here sound like a work of art."

"Isn't it? The work you do must require a sort of craftsmanship."

"True. Well, why don't I give you a bit of a tour. We do have an impressive testing area."

"That sounds like an excellent place to start."

Cole knew what room he was looking for as Dr. Ross led them through a door behind reception. He kept a mental image of the blueprints at the front of his mind as they moved through the corridors until they passed the room he was waiting for and cleared his throat to let Bristol know.

Dr. Ross stopped at the far end of the hall, next to a large window that looked into a plain white room with a wooden table. He swept a hand toward the window.

"This is one of our testing rooms. It's for preliminary testing as it's exposed to the hall. We have others with private viewing rooms specifically for extended observations."

"The room is completely white."

"We do our best to remove any obstacles to our results. White has its own problems, but you may note it's not strictly white, it's closer to cream. We chose the color after extensive testing. Even the table was carefully chosen."

"How clever." She pretended to be deeply interested, but they needed to move on.

As they turned the corner, Cole stopped abruptly and pulled his phone out of his pocket. "Excuse me, Miss Zimber, but I've got a call from the office."

"Yes. Go ahead and take it and catch up when you're finished."

He put the phone to his ear and walked around the corner. Bristol noted the confused look on Dr. Ross's face. "I apologize for the interruption, but we can continue."

"Yes." The furrow didn't leave his forehead, but he moved ahead. "I'll show you the more advanced rooms," he said slowly.

Cole dropped his phone into his pocket and went back to the unmarked door that he knew to be the archive room and set to work picking the lock.

Around the corner, Dr. Ross stopped again. "It's just. We don't get phone reception in here. It's specifically built to block all reception." His eyes narrowed. "Perhaps we should check on your assistant." He brushed around her, heading back the way they came.

"Excuse me, Dr. Ross." She grabbed his arm as he went past. "Are you suggesting something? Because if you are, *I* would suggest that you come out and say it."

His face was a mix of embarrassment and frustration, but at least he had stopped. "As you are aware, what goes on at this facility is highly sensitive and confidential."

"I am aware."

"And we are very protective of our work."

"As I would expect. But if you're going to accuse a potential client of sabotage, I *suggest* you have your facts straight before putting forward your speculations. It could be very damaging to the company." She raised her voice to carry around the corner to Cole but hid the exaggerated volume behind a look of distinguished outrage.

Dr. Ross's lips puckered, and his face turned bright red. It almost looked as though he stomped his foot before pivoting and hurrying around the corner with Bristol close behind.

She could knock him out if necessary, but that would have unfortunate consequences. This plan would work best if no one knew the documents were missing until it was too late.

The hall was empty and Bristol held her breath as Dr. Ross approached the door to the archives. She moved up to be directly behind him and ready to strike, but he marched straight past and sped down the corridor, finally turning into a dead-end hall that had a door with a sign that read *Maintenance*.

She found that very odd until she noticed the keypad with a blinking red light. He looked at it, then at her.

"If I was out of line, I apologize, but I have to check." He moved his body to block the keypad as he punched in a code, but Bristol, with her extra height, could see over his shoulder enough to memorize it. More out of habit than need.

Once Cole got that paperwork there was no reason to come back, but then a panel opened and Dr. Ross put his thumb on a fingerprint reader to open the door. That aroused her curiosity. What could they be hiding in there that they were desperate to keep people away from?

Bristol heard the click of the lock disengaging, and Dr. Ross opened the door. His stiff posture made it obvious he expected to find someone on the other side of the door. He took a few steps into the room and looked around, then turned abruptly to face Bristol, who had put on a look of insolent humor.

"My apologies." Pink blossomed on his cheeks. "Would you like to continue the tour? Or uh … " He laughed uncomfortably.

"I would like to continue, yes. Thank you."

They walked back past the archive door and around the corner.

"I appreciate your understanding in this matter," Dr. Ross said, fidgeting.

"Not at all. In fact, the information we want to gather is sensitive, and I'm happy to see you take excellent precautions."

Dr. Ross rolled up on his toes, bewitched once again. "That room has a number code that changes daily, and the fingerprint reader has a limited number of people who can access it."

"You remember a new number every day?"

"That's how my brain works." He almost giggled. "It locks on to things like that. My brain."

Mine too, Bristol thought.

"There are also lasers in there." He added as he continued down the hall. "If anyone moves — zap." He shot the word out with the end of his finger. "They're busted."

"Lasers?"

"You know, like motion sensors."

"Oh." Her laugh fluttered as she touched a hand to her chest. "I thought you meant real lasers that kill people."

"Oh no, no, nothing as dangerous as that. Although … " He tapped the side of his nose and winked.

Normally she would have rolled her eyes, but she smiled instead.

They continued the tour, visiting some slightly disconcerting areas of the building that included lockable evaluation rooms. The thought of being stuck in one of those rooms and monitored was a terrifying thought.

· · ·

With the tour finished, Dr. Ross escorted Bristol to reception, where they found Cole waiting.

Cole gave Bristol a grave look before his countenance changed. "Ah, there you guys are. We have these state-of-the-art phones that are supposed to get reception everywhere, but it cut me off as soon as I answered, so I came out here and then your receptionist wouldn't let me back in without you."

"Yes, that's our policy."

"I've been very impressed with their security measures," Bristol said to Cole. Then she turned to Dr. Ross. "Thank you for your time. It's given me a lot to consider. I need to have a conversation with a few people, but I expect you'll hear from me soon." They shook hands, and Bristol turned before stopping. "Oh, wait, do you have a card I could have?"

"Certainly." Dr. Ross pulled his wallet out of this back pocket and pulled out a card. "This is mine, personally. Call any time."

Bristol took it by the edge. "Thank you. We'll talk soon."

"Lovely to meet you, Miss Zimber. I look forward to discussing how we can work together into the future."

Bristol kept the serene smile on her face until they were well out into the parking lot. "You didn't get it," she said as she opened the car door.

"No, the files in there were all useless. I take it Dr. Ross wasn't suspicious when you yelled around the corner to warn me?"

"I was dignified in my volume. You covered it well out there."

"You gave me plenty of notice. So what do we do now?"

She set the card Dr. Ross had given to her on the dash. "You have anything in your stockpile that can create a fingerprint?"

Cole lifted an eyebrow. "Don't tell me you know where the file is."

"Our friend Dr. Ross didn't give a second thought to the archive room when he suspected we were doing exactly what we were doing. There was another room."

"Where?"

"Back the way we came, there was a dead end."

Cole's eyes flicked back and forth as he worked his way across the blueprint in his mind. He shook his head. "Maintenance closet."

Bristol leaned back away from him, impressed. "How do you do that?"

"I'm just that good."

"Well, anyway, the sign said it was a maintenance closet, but keeping their brooms and wrenches under fingerprint and motion sensor protection seems extreme, don't you think?"

Cole smiled. "Did you get a look inside?"

"Numbered archive boxes. There's a code that changes every day. I happen to have today's. So all that's left to get past are the fingerprint and the sensors."

Cole nodded slowly. "I always did like a challenge. All right then, I guess we go back in tonight."

Chapter 24

COLE PULLED into an underground parking garage in a part of the city that Bristol would have described as bland. All the buildings were the same ordinary linear design with small windows and a lot of concrete.

At first, she was surprised. She'd pictured Cole somewhere simple but trendy, until it occurred to her that this was the kind of place no one would notice because no one would care.

"Welcome to my office," he said when he turned off the car.

"You have an office in a parking garage?"

"Funny."

"Maybe I should get an office. It's so professional," Bristol said as they rode up the elevator to the twelfth floor.

The door opened into an alcove where Cole activated a retinal scan.

"An eye scan? What have you got stashed in there?"

"One of the perks of the trade. You get to try out the merchandise."

The door glided open, and they walked into an open room with windows that looked out at the other surrounding buildings. Bristol walked over to one. "You have security at the door, but anyone could send a drone up here and peer in."

"It's one-way glass." He walked over to a cabinet and opened it.

"Of course it is," she said as she walked up behind him.

"Have a look through here for anything you might like to bring."

There were a variety of weapons and gadgets. "What are you, James Bond? I don't know what most of this stuff is."

"One day I'll take you through all of it. You'd find some of that incredibly handy."

She picked up what looked like a walkie-talkie with four antennas. "What's this do?"

"Cell phone jammer."

She shrugged, put it back, then grabbed what she suspected was a key fob. She held it up to him and lifted her eyebrows in question.

"Credit card skimmer."

"So that's where you get all your money." She set it back with a grin. "I feel like a kid in a toy store," she said, picking up a knife and pointing it at him. "This is a weird knife. What's the button for?"

He took it off her gently and tucked it into the back

of his pants. "Haven't played with that in a while. Gas injection knife. It's messy, but useful."

She made a face. "For what?"

"I've seen people blow up soda bottles with it on YouTube."

"Nice. What if it blows a hole in your pants?"

"It's got a safety."

She lifted a ring with a large ruby. "You don't strike me as the jewelry type."

"Oh that? That's actually very useful."

"How so?"

"It's like you. It distracts people with its beauty."

"God, you're revolting."

"But you make it so easy for me."

She spun the ring around, holding it close to her face. There was a little catch on the bottom. After slipping it onto her finger, she flicked the catch with her fingernail and a small needle popped out. "Ooh, that's more like it. Is it lethal?"

"No, just a tranq."

"Is it loaded?"

"Yup."

"Sweet. I think I'll keep this one. It should help me keep you in line."

"Glad you found something you like. I'll go get started on the fingerprint." He moved to a closet built into the wall where there were various machines.

Bristol watched him move one carefully to a nearby table. "That looks like a printer."

"It is, basically." He held his hand out to her, and

she frowned. He couldn't help but laugh. "Dr. Ross's card?"

"It prints fingerprints?" She said, handing him the card.

He lifted the lid and placed it on the glass. "That would be a simple way to put it, yes."

After the machine processed the image, it brought the card up on a screen. Cole pushed a few buttons and highlighted several fingerprints.

He looked at Bristol. "You wouldn't happen to know which print is his?"

"When he handed it to me, his thumb was over the L in Lisco."

"You know, for a difficult woman, you sure make some things very easy." He made a box around the print they needed and set the machine into motion. "It will take some time to process."

"That's impressive equipment. You're like a real-life crime-fighting playboy. We should get you a superhero name."

"Only if you get one too."

She scoffed. "That's never gonna happen."

"Well, you're fighting crime right along next to me. Maybe we can give you a sidekick name."

"I'm going to sidekick your ass in a second." She watched the machine as it whirred. "So what do we do now?"

"I was thinking we should get something to eat. There's a little hole-in-the-wall place nearby that makes the most amazing pad thai."

"Sounds good. And what do we do once we've

finished our job tonight? Know any safe places to stay for the night?"

"I do." He went over to a dividing wall that didn't reach the ceiling. Bristol had noticed it when they walked in but didn't want to intrude on his privacy by going wherever she pleased.

Cole moved it aside to reveal a cot. It had a thin mattress on it that he pulled off onto the floor. "You can choose whichever one you're most comfortable on."

"It's a far cry from the bed at your dad's place. But closer to what I'm accustomed to." She sat on the cot and wriggled. "I think I'll take the one on the floor. You have a bathroom?"

"Through that door."

"Great. Now that that's taken care of, when do we eat? That pad — whatever sounds good."

"Pad thai. You want to come out for a stroll?"

"What, like a date?" The side of her mouth quirked up.

He raised his eyebrows at her. "Cute. But no, actually. When this is all over, I'm going to take you on a proper date whether you like it or not. Now, let's go. I'm starving."

◯◯

It was pitch black when Cole pulled the car over on a side road. Half a mile away was the back fence for the Lisco property.

They moved through the small wooded area quickly with the night-vision goggles and when they were crouched twenty feet away, Cole pointed up at a security camera monitoring that part of the fence.

"You've mentioned that breaking in isn't one of your strong suits, but have you ever done it before?"

"Not like this. I'm usually called in after there's been an incident. I have the pleasure of being escorted quickly and quietly to whatever situation they've gotten themselves into."

"It's a good thing you're a quick learner." He pointed at the corner of the fence. "There'll be a blind spot at that part of the fence. The trick is getting there without being spotted on camera."

"I assume you have a plan."

"How fast can you run?"

"You're not serious."

"No, I'm not. When we were at the building earlier, I added a little gadget to the power supply. It will give us a blackout period of a couple of seconds. We can only use it once, otherwise it will draw too much attention."

"Wait. How'd you know to do that? How'd you know we'd be back?"

"I didn't. But I try to be prepared for anything."

She gave him a quick nod of respect. "Okay. I'm ready when you are."

"When we get to the fence, don't touch it. It's electrified."

"Right."

He pulled his phone out of his bag and then slung the bag on his shoulder. "Ready, set … " Cole saw the red light blink off. "Go."

They sprinted across the lawn at full speed. The

grass was wet with dew and when they pulled up at the fence, Bristol's foot slipped. Cole's arm flew out, catching her on the neck and flattening her to the ground.

He dropped down to her. "Oh my god, are you okay?"

She coughed and rubbed at her neck. "Ye — " Was all she could choke out.

"I should have aimed my arm better."

"It — " She coughed again and swallowed. "It's fine. I'll be fine. Better than being electrocuted." She stood, took a steadying breath, then said, "What's next?"

Cole pulled a battery pack out of his bag with two cables and clips attached. He fastened them onto the fence. "I'll need you to lift the battery pack and follow me with it. It disrupts the flow through this section so I can cut it. Once I've cut, you need to move the clips so I can cut the next section."

"Got it. How do you do this on your own?"

"It's trickier and sometimes involves my teeth."

Once they got a large enough section cut out, they slipped through.

Cole motioned for Bristol to follow as he skimmed along the wall to a side door. Cole handed Bristol the cell phone disabler she had seen in the cabinet. "When I say, I want you to turn that on."

"Whose cell are we trying to interrupt?"

"Not a phone, a signal that would send notification to the security system that the door is being opened by an unauthorized person."

"Nowhere is secure with you around, is it?"

He blinked several times. "I think that's the nicest thing you've ever said to me."

"That's only because there haven't been that many." She jabbed him in the side hard enough that he flinched.

He got his lock-picking gear ready.

Bristol scanned the area. "I'm surprised that, with all this security, they have a standard lock here and not something fancier."

"Oh, don't worry, this is fancy. It's supposed to be unpickable."

"So how come you can pick it?"

He smirked. "Because nowhere is secure with me around. You ready?"

"Just tell me when."

He stuck the pick in the lock and another one underneath it. Then he took a third and put it in another hole she hadn't noticed. Cole bent down on his knee and put the third one between his teeth.

"You weren't kidding when you said you use your teeth. You want me to do something there?"

Cole pulled his head back. "No, I need to get the timing perfect. All you need to do is watch my face. When I look up at you, 'cause I won't be able to speak, you push and hold that button until I say stop."

Bristol nodded, and Cole put his mouth back on the pick. She watched him carefully maneuver each piece. Then he looked up at her and she hit the button, pressing it down harder than she needed. The door clicked, and he collected his picks.

"Keep holding it," he said as they went through the

door and closed it. He locked it from the inside. "Okay, you can let go now."

Bristol tucked the disabler in Cole's bag and rubbed her hands together. "What's your next trick?"

"Those lasers you mentioned."

"I was afraid to ask."

He pulled out a slim black rod. "This part is easy. Just point that light directly at the laser and it will temporarily blind it. You can stand at the door and I'll go in and get the records. Easy."

"Too easy?"

"Sometimes you get lucky."

"Then let's go."

∞

It was a simple thing, getting the door to the room open, but finding the origin of each beam was trickier. Bristol had lost track of time when Cole was finally able to move some distance into the room. She stood in the doorway watching him around the corner, when she heard a voice from behind.

"Don't move. I am a security officer with Lisco Pharmaceuticals. I have a taser, and you are trespassing. Please put your hands in the air."

Cole and Bristol looked at each other and Cole ducked to the side, out of the line of any lasers. Bristol swept her hand up, rolling the light across the room to him, and lifted her hands into the air as she turned.

The guard held the taser steady. "You're going to have to come with me."

Her lip curled up into a sultry smile and she stepped toward him.

He took a step back. "You can stay right there. You on your own?"

"Why don't you check for yourself?" Bristol said, hoping Cole had made it back to the door in time to ambush the guard.

The guard moved carefully around her and gestured for her to move back. He leaned into the door, scanned the room, and then moved back toward Bristol, who clicked her tongue. "So where are you taking me?"

"We've got lockable rooms in the east wing. You'll be comfortable there until the police arrive."

"Oh no, not those damned cells. The ones in the east wing, really?" she said loud enough for Cole.

Chapter 25

COLE WAS TUCKED behind the only cabinet that offered a hiding spot. He was lucky he got there before the guard looked in.

When Bristol had tossed the light to him, it hit a lip on the floor and changed direction. After Cole stretched out between beams to retrieve it, he was left with only enough time to hide again before the guard looked in.

It took him a while to get out, and he knew they wouldn't have long before the police arrived. One small mercy was that, from the position where he hid, his eyes locked on to a box with the documents they were looking for, so he didn't need to use up any time searching for those, or worse, leave them behind.

With Deb's salvation now tucked safely into his bag, he snuck along the corridor toward the east wing until he hit a dead end. He closed his eyes and pictured the blueprints. There were several doors, and he assumed Bristol would be in one, but he didn't know where the guard was and he needed to be ready.

He felt along the other side of the wall where he knew another door led to a section of the building that held offices, including security.

Running his hand along the wall, he felt a seam. It wasn't hidden, exactly, but it certainly wasn't obvious. Even when there was light, it wouldn't be noticed without looking for it.

He continued feeling around the door for some sort of keyhole when he heard, "Hey, what took you so long?"

He spun around and saw Bristol's face in a small window. "Where's the guard?"

"He walked through a door there, where you just were."

"We haven't got much time." He ran his hand across Bristol's door. "Dammit."

"What?"

"I can't pick this lock."

"Is that a joke? Because if it is, it's a bad one."

"No, there's no keyhole. How did the security guard open it?"

"He had something on a key chain. A button or something that slid the door open automatically. The door opens from the left if that helps at all."

"There's no panel that I can see. It must be built into the wall." He rapped his knuckles on a few spots around the door, hoping for any indication of anything. All that he could tell is that the door wasn't solid.

"I thought you said you could open every door."

He sighed loudly enough he hoped she could hear it. "No, I said I can pick every lock. This door doesn't have a lock." He ran through the inventory of what he had in his bag. There was nothing. It was a flimsy door. It would have been simple with a small explosive, but as it was, there was no way in or out.

Bristol tapped her fingernail on the window. "You should go."

"Go where?"

"Just go."

"I'm not — "

"You have to. There's no sense in both of us getting arrested." He leaned against the wall. There was no point arguing with her, and there was also nothing she could do to make him leave.

Something dug into his back. He reached his hand around. "Well, I'll be damned," he said with a laugh.

"What?"

"I've got it." Swinging around, he pulled the gas injection knife out.

Bristol pushed her face into the glass but couldn't see what he had. "What is it?"

He held it up for her while he judged where the locking mechanism most likely was.

"Where'd you pull that from?"

"When I took it off you, I put it in the back of my pants, remember?"

"You forgot you had that in the back of your pants? How do you not notice something like that?"

"I've always got something back there, gun or whatever. I just stop paying attention. Now, do you want me to get you out of there or not?"

"I wish I had something quippy to say to that. It

deserves a smart comment. I think I'll mention it to Michael next time I see him. He'll think of something."

"You might want to stand back, I'm not sure what this is going to do," he said, then jammed the knife between the door and the wall as best as he could.

Bristol moved to the side of the wall. Cole braced himself then pushed the button. There was a hiss and a bang and the area around the knife exploded. It would have burned his hand if he weren't wearing gloves.

"That's hot," he said, examining the burn mark on his glove. He shook his hand out then tested the door.

"You okay?"

"Yeah, fine." He pulled at the door, and it moved a little.

Bristol's face appeared at the hole, checking it out. "Not bad. But I don't think I'll fit."

"Then get that pretty mug of yours out of the way so I can make the hole bigger."

She moved back as he gripped the door with his gloved hands and anchored a foot on the door jamb. He yanked once and felt it give slightly. He pulled again but still didn't get it to move much.

"Here, let me help," Bristol said, slipping her hands over his.

"Okay. On three. One, two, three." The two pulled together, and the door ripped open partway and then jammed at an angle.

Bristol wedged herself through the space. "It would have saved us a lot of time and trouble if you had been ready back at the archive door when I sent the guard in to look for you."

Cole reached down for her hand to help pull her through. "You know what would have saved us a lot of time and trouble?" he said, lifting her hand and twisting it in front of her face. "If you would have remembered your fancy ring."

Bristol looked at the ruby. "Shit. I completely forgot."

"I hope there are no fingerprints in there we need to wipe down."

"No. I kept my hands to myself."

"Then we'd better go. We don't have much time."

The door behind them slid open, and the guard stepped out. It only took him a fraction of a second to take in the broken door, but even with his taser ready, he couldn't keep both Bristol and Cole in the taser's sight at the same time.

Bristol knew he'd retreat, and so took the opportunity when he was focused briefly on Cole to charge him. As she leapt for him, he swung around with the taser and pulled the trigger. She threw herself back to avoid it and smashed her head on the wall. There was a burst of light and then darkness.

Cole saw the taser discharge past Bristol and jumped into action. He went straight for the knockout punch, but the guard dodged far enough that he didn't go down. Cole got around behind him and wrapped an arm around his neck, keeping his face out of the way of the guards grabbing hands until he passed out.

Cole eased him down, then reached for Bristol.

He tapped her cheek lightly. "Bristol, you with me?"

She groaned. Cole put a hand to the back of her head and felt it was wet with blood.

"I can't believe I did that to myself."

"Oh good, you're conscious." Cole ripped a piece from his T-shirt and wiped the blood off the wall then pressed the cloth against Bristol's head. "I'll need you to hold this here. Can you walk?"

He helped her stand, but she had to lean on him heavily. "The room is spinning."

"Just don't throw up. I can handle blood. I can't handle puke."

"I'll do my best."

They limped their way out, and because the police would already have been alerted, he used his phone to short out the camera on the fence and left it off while they limped across to the woods. The flashing lights appeared as Cole and Bristol drove off in the opposite direction.

Back at Cole's office, Bristol lay on her stomach while Cole assessed the wound. "It's not too bad, but you'll have a lump. You should be fine to have a shower and wash the blood out. Just be gentle."

"Shouldn't you check my pupils or something to check for concussion?"

"I could, but I have no idea what I'm looking for, so there's no point. I'd take you to Eli, but I'd expect someone to be watching for you there."

"I don't want him involved, anyway. I'll be fine. I

didn't vomit, like you asked, so I should be fine. I only lost consciousness for a second."

"Great," Cole said flatly.

"I'll just have a shower and a good re — shit."

"What?"

"We didn't get the files."

"Hmm."

She could hear Cole rustling around and she sat up. He pulled a folder out of his bag. "Go ahead and gush."

She dropped her head into her hands. "Thank god." She mentally blamed the head knock for the tears that burned her eyes and took a deep breath to clear them. "I assume you have a scanner among your treasures?"

"I do."

"Good. You can scan them while I shower, and I'll send them to Deb." She lifted a hand up to Cole. "Help me up, please."

"You sure you're going to be well enough for our trip to the bank tomorrow?"

She grabbed Cole's shoulder and shut her eyes while she waited for the room to stop spinning and her blood pressure to return to normal, then looked at him and said, "We don't have a choice. You know that. I'll be fine. And can you do one more thing for me?"

"What's that?"

"Stop asking me questions you don't want me to answer."

"Go have your shower." He kissed her on the forehead before he realized what he was doing. It was a simple gesture, but the intimacy of it startled them both, and sent Bristol hurrying for the shower.

While the scanner hummed through the pages of the file, Cole stared out the window at nothing. He considered his options with Bristol. Deb would be fine, and after their visit to the bank, Eli had a good chance at saving his gym. That only left Tesco.

He briefly considered the possibility of simply kidnapping her. He had contacts in different parts of the world where they could disappear. But that would leave Mick and Lila exposed to retribution from Tesco, and although he loved Bristol, he not only would never do that to them, but she would never forgive him.

There was a slight chance that Tesco would take the bait of what the invoices and ledger showed, but like Bristol said, he wasn't stupid. They needed better proof. Cole felt a dark sense of dread about what lay ahead of them. And the only thing he knew for certain was that he had no idea how he'd react in the end. He was a man in control, certainly, but he also knew, if it came to it, he'd sacrifice everything to protect her.

Chapter 26

"I NEED you to stay out here for this one," Bristol said as they walked up the wide steps of the bank.

Cole stopped. "Why?"

"That way I can explain that the information I have about Silas is highly sensitive material for his ears only. It sells the illusion better. And I need as much leverage for that as I can get. I've only got one shot at this, but you'd be surprised at how many people like to know things that others aren't allowed to know. They can't help but be swept up by the drama of it."

"All right. I'll be right here."

Bristol stepped through the sliding door into the large marble reception area that was buzzing with the Monday morning activity. Behind an elevated desk stood a thin woman with a smile to match and horn-rimmed glasses. "Good morning, how can I direct you?"

"My name is Melissa Zimber. I have an appointment."

The woman typed something into a computer then

looked up. "If you'd like to have a seat, Mr. Beacon will be with you shortly."

"Thank you."

Bristol sat with a straight back on the elegant leather couch next to a man who was dressed in an expensive suit, but the dark circles under his eyes said he had had a rough weekend.

Cole had briefed Bristol as to where the cameras would be situated, and she kept her face tilted away.

All she had to do was plant the notion that continuing business with Silas was a bad idea. And with the encouragement that Miss Zimber and her daddy's company were out bank hunting, it would hopefully be enough to get them to recall the loan on Eli's property. That would be everyone taken care of with only herself left.

A man with broad shoulders and a loping gait came charging out toward her with most of his face taken up in a smile.

"Ah, Miss Zimber. What an absolute pleasure." With genuine delight, he kissed each of her cheeks when she stood up to greet him.

"Thank you for seeing me on such short notice."

"Not a problem at all. What more could I ask for on a day like today than to spend some time with an exceptional person such as yourself?"

Bristol felt her cheeks redden at his authentic gushing. It made her feel ill at ease for playing a part while his joy seemed so unadulterated, even though she was sure it couldn't be.

At least Bristol could tell the smile the receptionist

gave them as Mr. Beacon led her across the floor wasn't real.

"Please come this way and we can have a proper chat. Can I get you anything to drink? Coffee?"

"No, thank you."

He punched in a number on a keypad and they went through a series of halls and into a conference room. "Please have a seat."

She sat, but he didn't. The door opened behind her and a plump woman came in carrying a tray with three glasses of water. She smiled pleasantly at Bristol then nodded to Mr. Beacon. When she left the room, the slight smell of lavender lingered.

Bristol blinked at the tray. "There are three glasses of water. Is someone joining us?"

Mr. Beacon shook a finger at her. "Very perceptive. I knew you would be. I could tell the moment I saw you."

The door behind her opened again and Bristol turned, then shrank into the seat. She knew she shouldn't show weakness, but it was so unexpected. There was no way to stop the blood draining from her face.

Bristol cleared her throat and turned back to Mr. Beacon. "What is he doing here?"

Mr. Beacon looked suddenly flustered as Silas walked around the table to stand next to him.

"He … he's a valued client of this bank, just as we hope you will be."

Silas put a long-fingered hand on Mr. Beacon's shoulder. "By a funny coincidence, I called not long after you did, Miss Zimber. I explained to him how we were old friends and asked if he would allow me to join you and put my weight behind persuading you to bring your business over to his bank."

Mr. Beacon was watching Bristol closely. "I'm sorry, are you okay? You look pale. I realize I took liberties, but Silas assured me — " He looked at Silas, who smiled soothingly.

"It's just been a while, that's all." Silas clasped his hands together. "You know, with her father's illness and the responsibilities she's had to take on, Miss Zimber has an immense weight to carry these days. You have nothing to worry about. But would you mind leaving us for a few minutes? I'd like to have a quick chat on a personal level. See how things are going." He leaned into Mr. Beacon and dropped his voice. "Don't worry, I'll convince her to bring her business here." He winked and Mr. Beacon nodded, apparently satisfied, or too afraid of Silas to pursue the matter further.

Still unsettled by the unexpected tension, Mr. Beacon moved to the door. "I'll be just down the hall. Let me know when you're ready to discuss business."

The door closed gently, and the room fell silent. Bristol didn't take her eyes off Silas, but she spun the ruby ring around her finger, touching the catch each time it slipped past.

Silas pulled a chair out and sat down. "Fancy meeting you here."

"How did you know?"

"Come on, Bristol. You're a clever little rabbit. It didn't occur to you that I'd be watching you? Watching for every move you might make? When I purchased the building where your friend has his gym, I knew there were only a few options available to you. So I've been monitoring the bank for anything out of the ordinary. When I discovered Melissa Zimber was suddenly interested in my bank, I found that rather curious. And I will say, I'm impressed."

"And what if the real Melissa had come in?"

Silas shook his head. "Then what difference would it have made?"

"So you used Eli to lure me out. What about Deb and Mick? Why'd you go after them?"

"Deborah was a favor for a friend."

Bristol leaned forward and rested her arm on the table. "Phillip Ryder."

"We go way back."

"And Mick?"

"I don't consider myself to be a petty man, but Mick helped you save my wife all those years ago. He deserved a good beating."

It was everything Bristol could do to keep her temper in check. "So what is it that you want?"

Silas linked his fingers together and rested his elbows on the table. "What I've always wanted, Bristol. We have a game to finish."

"Not interested."

"No? You sure don't act like it."

Bristol shook her head. "If you're so keen to play the game, then why'd you send someone to my apartment to kill me the other day?"

"Did he try to kill you?"

"I don't know why else he would have shot me."

Silas sighed deeply, pressing his fingers into his temple. "It's so hard to find good help these days. Killing you was not my intention. I apologize."

"Apology not accepted, I'm afraid."

He tsked. "Speaking of apologies, when you agreed to help the FBI, that really hurt."

"Well, gee, Silas, I'm so sorry I hurt your feelings."

He slammed his hand on the table, making Bristol jump. "It didn't hurt my feelings. It hurt that such a beautiful specimen of a woman would stoop so low." His voice softened. "I thought you were better than that."

"I'm sorry to disappoint you."

"It was a weak move, Bristol. That was the whole reason I brought Eli into the picture. I needed to get you back into the game where you belong."

"I told you. I don't want to play your game."

"And I told you, I don't believe you." Silas splayed his fingers out toward her. "I merely set the chess pieces on the board. You're the one who chased after them. Like a novice, I might add." His eyes narrowed. "But while it's been fun, I've grown tired of the whole thing. I don't enjoy playing with sore losers, so it's time for the endgame."

"So it *is* meant to end."

"All games end, Bristol. In so many ways, you had great potential. If I could have enticed you over to my side, you would have gone places. But there's too much holding you back."

"There's not much holding me back from jumping across the table and beating the hell out of you."

Silas chuckled. "That's exactly my point. You let

your emotions dictate too much to you. When I first met you, I thought the warmth that still flowed through your veins would make this more thrilling, but the truth is, it's the ruthless who truly make a game worth playing."

Bristol picked at the skirt of her dress. She knew Silas was right. She'd do her job a whole lot better if she didn't care. "So, you've been vague on the details of what the next move is."

Silas breathed deeply in pleasure. "I see your boyfriend is waiting for you out front."

"He's not my boyfriend."

"I saw the look on your face when you shot him the other night. You're not the devil you pretend to be." Silas shrugged. "But if what you say is true, then this next part should be easy for you. I want you to get rid of him."

"You want me to kill him?" Her chest tightened.

"We've already established that you're willing to do so if given the right incentive. But no, I've found a much better use for him. I don't want him dead. I want you to make it clear to him that you don't want to see him again. Wonderfully torturous for you both."

She couldn't help the wash of relief that flooded her, but a knot remained. "That's it? That's your big finale?"

"Finale? No." Silas leaned back in his chair. "Have you ever watched a boa constrictor catch and eat its prey?"

"I think I saw it on a nature program once."

"The snake wraps around its dinner, and each time the animal breathes out, the snake squeezes tighter and tighter until there is no breath left."

Bristol shook her head. "I'm not following."

Silas stood and walked around his chair, gripping the back. "When I told you why I went after your friends, I wasn't being completely honest. You see, I have no doubt that you have a high pain threshold. But when it comes to the people you care about, their lives are the real torture. And the tighter I squeeze your friends, the more breath I squeeze from your lungs." Silas licked his lips. "You love Cole."

Bristol couldn't help the curl in her lip. "That's ridiculous."

"Love is ridiculous, and it's dangerous. It makes you do things you wouldn't normally. It's an emotion that is the downfall of many, and it will be yours."

Bristol scoffed. "I don't love Cole."

Silas spread his hands wide. "Then we will have to agree to disagree, but the fact remains, if you don't get him out of your life — permanently — I will. And don't forget, I've got eyes everywhere, and I know Cole is not a stupid man. If you don't do a convincing job, he'll know, and so will I, and he will die."

Bristol stopped breathing, waiting for the panic to pass. She stared at one of the water glasses, watching the condensation drip down the side and connect with other droplets of water until it hit the tray.

She sucked in her cheeks. "And then what?"

"That depends on a few things. The pieces have to settle on the board. I can't say my next move until I see where things end up."

"But your plan is to eventually kill me."

"Yes, well, the whole reason for the squeezing is to devour." He chuckled like he was innocently amused.

She had already given herself up to Tesco. Maybe Silas was doing her a favor with Cole. If he didn't think she cared about him, it would be easier to leave … or die. She stood up quickly from the table. "Fine. Just make sure you watch yourself."

Silas yawned behind the back of his hand, which Bristol thought was juvenile for a man like Silas. She didn't say another word as she left the room.

The tips of her fingers were tingling when she went into the ladies' bathroom before facing Cole. He'd never leave her alone. The harder she tried to push him away, the harder he'd fight back. She looked in the mirror as she rubbed her hands together. "You can do this. You're talking to yourself in a mirror, so you're crazy enough to convince Cole that he's a fool." She slapped her face a few times to bring color back into her cheeks then took a deep breath and set her face to stone.

Chapter 27

BRISTOL WALKED out the door of the bank, looked Cole in the eye, and smiled widely. When she reached him, she slipped her arm through his and led him down the steps.

He stopped her at the bottom and turned her to face him. "Did everything go okay in there? Something seems off."

"Oh no, everything went perfectly. It's just this charade. It makes me weary sometimes. Especially when I have to disappoint really nice guys."

"So the manager was a nice guy? He'll get over it."

"Not him, Cole." She pulled away, her lips pouty. "The nice guys always get the raw end of the deal, don't they? You poor thing." She patted his cheek.

Cole's face darkened. "What are you talking about?"

"We've had fun though. Unfortunately, I think you've let yourself get a little too attached." She tipped her head to the side. "It worked to get me the outcome I needed, but honestly Cole, you should know better."

"What are you talking about?"

Her smile vanished. "You really are thick, aren't you? I've been playing you, Cole. I figured out early that Silas was after me way back when we first met, and I knew your dad was involved with him, so I needed to find a way to get to him if necessary. You suited the situation perfectly. And all I had to do was the damsel in distress act."

"Bristol." He looked back at the bank and lowered his voice. "I know you're lying. Why don't you tell me what's really going on?"

"Cole," she said, getting aggravated. "I manipulate for a living. People, scenes, everything. Why do you think we found nothing solid for Tesco? He's all part of my plan. He agreed to help me suck you in. I couldn't have gotten into Lisco without you, and I mean that. You've helped me a great deal, but I don't need your help anymore."

Cole took a step back. "I don't believe you."

Bristol faltered for a second. She knew he would try to resist. She had to hurt him. "You just don't get it, do you? Why do you think I told you I wouldn't sleep with you? Because I was protecting myself? Please. I cross a lot of lines in my business, but sleeping with someone I care nothing about?" She huffed. "I told you that whole dramatic story, and you lapped it up. You can't help yourself."

She took a step up to him and fixed the collar of his shirt. "You've served your purposes. Now I can go after Silas without you. If you'll excuse me. I've got things to do." She rested a hand on his chest. "Maybe next time you'll be a little more careful who you fall for. And don't worry, you've got Elly as backup, so I'm sure you'll be fine. She loves you, you know. That's a lot more than you'll ever get from me."

Bristol wasn't sure who she had hurt more at that moment, her or Cole. She leaned in and kissed him on his cheek. The part where she could feel his jaw clenching. "See you around."

She turned on her heel and strode to the street hailing a taxi, a tear escaping as she pulled the door open, and then she was gone.

◯◯

Cole found it hard to breathe. He wanted to go after her. To shake her. Had he missed it the whole time? He needed to sit down, but he also needed to move. His mind felt as though it would explode if he were to stop moving. He took long loping steps down the sidewalk, shaking out his arms as he went. He got a few odd looks and almost wished someone would have a go at him so he could fight.

His phone vibrated against his leg, stopping him mid-stride. He pulled it out and read the text message: *Where are we up to with that rain check on dinner? Elly*

He stared at the text, his jaw sore from clenching. Finally, he texted back: *I'm free now if you are.*

◯◯

Bristol gave Deb's address to the driver and held onto the murky cloud that had settled on her, wrapping it around herself like a cold wet blanket. When the time came, she'd let it envelop her completely, but she had a few things to do first.

She watched the city go by, surprised by the ache thrumming through her body. She hadn't expected it to hurt so much. That was the price she paid for opening up. She'd spent a lot of years perfecting numbness, and she gave it all away only to remember why she had done it in the first place.

But she was confident that, because of how she felt about Cole, she had done the right thing. Letting herself feel again meant that now she understood — you give away the things you love if it means keeping them safe.

"Mom," she whispered. The word floated from her lips and dissolved into nothing. She had hated her mom for a long time. Never forgiving her for being absent from her life. She hadn't disappeared physically at the time, but she may as well have.

There was a sob menacingly close to slipping out of Bristol's throat. She shook her head to knock away the thoughts. She couldn't allow emotion any room right now. She had things to take care of.

The cab stopped, and she got out, barely seeing the driver as she paid him.

He drove off before she could get herself to move toward Deb's office. She tried the door knowing it was locked, but she was equally confident her friend would be there. The woman practically lived there. And after receiving the information about Lisco, she'd be putting her case together to negotiate with the FBI so she could get the doors opened again.

Bristol banged on the door until Deb came into view. The look on her friends' face changed from outrage to concern so quickly Bristol almost smiled.

Deb wrestled with the lock on the door, speaking a solid line of cursing until it finally gave and she yanked the door open.

Deb grabbed Bristol's hand and pulled her in. "Oh my god, you look like hell."

Bristol just nodded and walked past Deb. Her legs felt like jelly when she reached Deb's office and she fell onto the chair.

Deb walked attentively around Bristol, studying her face, then leaned back onto her desk, crossing her arms.

Bristol couldn't meet her eye, so she picked at a fingernail instead. "How did you like that information I got for you?"

Deb responded cautiously, "It's good. It's very good." She wasn't her usual exuberant self. "I'd be celebrating with you right now if the look on your face didn't say you'd just seen the devil himself."

"I have. So the information will get you out of trouble?"

"Oh Bristol. It made me so excited I almost peed a little like a tiny excitable dog."

Bristol managed a weak laugh. "I'm so glad things have worked out for you. Can you do me a favor and see what you can do to help Eli find a new gym?"

"Me? Why me?"

"Because you're a lawyer and you're a good negotiator." Bristol shook her head. "Just do me that favor."

"What's going on? Something is going on."

"Nothing. It's nothing."

"It's not nothing. You're talking like someone who's about to jump off a bridge."

"I've just had a bad day. A very bad day." She sighed and rubbed the back of her head. "And I gave myself a concussion yesterday, so I've got a terrible headache."

Deb jumped up and ran around her desk, ripping open a drawer. "I've got a few things in here for a headache." She shook a tiny white unmarked bottle. "But I need to know if you'll be operating heavy machinery in the next few hours."

"No, I've taken something, it's fine. I have a lot going on and just wanted to make sure you were safe and that Eli had someone on his side in case I can't help him."

"All right." Deb nodded. "Fine. If you don't want to tell me what's eating you up, fine. You got Phillip for me. I'll definitely help Eli. But there is no point lying to me. I am the queen of lies and I can sniff them out faster than a bloodhound in heat."

Bristol laughed. "That doesn't even make sense."

"At least I got a smile out of you. Listen. I know you're a loner, but you know I'd do anything for you. So if you ever decide to let someone help, let me know. Anything."

"Thank you." Bristol needed to leave before Deb pressed any further. She didn't know what Tesco would require of her, but she had a feeling she wouldn't be seeing any of her friends again. And after what she did to Cole, she wasn't sure she could look any of them in the eyes again anyway.

She stood and gave Deb a big hug. When she let go, Deb's eyes were as big as saucers. "You just hugged me. Like a *for real* hug."

Bristol turned and rushed out the door with Deb hot on her heels.

Deb grabbed her arm and pulled her around before she could go. "I know you're not going to tell me what's going on, but Bristol — "

"I thought we just talked about this. Please, I've got to go." Bristol pulled free and made it out the door before Deb grabbed her hand and squeezed as Bristol raised her other arm to hail a cab.

When a cab pulled up to the curb Bristol tried to free her hand but Deb wouldn't let go. "Please, just promise me you won't do anything stupid. If you need help, ask for it before you do something you'll regret."

Bristol smiled at her friend. "You've always been good to me, Deb." She squeezed Deb's shoulder then slid into the cab.

Cole arrived at the restaurant and saw that Elly had already gotten a table. As he wound his way to her, he noticed two large men seated at a table against the wall. They were perusing their menus.

Elly smiled and bit her lip when she saw Cole. He leaned down and kissed her on the cheek before sitting.

She reached across the table and took his hand. "I appreciate your being available so quickly."

He pulled his hand back and dropped it in his lap. "My schedule suddenly opened up, and I thought there were a few things we needed to talk about."

"Yes, I'd like that." She blushed. "I don't feel like I can say sorry enough for what I did to you all those years ago. I know I've never forgiven myself."

"I appreciate your concern, but honestly, I have no hard feelings."

"But it was a mistake," she gushed. "The biggest mistake I have ever made. I was afraid of what I was stepping into, and the best way I knew how to deal with that was to run away."

"I know. But things worked out for you, right? You've got a great job. You're successful."

"But I don't have you."

Cole glanced over Elly's shoulder briefly, catching the eye of one of the men he had noticed, but the man quickly dropped his head into his menu.

Cole reached across the table to take Elly's hand. "You are a lovely woman, who I'm sure will make someone very happy."

Elly frowned and pursed her lips. "But not you?"

"There is a part of me that would love to say yes to you, but that wouldn't be fair."

"Why?"

Cole looked down at Elly's hand in his. It was smaller than Bristol's. "There's someone else."

Elly let out a breath. "That woman from the café. I thought so. So you're with her?"

"No, no, I'm not. But if I were to just jump into your arms, it wouldn't be with my whole heart." It wouldn't be with any of his heart, Cole thought.

"What if I said I didn't care?"

Cole smiled. "Tempting. But you'd change your mind, eventually."

"What if we just gave it a chance? I came all this way."

"You moved to LA on the off chance that I'd be available?"

"Well, no. But … I don't know. I just don't want you to give up on me because of some woman that doesn't share your feelings."

Cole knew she didn't say it to be harsh, but it felt like a knife to the gut. "I'm just not ready."

He kept his eyes on Elly, but he saw the two men shift behind her. He reached up and put a hand on her face. "I'm sorry, Elly. I'm not going to do that to you."

She nodded. "Well, if things change, you know where to find me."

Cole kept the rest of the conversation steered toward Elly's new job as they ate lunch together. He finished his quickly and then waited patiently — at least on the outside — for her last bite before saying, "I hate to leave you so quickly, but I've got some loose ends I need to tie up."

Elly took the napkin off her lap and laid it on the table. "I won't keep you then," she said as she stood and reached for Cole. He took the opening, leaned in and kissed her on the cheek, longer than necessary. When he pulled back, he put a hand on her cheek and rubbed his thumb across it. "See you later."

"I hope so."

He turned. The sad smile that had lingered on his face slid off as he headed for the door. He'd need to stop back at his office for his gun.

Chapter 28

BRISTOL HAD TAKEN the cab to get her own car before heading for Eli's, where she now sat gripping her steering wheel, afraid to get out. All she could do was be honest with him, because he'd know if she weren't.

She finally got as far as the gym door where she stood for a while, trying to memorize everything about it, from the water-stained ceiling to the old wooden bench where she had scratched her name underneath when she was a teenager. It had been a place that was more like home to her than anywhere else.

She'd failed to help Eli. Somehow, Silas always managed to be one step ahead. But Eli was a good man, and he was smart and resilient and would be able to start again. She was confident of that. Maybe her move over the border for Tesco would be the best for her and everyone in her life. It would keep her friends out of the line of fire and could be a fresh start for her in a way. Even though it meant being in Tesco's employ.

She grimaced. Tesco hadn't been clear about what

he wanted her to do, but it was most likely moving drugs. And after watching what had happened to her mom, drugs were the last thing she wanted to be involved with. If it weren't for the risk to Mick and Lila, she'd just disappear. But if she went against her word to Tesco, she knew he'd take it out on them.

She could see Eli watching her out of the corner of his eye while he gave instruction to a short, stocky woman. Bristol attempted to lift her leg to step into the room but couldn't make herself move.

Eli nodded to the woman then walked over to Bristol. He squeezed her arm when he reached her. "I'll find a new place."

"I tried to fix it."

"I know."

"I wanted you to know that I've forgiven my mom."

Eli ran a paternal hand down her hair. "That's the best news I've heard in a long time. It makes everything else that's going on pale in comparison."

"Then I guess it's a good time to tell you that I'm going away for a while."

"What about Cole?"

She cleared her throat. "What about him?"

Eli sighed. "Is this what you want?"

"When we care about people, sometimes we do what we don't want to in order to protect them. I learned that from my mom."

Eli pulled her into a hug. "I'll miss you. Desperately."

"That's it? You're not going to ask me any more

questions or try to talk me out of it?" she asked while he held her tightly.

"Would it make any difference?"

She coughed out a sob and buried her face in his chest. "I love you, Eli."

"Oh dear. You're not going to do something stupid, are you? Something you'll regret?"

"I'll do what I have to do."

"That's a yes, then. I love you too, Bristol."

"I'll send you a letter now and then so you know I'm safe." She pushed away and turned quickly, running for her car as the tears burned her eyes. Eli didn't try to stop her, but he stood at the door a long time before he was steady enough to move.

Cole tucked the gun into a holster at his back and flicked his jacket over it. His stride was purposeful as he walked the block and a half toward the building that Silas Lincoln worked out of. It wasn't one of the taller buildings in LA, but it was one of the most striking. The architecture was similar to the Sydney Opera House with its waves, but it was set apart by the stacked concrete blocks and mesh windows that let hexagonal light stream through into the reception area that he now entered.

Cole had been to the building before but had never been to Silas's office. He hadn't studied the floor plan and didn't know where the security cameras were, although he noted them all as he marched through the large lobby. He wasn't trying to hide.

The slim young man at the front desk smiled as he approached, but the smile faltered when Cole reached him. "How can I help you, sir?"

"I'm here to see Silas Lincoln."

"Do you have an appointment?"

"No."

"Well, I do apologize, but Mr. Lincoln insists on an appointment."

Cole reached across the desk and grabbed the man by his tie, pulling him forward. A security guard approached at a half run. "You call Silas and tell him Cole Sullivan is here to see him." He let go of the tie as the guard arrived. His hand was on his gun.

"Is there a problem?"

With the arrival of the guard, the receptionist gained some pluck. He looked down his nose at Cole then turned to the guard, but when he opened his mouth to speak, Cole beat him to it.

"Just call him." Cole turned to the guard. "If Silas won't see me, I'll leave without further incident." Cole watched as the guard attempted to work menace into his face, but it ended up looking more like a grimace.

Cole tsked. "If you'd rather, I could make a scene. Your choice." He waited, and finally the guard nodded to the other man who looked offended but picked up the phone and dialed a number.

"Yes, hello. This is Marcus in the lobby. There is a man here to see Mr. Lincoln … No, he doesn't have an appointment … Yes, I know, but — " He dropped his voice. "He's being abusive … He says his name is Cole Sullivan." His eyes dropped as he listened. "Yes, but … Yes, I understand. Thank you."

One of Cole's eyes twitched in irritation. "Well?"

The receptionist sneered. "Please, come this way, sir."

He led Cole to a private elevator. "Mr. Lincoln will call the elevator momentarily."

Cole stepped in and turned. Marcus didn't wait for the doors to close before scurrying back to his desk.

As the elevator rose, Cole considered himself in the metal reflection.

He felt nothing as the doors opened onto an impressive glass walkway that looked down on the pedestrians below. Despite the warm sunlight, the hall was cool. If he weren't so angry, he'd have been impressed.

As he approached the end of the corridor, a door slid open to a U-shaped reception space with two glass-fronted rooms on either side of a solid wall that looked like it was made of obsidian. The room to the left was a conference room, judging by the marble table that nearly filled it. On the right sat a well-groomed man behind a desk. He waited for Cole to make eye contact then nodded briefly, glancing toward the middle room before dropping his head back to his work. A nameplate beside the door read *Cecil Bryant.*

Cole headed for the wall of obsidian and pushed a silver button at the side of the door. It slid open noiselessly.

Silas stood behind his desk, his fingers pressed into the top. His lips weren't smiling, but his eyes were.

Cole pulled the gun from his back, aiming it at Silas. Two guards appeared on either side of the doors with their guns ready.

Cole ignored the men and held his gun steady, walking toward Silas who held up a hand for the men to hold their fire. When Cole reached the desk, he lowered the hammer and set the gun on the desk. "I'm not here to kill you."

"No. I didn't think you would be that reckless." Silas nodded for his men to stand down. They returned to their positions against the back wall. "Please, have a seat."

Cole sat down and crossed his legs as if it were a casual meeting. "So."

"So, indeed. I must say, I was surprised to hear you came to pay me a visit. Surprised and pleased. Is there something I can do for you?"

"You slept with my mother."

Silas frowned. "Is that what this visit is about? If so, I've misjudged you."

"She stopped being my mother a long time ago. My point is that you understand how women can be. The reason I'm here is that I recently discovered that Bristol has been playing me."

The delight in Silas's eyes was tangible. "Now that's more like it. And unfortunately, does not surprise me. She has a way of doing that. But then, she does have a particular talent for it."

"I just want to make it clear that I don't care what you and my mother did. But I want your help with Bristol. Obviously you are already after her."

"Obviously."

"And her presence is keeping me from moving on. I need her out of my life."

"Indeed." He tapped a finger on his chin. "You're not satisfied just never seeing her again?"

"There's someone else. Elly. An old girlfriend who's come into my life. But Bristol has messed me up and I can't move forward with Elly until I get rid of Bristol."

Silas breathed in deeply and leaned back. "Yes, I was told of your rendezvous with Elly today."

"I thought that was you."

Silas flinched. "You saw my men."

"They may need a bit of training in the art of blending in. Perhaps after this is all over, I can offer you my services."

"Yes, I believe working with you will be much more satisfying than working with your father. So, what do you want from me with regards to Bristol?"

"Just a piece of the action. What's your next move? I'm in."

"I hope you aren't disappointed to hear that I've had my fun with her, but her time is up, I'm afraid."

"That's fine with me as long as I get to be there when it happens."

"Very well. I'm headed to collect her shortly. Your involvement will certainly bring another level of satisfaction to the completion of this game."

"Let me pick her up. I've got a guy I can use."

Silas's eyes narrowed. "I only use my men."

Cole shrugged. "My man is better, and I trust him. He had a run-in with Bristol a few years ago, and I just thought he'd enjoy being a part of it." Cole smiled but shook his head. "But it's not important. If I'm there, that's enough for me."

Silas ran his hand along the edge of his desk, thinking. "No. I think for this one, the more the merrier. Just be aware, I won't hesitate to kill you, even if it's just an inkling that something's off."

"I wouldn't have expected differently from you."

"You'll wear a mask when you collect her, you and your friend. I don't want her to know it's you until I'm there for the big reveal. And you'll take these two with you." Silas pointed behind Cole.

Cole turned and waved at the men. "Great."

"Go get your guy and meet back here in an hour."

"You know where she is?"

"We've got eyes on her."

◯◯

Bristol buzzed Mick's apartment.

"Yeah?"

"It's me."

The door clicked, and Bristol prepared herself to say goodbye to Mick and Lila.

Mick hugged her as soon as she walked in, and Lila practically dive-bombed her. Bristol picked her up and squeezed her hard. "How are you doing, little miss?"

"Good."

She put Lila down. "Your eye is looking better," she said to Mick as she reached out a hand toward his face.

"Now that Tesco is taken care of, things should quiet down for you two."

"Yeah, I'm being very selective of what work I take on right now. Can I get you a cup of tea?"

"Uh." She almost said no, but this would be the last time she got to see the two of them. "Yeah, that would be great, thanks."

Bristol sat down with Lila on the couch, looking at some pictures she had made. Lila slid one out from the bottom of the pile. "That's me and you," she said, pointing at the two figures walking hand in hand. The side of the picture that Bristol was on was dark, but on Lila's side a yellow and orange sun shone. "It's a picture they had me draw after what happened before. You're in the dark because you kept me safe from the bad people." Lila's voice was light, and Bristol was relieved that her memories didn't haunt her.

Mick set a cup on the coffee table in front of Bristol. "I don't think I could ever thank you enough for protecting Lila. Not just physically, but — " He pointed at the picture. "It's been hard without Lucy around, but you've meant so much to Lila and me."

Bristol picked up her mug. "God, I miss Lucy so much sometimes. She always gave me such great advice."

"She was a very good woman. A lot like you."

Bristol smirked. "No, not like me. She was one of a kind."

They spent the next half-hour reminiscing about Mick's wife. Even though Lila had been a baby when her mother died, she still added her own bits that she had heard over the years.

Bristol set down her mug when it was empty. "Look, I've gotta get going and I'm not sure when I'll see you next. I was thinking of doing a bit of traveling. Get out of here for a while."

"You okay?"

"Yeah. Just tired. Really, really tired."

Lila jumped on Bristol's lap. "You can't go."

Bristol wrapped her arms around her tiny friend. "I won't be long." She hated lying but couldn't bear to tell her the truth. "You draw some pictures for me so I can cover my fridge with them when I get back."

"Okay." Lila moped.

Mick stood and pulled Lila off Bristol, then grabbed her hand and pulled her up into another hug. "You take care of yourself."

Lila wrapped herself around Bristol's leg. "Don't go."

"Oh Lila, I'll see you when I get back. I'll send you a postcard."

"No! I don't want you to go."

"Come on, Lila," Mick said as he pried her off Bristol's leg. "She'll come back."

"But you're not coming back." Tears streamed down Lila's face.

"Of course I will, sweet pea." She was so tired of lying to the ones she loved the most. At least she wouldn't have to do that anymore. Just this last one. "I'll be back before you know it."

When she got out the door, Lila wouldn't let Mick close it, so Bristol hurried out of sight before she allowed herself to cry freely, but only until she reached the front door of the building. When she walked back out into the fresh air, she stopped to take a breath and wipe away the tears.

Now that she had said goodbye to everyone, she was ready to face Tesco without fear, and she was determined not to regret the steps she had to take to protect the ones she loved.

Chapter 29

BRISTOL STARED at the ground as she walked to her car. There were no weeds pushing out of the cracks in this sidewalk like there were at her apartment. She looked up as she approached her car and noticed a black van parked on the side of the road.

She paused when it pulled out and drove toward her. Her muscles flexed. If the FBI thought they would pick her up before she could go square things with Tesco, they hadn't seen her fight yet.

The van's door slid open before it pulled to a stop. Bristol kept her stance casual with her hands on her hips. Punching Agent Tellis in the face when he wasn't expecting it would allow her to release a bit of tension.

But when the door opened fully, she saw the men inside wore masks and her heart skipped. Weapons were already trained on her.

She put her hands up halfway. "Are you with Tesco? Because he gave me seventy-two hours and I still have a few to go."

In answer to her question, the front passenger door opened and another man with a gun got out and walked around behind her. "Just in case you get any ideas." He pushed his gun into the back of her head to encourage her forward. "You're going to let the gentleman in the van handcuff you, and if you try anything, I'll blow your head off."

"Gentleman?" Bristol sneered. She held her hands out and walked forward, looking up and down the road as she went. The street was empty besides them and as the cuffs closed around her wrists, she prayed Tesco was behind this.

She climbed inside as best she could with her hands locked in front of her and was pushed up against the window in the middle seat. There were four men altogether. Two in the front, one guy beside her and another one behind, pressing a gun to her neck.

"I'm handcuffed and surrounded by four armed men. Don't you think holding a gun to my head is a little overboard?"

The guy in the front said, "If she so much as sneezes, shoot her."

"You're not going to blindfold me? What kind of amateurs are you?"

"Honey, where you're going, you're not coming back."

"Seriously guys, does Tesco really think I won't turn up?"

"We don't work for Tesco."

A chill went down her spine. Hopefully, it would be a quick death. But her luck had run out a long time ago.

To keep the panic at bay, she focused on where they were headed. Not that it would matter, but she didn't like surprises.

At one point she looked over at the man next to her who hadn't spoken. He was staring at her. There was something familiar about his eyes, but she was too wound up to figure out what. She'd seen a lot of eyes. They were probably the same color as someone whose life she had destroyed.

When they pulled into an abandoned shipping yard, Bristol kept up the appearance of an attitude. She felt anything but confident, but pretending she was helped in a small way.

"This is so cliché. A shipping yard? Really? One day, I'd like to see you guys be a little creative. What about abducting someone and taking them to the mall or something? At least it would add a bit of a challenge."

The man who sat next to her dragged her out of the car. She fell hard onto one knee. Pain exploded up into her hip, but he yanked her up.

She kept her eyes forward as she limped into a large warehouse room. Lights illuminated the center, leaving the rest of the area in shadow.

The man with the familiar eyes shoved her into a metal seat at the center of the light and tied her to it, then walked around to the front and gave her a cold, calculated grin. Whoever he was, he enjoyed his job. He adjusted the light so she had to dip her head and squint.

"Very theatrical," she mumbled.

The other three men took up positions they had obviously worked out ahead of time.

The one with the eyes stood next to another who had a similar build but was slightly shorter. The other two, bigger guys, stood on her other side. She almost smiled at the irony of it, thinking back to her conversation with Cole about the size of bodyguards. They all handled themselves well enough. It would take a miracle to overpower them all, if given the chance. She tested her restraints. They were tied well. If the opportunity to escape arose, her only hope was to manage a quick death. Maybe she could even take one of the men down with her.

A door clanged behind her and Bristol turned as much as she could, but the light kept her from seeing who had entered.

A voice came through the shadow. "Our time is drawing to a close."

Bristol stifled a groan even though she already knew whom to expect, her mouth felt like sand. "Silas. I did what you asked."

"Oh, I know you did. An excellent job too, but I don't want to talk about that right now. I want to talk about where we go from here."

"I thought kidnapping me like this would be considered cheating. There's no sport in it at all."

"Cheating? When I hired you to kill my wife, I looked forward to a very prosperous relationship. Then you double-crossed me. You're the one who cheated."

He shrugged. "I was very hurt by that, Bristol. Very hurt."

"God." She threw her head back in disgust. "Are you listening to yourself? Just get over it already. Man, you sure know how to hold a grudge."

"Not a grudge. I saw so much potential in you." He walked closer to her. "What hurts me the most is the lengths that you seem to go to disappoint me. I never had children of my own, but I know how parents must feel when their kids let them down."

"You're a lunatic."

"Perhaps. But only because I thought I could mold you into something better."

"Better?"

Silas smirked. "It took me a while, but I finally realized that you're like a wild horse, a brilliant wild horse. The only way I could turn you was to break you. But some horses won't be broken."

"I'll take that as a compliment."

"Do you know what we do to horses that won't yield?"

"Turn them into glue?" She snorted. "If you're going to kill me, just get it over with. You obviously have more important things to do with your time."

He walked around into the light before responding. "A cat always toys with the mouse before he eats it."

Bristol shook her head. "You've got a thing for animal metaphors, don't you? You'll never get away with it."

"Oh Bristol, now you're just being generic. Of

course I'll get away with it. You've just said goodbye to everyone you love, so no one will miss you. And when I bury you in the cement of the new building I'm erecting in place of Eli's gym … ah, but I'm getting ahead of myself."

Bristol pulled again at her restraints as Silas took another step closer. "I see you are trying to loosen the rope. But you'll never get out of those knots," he said, leaning toward her. "They were tied by a SEAL."

"What?"

Silas stepped back, sweeping his arm out like a ring-master. "If you would like to do the honors, sir?"

"Technically." Cole pulled off his balaclava and scowled at Bristol. "I only trained with them."

"Cole?" Bristol was suddenly breathless. "Cole, what … what are you doing?"

"What I should have done from the beginning, bitch."

Bristol flinched. "Cole, I didn't — "

"Now, now," Silas said, dropping behind Cole and pointing a gun at his head. "Don't say anything you can't take back."

Bristol sucked in a breath, then whispered, "I'm sorry." She wasn't sure whom she was even saying it to.

"You will be when I'm done with you," Cole growled.

Silas tucked his gun into his belt. He wasn't finished with the torment. "You know, Bristol, my men had the pleasure of seeing the reunion of Cole and Elly earlier today. They make quite the couple." Bristol couldn't help but recoil. "Didn't take him long to move on, did it? So it's all for the best that you turned on Cole. I expect they'll be very happy together. Now — " He clapped his hands together. "Let's get on with it then shall we? I am eager to hear your thoughts, Cole. A man in your position would have any number of macabre ideas, I imagine."

Cole stepped forward into the circle of light and the guy next to him followed. "I'm a simple man, actually. One bullet will do it." He looked at Silas. "Or is that not gruesome enough for you?"

Silas crossed his arms. "I hoped for something more creative. I'm enjoying this so much, I'd hate for it to end too abruptly."

"I suppose the simple route wouldn't be right for Bristol anyway. Not elaborate enough. Perhaps something closer to what you did to Jimmy, eh Bristol?"

"Jimmy?" Bristol breathed. "What about Jimmy?"

"That act won't cut it anymore, Bristol. I'm on to you now. It's all just smoke and mirrors, right?"

She shook her head, confused.

Cole stomped forward and slapped her across the face. When her head stopped spinning, she touched her tongue to her lip, tasting blood.

Cole leaned in further. "Smoke. And. Mirrors." He stared into her eyes. "Right?"

The guy that had been standing beside Cole stepped forward into her line of vision. He rubbed his hands together and sucked on his tooth. The light glinted off the gold and Bristol nearly hiccupped. She stopped herself short of yelling out Jimmy's name as an expletive. Her eyes darted between Cole and Jimmy.

She nodded lightly, tears brimming in her eyes. She blinked them away as Cole spit on the floor next to her. "That's what I thought. Time for a bit of payback for me and for Jimmy."

Bristol breathed in, and her face went hard. If she was wrong about what just happened, what difference did it make? She looked over at Silas, her mind racing until it settled on what she needed to do.

She lifted her chin. "Do what you want, but there's one person who will miss me. I've got a meeting with Tesco tonight and you're going to make me late, so you'll be answering to him when this is all over."

Silas's head jerked a little. "Tesco?" he said with what sounded like a laugh.

"Yeah, I wanted to have a chat with him about what he did to my friend Mick."

"I thought I already told you it was me."

"Tesco is a grownup. He makes his own choices."

Silas laughed. "Maybe you're right, Cole. Maybe we should put her down quickly. Put her out of her ignorant misery."

Bristol leaned forward as far as she could. "What's that supposed to mean? Just because he does dirty work, doesn't mean you own him."

"I wouldn't call what Tesco does dirty work, but he is good for the more … obtuse jobs. I prefer to work with professionals such as Cole for minutiae. And I can assure you that I do in fact have Tesco on a leash."

"God, you're so superior. You think you're so above everyone else."

"That's because I am, my dear. I have yet to meet my match. I thought you came close, and I appreciate this last little burst of contempt, but I see more and more now that ultimately, I was wrong."

"Well, I heard Tesco runs quite a good business around here. He's even venturing across borders."

Silas nodded. "He likes to think much of himself. But like you, he's a pawn."

"You mean like his demolition of that empty lot on Mocrossen?"

Silas lifted an eyebrow. "You've been busy."

"I was going through some of Cole's dad's paperwork."

Cole's head twisted hard toward her. "What? You went into my dad's things?" He pointed the gun at her.

She shrugged and looked back at Silas. He was enjoying this. "I found the invoices for the demolition on that vacant block. You and Sullivan had quite a little scam going on there. You say that Tesco's close to worthless, but you gave him a big cut of the action."

"It wasn't as big as it looked. The thing about a guy like Tesco is, he's a small fish in a big pond, and if he gets to play with the big boys, he's too dazzled to recognize when he's getting ripped off. It's a cheaper way to go than hiring someone with half a brain. If Tesco is disappointed at missing his meeting with you, I'm sure I can find a morsel to throw his way to keep him happy."

"Well, this is it then. I guess I lose."

"You lost a long time ago. Cole, we will go for the

one shot, but make it a gut-shot. I want her to bleed out and watch you enjoy it."

Cole and Bristol were watching each other. Cole's face was unreadable, but he didn't take his eyes off her. "I don't think so."

"I beg your pardon?" Silas said, stiffening.

Chapter 30

COLE TURNED his gun on Silas, and as Silas's men lifted their guns in defense, Jimmy took both men out before anyone could blink.

"Holy shit, Jimmy." Bristol sat up straight. "Where'd you learn to shoot like that?"

"Hey, I'm not just a pretty face."

Silas turned and looked at his two men, dead on the floor. He put his hands up toward Cole. "You don't want to do this."

"Like hell I don't."

"I am the FBI's greatest asset. You think they'll let you just kill me and walk away."

"Killing you is tempting. But I've got other plans. More suited to a guy like you." Cole nodded at Jimmy, who pointed his own gun at Silas so Cole could disarm him and then he went to untie Bristol.

"I'm so sorry, Cole. I'm so sorry for what I said."

"Don't worry about it."

"Are you mad? I was horrible, but I didn't mean any of it, and I don't blame you for going to Elly."

"Bristol," he said as he got her hands free. "I'm not as stupid as you seem to think I am."

"What?"

"I never believed a word you said. You were convincing, but I knew something was going on. I knew that wasn't you. And if I've learned anything about Silas, it's that if something seems off, he's involved." He took her hands and pulled her off the chair. "I tested out my theory by meeting up with Elly. I know how Silas likes to torture you and when I saw they were watching me with her, I figured I'd give Silas what he wanted." He turned to Silas. "You should have seen the look on your face when you thought I had turned against Bristol. You wanted it so bad you couldn't even think straight, otherwise, I reckon you wouldn't have fallen for it."

Silas was simmering, but his voice was cool. "You really are a cut above the rest. It was worth it — the interest I took in your family."

"You call sleeping with my mom, 'taking an interest'?"

"Don't tell me you're actually upset about that. I only sent her to you to see how you'd respond. It wasn't that hard for me to convince her to tell you either."

"No? You just told her you'd kill her if she didn't. How odd that she would do what you asked."

"Actually, it was more pathetic than that. I don't know how you do it, Cole. These women in your life will do anything to keep you safe." Silas crossed his arms. "I told her I'd kill you, the son she barely knows. She begged me, Cole, not to kill you. She always was a weak woman. That's why it was so easy to get her into bed the first time. But you, Cole. You're something special. You should reconsider working with me. The things we could do, you and I."

"Cole." Bristol grabbed at his arm to stop him, but it was too late. He marched over to Silas and punched him in the face. Silas made an effort to stand his ground, but the punch knocked him flat.

"Hey!" A voice called out of the shadows.

Silas jumped up, his hand pressed against his face and took a step back so he could keep Cole in his sites.

Tesco walked into the lighted area with three armed men behind him.

Silas stiffened. "Jacob. When did you get here?"

"Just now. What's going on?"

Silas chuckled. "You always did know when to make an entrance."

Cole walked forward. "Tesco, thank you for agreeing to meet us here."

Silas smiled and shook his head. "Jacob — " He walked over and shook Tesco's hand. "I've never been more pleased to see you."

Bristol watched as Tesco stood a little taller at the compliment and a shrill of fear passed through her. But only for a moment.

"What's going on?" Tesco asked again.

Silas spoke first. "I'm taking care of a little business. But it turns out, I've put my trust in the wrong people." He motioned toward the two dead men.

"And so has Tesco." Bristol said, stepping forward. "You just admitted that you double-crossed him."

"Oh, now I see." Silas hooted. "You brought Tesco here so you could make up scenarios. You greatly underestimate his intelligence." Silas put a hand on Tesco's shoulder. "I'm sorry for all of this. It's really an enormous waste of your time. If you'll allow me to borrow a few of your men, I'll take care of it. And if you have some spare time, there's a very profitable job I wanted to talk to you about."

Jimmy stepped forward and pulled off his balaclava. "I heard the whole thing."

Tesco turned away from Silas. "Jimmy. There you are. Cole said you'd be here."

"Silas has been cheating you."

Silas's face was murderous. "This is ridiculous. Tesco, we've known each other for a long time. Don't tell me I haven't made you a lot of money. Don't insult me by listening to their lies."

"Actually," Cole said, sticking his hand into his pocket. He pulled out his phone. "I've got another recording. Lucky for me, I don't think Tesco will be too worried about how I got the evidence."

Silas lunged toward Bristol. He was surprisingly agile. As he swung around, he slipped a gun out from under his pant leg and held it to her head. "Sorry, Tesco. I can't help it if you're an imbecile. But your usefulness is over for me now. Bristol, it looks like *you* will come in handy after all."

Bristol grabbed at his arm that was locked around her throat. She looked at Cole who widened his eyes, looked down at her hand, then back at her face. She shook her head. He was trying to say something, but she had no idea what. Silas was close to choking her. She could sacrifice herself and save them all.

"Bristol," Cole said when he saw the look of defeat on her face. There was no point being coy. He lifted his hand and splayed his fingers, pointing exaggeratedly at his ring finger.

"Time to go, Bristol." Silas hissed in her ear.

"No," Bristol choked out as she spun the ring around her finger. "You were right the first time. You're better off without me." She flicked the catch and swatted her hand around behind her like she was smacking a mosquito on Silas's neck.

He barely noticed the prick, and for a moment, continued to pull her back into the shadows. Then his grip loosened, and he dropped to the ground.

Cole raced over. "Geez, you're thick sometimes."

"Give me a break," she said, looking down at Silas's unconscious body. "It's hard to think straight when your airway is being cut off." She considered Silas for a moment while she rubbed her throat, then looked up at Cole, swung around, and grabbed him hard around the neck. He wrapped his arms around her and lifted her off the ground until Tesco joined them.

"You must be some bodyguard," he said, giving Silas a testing kick as Cole and Bristol awkwardly separated. "The recording wasn't really necessary. I'd have taken Jimmy's word over his."

"That's good. I was bluffing about the recording."

Bristol ran her hands down her face. "I can't believe you. You are obviously way better at this than I am."

"Give yourself a little credit. You got Silas to admit with his own lips what he'd done to Tesco."

"It's not hard to get Silas to boast about himself over someone else."

Tesco called his men over, then shook hands with Bristol and Cole. "I assume you're happy to let me take out the trash?" he asked. "He did make me a lot of money, but I can't ignore being dishonored."

"He's all yours," Bristol said as they dragged him away.

"No one's gone through this much trouble to convince me of something before. I'm impressed. But then, you always did go the extra mile."

"I do what I can."

"I will admit, I'm a little disappointed. I was looking forward to having you on my team."

"I don't work well with others. But if you ever need help with anything, let me know. Just understand, I've become very picky about what work I do."

Tesco nodded. "I guess we're finished here."

Jimmy slapped his hands together. "Guys, it's been fun. But I've gotta get going."

Bristol pulled him into a hug. "Thanks again for your help. We couldn't have done it without you."

Jimmy grunted. "Hugging you is weird, Bristol." He pulled back and looked at Cole. "Does she do this sort of thing to you?"

"Oh, all the time. It's awful."

"Right?" He looked back at Bristol. "Give it a rest. See you around." He slapped her on the shoulder and walked off.

"Yeah, see you around."

Bristol looked at the two dead men lying in their own blood on the floor, then down at Cole's gloved hands. She walked over and grabbed a discarded balaclava off the floor and wiped down the chair.

Cole walked over. "What are you doing?"

"Fingerprints. The FBI have mine. They don't need to find them here with these two dead guys."

Cole said nothing, just watched her do what she did best. When she had finished, they went outside into the dark.

Bristol moved across the threshold and leaned on the outside of the building. She bent over with her hands on her knees. Cole put a hand on her back. "You okay?"

"Tesco will kill him," she said with little conviction.

"Yes, he will."

She stared at the ground. "So much of what I've done has been connected to him and now it's over."

"You say that like it's a bad thing."

"Not bad, just … it's like a big black hole."

"Think of it this way: now you can make decisions knowing Silas isn't connected to them. That's a really good thing."

"She stood up straight and looked at Cole. "How'd you get so grounded? I take it that's not something your dad taught you?"

"I trained with the SEALs remember? I learned

control. I learned how to think straight under pressure. Now let's get out of here. I'll buy you a cup of tea."

Bristol looked over at the van they arrived in. "We'll have to get rid of that."

"I've already got that sorted. You can turn off now."

"Right. Like that's gonna happen."

Chapter 31

BRISTOL LEANED her head back in the seat now that they were in Cole's Mustang. With the van taken care of, she felt a little more steady.

Cole focused on the taillights of the car in front of them. If he hadn't been able to read her so well when she blew him off at the bank, they wouldn't be sitting there together right now. Then he thought of something. "Has it occurred to you that with Silas gone, we may be able to save Eli's gym?"

Bristol closed her eyes. "I didn't even think of that." Maybe she could have a rest after all. "I'm so glad Silas is gone."

"Me too."

"So where exactly are we going?"

"Do you want me to take you home?"

She looked down at her watch. "Is it only ten?"

"Really? After all that? It feels later."

"Take me to see Eli. He's expecting to never see me

again, so it would be good to stop in and tell him the bad news that I'm sticking around."

"You sure you want to ruin his night?"

"Well, I can follow it up with the news that his gym should be safe."

Bristol drifted off as they drove. When the car stopped, she was startled awake.

"We're here."

"Did I just sleep?" She rubbed her face and looked across at the gym. The door was open.

"How long does he usually stay open for?"

"He'll be open for at least another hour."

Inside, there were more people standing around than working out.

"Eli, what's going on?" Bristol said as she walked up to him.

"Bristol?"

"Yeah, I'm still here. I changed my mind."

His face was hard to read. He nodded slightly and then turned his attention to Cole. "It's good to see you, Cole." The two men shook hands. Both were so stoic looking that Bristol rolled her eyes.

Eli moved closer. "I assume, Cole, that you have something to do with the fact that she's standing here right now?"

"He saved my life. Again."

"That's a nasty habit you're forming." Eli laughed.

Cole nodded. "What's with the crowd?"

"I gave these guys the bad news. I thought it would motivate them to work harder, but now everyone is trying to solve my problems for me. It's like I've got a room full of Bristols."

"God forbid." Cole murmured under his breath.

Bristol elbowed him then said, "I'm not surprised. Everyone loves you. But some things have … uh … changed. It may be that Lincoln Enterprises pulls out. I can't confirm it, but just don't do anything drastic."

"I'd say thanks, but I'm concerned that whatever has changed has been done illegally."

"What? Me do something illegal? Come on, Eli. You know me better than that."

"You know about this, Cole?"

"I don't like to miss out on the action. But at least I can confirm that Bristol is safer than she's been in a while."

"Good."

Bristol crossed her arms. "Are you two ever gonna stop?"

"Probably not," Cole said as he reached into his pocket and pulled out his phone. "Sorry, I've got a call." He turned slightly as he answered it. "Andrew?"

"So you've decided to take a risk," Eli said, nodding toward Cole.

"Turns out he's a pretty good guy after all. And unfortunately, I also like him."

"What a pain."

"Totally. Life would be a lot easier without feelings."

"Easier, yes, but not good. You've had enough not

good. It's time I saw you smile more." He rested a hand on her shoulder. "I better let these guys know they can settle down. We'll just ride it out for now and see what happens."

Bristol turned to Cole. He hung up his phone with the dopiest look on his face.

It made Bristol nervous. "What's that look about?"

"Andrew has a baby girl."

"Oh." Bristol felt a thrill of excitement but squashed it, then rebuked herself. It was hard to give herself permission to feel the good stuff.

Cole grabbed her hand and pulled her through the crowd. "Come on. We've got a baby to visit."

She allowed herself to be dragged along, but when they got outside, she pulled back. "I don't really do the baby thing well."

Cole ignored her and pushed her the rest of the way to the car.

"Isn't it past visiting hours?"

"Andrew said he'll make sure they let us through."

"Fine." She sulked as she got in.

"You're safe from Silas now. We are about to go see a brand new person. Cheer up."

"I don't know why you're so excited to see a baby. I thought guys weren't usually that into it."

"Are you kidding? This is a person that's been out in the world for only a couple of hours. You don't think that's wild?"

"You're very strange."

"So are you. That's why we get along so well."

At the hospital, Bristol hung behind Cole as they walked along the antiseptic hallways to the maternity ward.

A woman in scrubs gave them a disarming smile as she told them the room number they were looking for, and Bristol wanted to growl at her when she pointed them down a hall with a look on her face that said she expected to see the two of them in there one day with their own little bundle. *Must be a nurse thing* Bristol grumbled to herself. Sometimes, her ability to read people was a real problem.

When they reached the door of Jenny's room, Bristol froze. Cole turned to her. The smile on his face fell away when he saw how pale she was. He pulled her aside. "You don't have to do this if you don't want to. I didn't realize it would affect you so much. I thought you were just being difficult."

Bristol breathed out slowly. "The last time I was here was when Lila was born. Her mother died from complications."

"Oh, I'm sorry. I didn't realize. We don't have to stay."

"No, I need to face this." She swallowed hard. "Okay. Let's go."

"You're sure?"

Bristol nodded but gripped the door as she walked through. She had to make a conscious effort to let it go. Cole announced their presence, and the curtain was pulled back by a beaming Andrew.

When Bristol saw Jenny, Andrew, and the baby, the pressure eased and gave way to a lump in her throat.

Andrew hugged both of them at the same time. "I'm so glad you guys could come. I thought with everything you've been through, it would be good for you to see what you had a part in protecting."

"You want to hold her?" Jenny angled the baby toward Bristol.

"Uh, no. I'm not really a baby person."

Andrew stepped forward. "Her name is Chloe. Chloe Bristol Turough."

Bristol grunted. "What?"

"Yeah well, like I said, if it weren't for you, I wouldn't have been here to see the birth of my baby girl."

Bristol felt the burn at the back of her eyes. She couldn't understand why it affected her so much. It was annoying.

Andrew put a hand on her arm. "She won't break if you hold her."

Bristol looked down at Chloe who was asleep, wrapped up tightly with a fist in her mouth. "Come on, be brave." Andrew nudged her.

She gave him a sulky look, then smiled. "Okay."

She took the baby in her arms and scanned the space around her for anything that might be a trip hazard, then decided her best option was to sit in the closest chair.

As she settled into the seat, she pulled Chloe close to her chest and felt an ache ripple through her body. It was odd and unexpected, but strangely alluring. She ran a finger down the sleeping girl's cheek. Chloe had everything ahead of her, and because Bristol had made the right decisions, this girl got to grow up with her mom and dad.

"Babies aren't so bad," she said when she noticed everyone watching her. To their credit, they didn't comment.

The moon was high and the air had a chill when Cole and Bristol left the hospital. Cole took her hand and was half surprised when she didn't pull away. "That wasn't so bad."

"No, it was a great way to finish a really sucky couple of weeks," Bristol said, then breathed out to see if her breath would cloud under the copper glow of the parking lot lights. Not cold enough, but close.

"Has it only been a couple weeks?" Cole shook his head.

"I know. It feels like years. It's amazing how much can change in such a short time."

"We should get married."

"What?" Bristol tripped on her own toe and yanked Cole to a stop. "We can't get married."

"Who says?"

"Me, for one."

"That's fine. Just let me know when you change your mind."

"You're terrible. I can't even tell if you're joking."

"How about that? My girlfriend can't even tell if I'm joking."

Bristol groaned. "Don't call me your girlfriend."

"What should I call you then?"

"How about tired and hungry?"

"You're never going to make things easy for me, are you?"

"What would be the fun in that?" She started walking again, but he pulled her back.

"I'm serious. I don't want to be with anyone but you."

Bristol felt a little light-headed. She looked at the ground. "I don't want to be with anyone else either."

"Good. Then we're going steady." Bristol made a gagging noise and tried to push him away, but he wrapped an arm around her shoulder and pulled her forward as he laughed. "I'll find you something to eat and then I'm going to put you to bed."

She allowed herself to be pulled along while she tried to think of a proper come back. Nothing came to mind.

When they got to the car, Cole opened her door, but before Bristol got in, she put a hand on either side of his face. She looked at him for a moment then took a deep breath, and as she exhaled she whispered. "I love you." Then she ducked down and got in the car, pulling her door shut.

Cole stood stunned for a moment until Bristol called through the window. "Are we going or what? I'm starving."

Cole chuckled to himself as he walked around to his side of the car. "Wouldn't have it any other way."

THE END

Enjoy the book?

Book reviews are the most powerful tool I have as an author to grow my readership. If I had the sway of a New York publisher, perhaps it would be easier to gain attention, but a simple reader review is way better than what any top publisher can offer…

Readers like yourself are what make the biggest difference to an author, and if you've enjoyed this book and wouldn't mind spending a few minutes leaving a review, it would help me out immensely.

Free Novelette

One of the best things about being a writer is that I get to build relationships with my readers. And one of the best ways to do that is through a newsletter. I'm not a prolific emailer, but I will occasionally send out a newsletter with details on new releases, special offers, and anything else I have that might be of interest.

And to say thanks for your interest, you'll get the prequel to Sleight of Hand, free (as well as an extra bonus you'll find out about in the email.

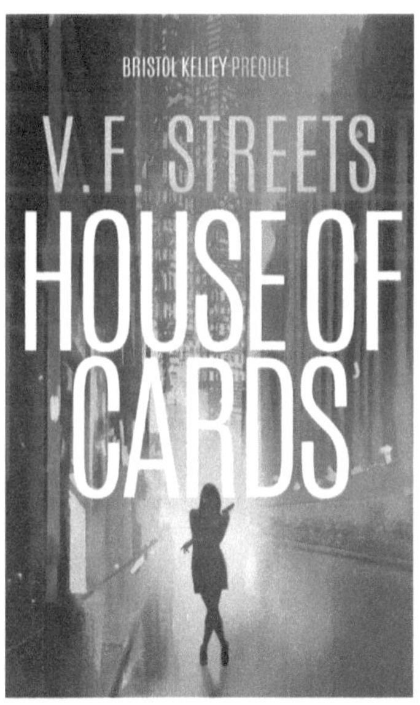

GET YOUR FREE EBOOK NOW

visit www.pgturners.com/books

Also by V F Streets

OUT ON A LIMB (Erin Hart Book One)

For Erin Hart, burglary is a means to an end. She also happens to be very good at it. But when her brother is sentenced to decades in prison for a crime he didn't commit, she risks everything to give him back the life that was stolen.

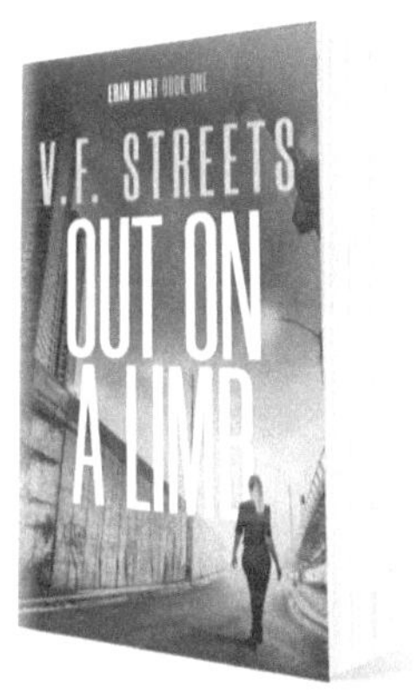

About the Author

V F Streets is the author of the Vigilante Justice Series. You can find her on www.pgturners.com or feel free to contact her by email at vfstreets@pgturners.com. Otherwise you can connect with her here -

Acknowledgments

I have begun an incredible journey that I never could have imagined, and there have been numerous people who have been a great support to me along the way.

As always, I have to give thanks to God who set me along this path in the first place. To Matt and the kids for being excited about it all. To mom and dad for always being behind me. To Jenni Fry, once again for your hard work on the manuscript and your enthusiasm for this project. And to friends like Donna and Moira for getting your hands dirty to help me make the story better than it was. And to all those who have read my books and given me the encouragement I needed to keep going.

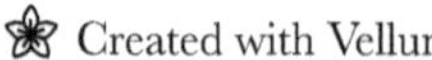 Created with Vellum